TWICE PROMISED

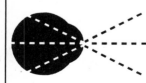

This Large Print Book carries the
Seal of Approval of N.A.V.H.

TWICE PROMISED

MAGGIE BRENDAN

THORNDIKE PRESS

A part of Gale, Cengage Learning

GALE
CENGAGE Learning®

Detroit • New York • San Francisco • New Haven, Conn • Waterville, Maine • London

GALE
CENGAGE Learning

© 2012 by Maggie Brendan.

Most Scripture, whether quoted or paraphrased by the characters, is taken from the King James Version of the Bible.

Scripture quotations marked NASB are from the New American Standard Bible®, copyright © 1960, 1962, 1963, 1968, 1971, 1972, 1973, 1975, 1977, 1995 by The Lockman Foundation. Used by permission.

Thorndike Press, a part of Gale, Cengage Learning.

The internet addresses, email addresses, and phone numbers in this book are accurate at the time of publication. They are provided as a resource. The publisher does not endorse them or vouch for their content or permanence.

Thorndike Press® Large Print Christian Romance.

The text of this Large Print edition is unabridged.

Other aspects of the book may vary from the original edition.

Set in 16 pt. Plantin.

LIBRARY OF CONGRESS CATALOGING-IN-PUBLICATION DATA

Brendan, Maggie, 1949–
    Twice promised / by Maggie Brendan.
        pages ; cm. — (Thorndike Press large print Christian romance) (The blue willow brides ; book 2)
        ISBN 978-1-4104-5423-2 (hardcover) — ISBN 1-4104-5423-1 (hardcover)
    1. Mail order brides—Fiction. 2. Large type books. I. Title.
PS3602.R4485T95 2013
813'.6—dc23   2012044205

Published in 2013 by arrangement with Revell Books, a division of Baker Publishing Group

Printed in the United States of America
1 2 3 4 5 6 7 17 16 15 14 13

For my niece Kathy Hardison Wells,
who stays focused on the Lord.

"All this," said David, "the LORD made me understand in writing by His hand upon me, all the details of this pattern."

1 Chronicles 28:19 NASB

PROLOGUE

August 1887
Outskirts of Fort Bridger, Wyoming

Keeping his eye along the steep ridge above him, Sergeant Bryan Gifford clutched his Sharps carbine next to his hip. He hunkered among the thickets of scraggly sagebrush, which wouldn't allow much protection from the renegade band of Sioux who bore down on his unit in a surprise attack. The sagebrush's pungent smell tickled his nose, and its yellow flowers were bright against the brown earth, but he had no time for enjoyment of the surrounding kinnikinnick, the evening star, or the wintergreen that crept over the warm rocks. For just a moment, he thought of when he'd played soldiers with his two brothers, but this was no game. This was the real thing, and if he made it out alive, he'd run, not walk, to the nearest train headed to Cheyenne, into the waiting arms of his true love.

9

Bryan thought about the recent unrest among the different tribes. After the government passed the Dawes Act in February, they had taken away the land of the tribal communities. *Maybe they have a right to be angry,* Bryan thought. Their land was going to be divided up into parcels of 160 acres for families and eighty acres for individuals. But it was up to him to follow the orders of his superior, not disobey them, and right now he didn't care who was right or wrong. He just wanted to win this attack and save his men . . . and his life.

Bullets whizzed past him from Private Charlie Foster shooting in the direction of the jagged rocks above him. Charlie signaled to Bryan from another group of rocks, indicating that he'd cover him. Crouching low, Bryan made a beeline for the safety of the rocks, his boots stirring up the dry dust.

When he was only a foot away from Charlie, he felt an arrow pierce his heart. He knew he was mortally wounded. For a moment he wavered sickeningly, feeling the sharp pain, then he lunged for the shelter of the outcropping of rocks.

"Sarge!" Charlie yelled, dragging Bryan next to him. Charlie cradled his upper body, and Bryan heard the ripping of his shirt as Charlie quickly yanked the fabric free, exposing the embedded arrow. His voice seemed distant now, but Bryan saw Charlie's frantic eyes look around for help when his hand came in contact with blood. "I need to get this out."

Bryan's hand stayed Charlie when he reached for the arrow. He lay helplessly, knowing that his life's blood pumped from him, soaking his chest. The yelling of victory from the Indians seemed distant, as did the silence of his men around him. He reached for Charlie's hand, and the private paused, fear etched in his young face. Charlie was barely old enough to be in the Army, and this was the first scrimmage of any kind he had encountered. Up until now it had all been drills and make-believe.

"Charlie, listen to me," Bryan said, his voice barely above a whisper. "You must leave right now or you won't make it!" Bryan gasped for breath, his sight becoming fuzzy. "I'm not going to make it . . . but I'll fire into the air until you can scamper out of sight . . . They'll think you're dead." He winced, forcing down his pain, then stared at Charlie, seeing the fear reflected in his hazel eyes.

Charlie shook his head. "No, I can't leave you like this."

Bryan mustered all his strength to grab

11

the private by the collar of his uniform and pull him closer. "You have . . . no choice. All the others are dead . . . You have to obey my orders while there's still time!"

"Yes, sir." Charlie's eyes filled with tears, and he was shaking.

"One other thing . . . I need you to do." He released Charlie's collar. He was becoming light-headed now. He must try to concentrate. "Go to Cheyenne and find Greta Olsen. Tell . . . tell her . . . I love her and we'll meet . . . in heaven." He gasped, trying to clear his throat, and tasted blood on his tongue. He had to say this before he died. "And tell her for me . . . that there's only one other man worth her love . . . my brother —"

Suddenly Bryan stopped and looked heavenward as the midmorning clouds scattered, revealing the brightest of skies and the most glorious of gardens . . .

1

August 1888
Central City, Colorado

Greta Olsen perched primly on her seat, clutching her Bible as the train headed to Central City, Colorado. She stared out a smudged window at the moving landscape of canyons and mountain ridges, where snow capped the distant purple peaks. The ride was somewhat thrilling, as well as frightening. The Colorado Central chugged up its winding tracks around the Rocky Mountains and the sparkling Clear Creek. Greta held her breath at their incredible beauty, wincing as her ears popped with the change in altitude. The further up the mountains they traveled, the chillier and drier the air became. Greta pulled her woolen cape tighter about her shoulders, thankful that she hadn't packed it in her case.

She contemplated the new venture she'd

thrust herself into. The advertisement for a mail-order bride was tucked safely into her reticule. Greta had hated leaving the crowded farmhouse outside of Cheyenne where she'd lived since coming to America. After saying goodbye to her only family, she'd watched as the wheat fields, already ripe with promise, were soon gone from her sight. Her eyes had flooded with hot tears, and an ache planted inside her chest.

But that was yesterday, and today there would be no tears. In fact, she was excited about living this deep in the mountains, even after hearing the rumors of the cold and snow and the rugged life where miners were as thick as fleas on a dog's back, as she was informed by Peter, her brother-in-law. But that hadn't deterred her. Greta wanted adventure and had closed the door to her heart on love once and for all. She had no illusions when it came to love. It may have finally worked for her sister and Peter, but just look what had happened to Clara, Peter's mother! Greta decided that when she wed, her marriage would be one of mutual love and respect.

Greta caught the gaze of a young lady with big brown eyes sitting across the aisle, so she smiled back at her with a nod, thinking maybe the lady might be a new friend here in the Rockies. The lady's lips lifted slightly at the corners, then she turned to look out the train's window, keeping her hands clasped together in her lap. Greta guessed her to be about the same age as herself and wondered where the young woman might be headed. She glanced down at the lady's left hand, noticing it was devoid of a wedding band.

Through the entire trip, the young woman had not moved from her stiff sitting position, nor had she spoken to anyone. She simply handed the conductor her ticket when asked. Her hourglass figure was smartly dressed in a dark navy traveling suit with black velvet trimming, and the matching hat sported a long-plumed black feather at the band. Apparently she was well-bred — Greta noted her poise and secretly admired her fashionable attire. The few dresses Greta owned now were beginning to show wear. She looked down at the frayed cuffs of her traveling dress and crossed her arms at the wrists, hoping to hide them.

Knowing they had only a little time left on the train before reaching Central City, Greta turned her attention to her open Bible, her sister Catharine's parting gift before Greta left Cheyenne. It had belonged to Catharine, and their mother before that.

Greta remembered her sister's words before she left: "Greta, you take Mother's Bible — I want you to have it. Remember to let it guide all that you do. And remember us when you read — it can be the connection we have when we're apart, until we meet again."

A newspaper clipping fell into her lap, and Greta carefully opened the folded paper, now browning with age. She recognized it — Peter's ad that Catharine had responded to when they were still in Holland and thoroughly adrift as to their future. Catharine must have forgotten she'd placed it there. She'd read it to Greta and Anna a dozen times, and now its creases were worn through with use. Greta remembered how God had been faithful to Catharine, Anna, and herself, providing Catharine a good husband and a fine home for all of them. It was a good life . . . for a while.

Lord, what's in store for me now? No one but Bryan will ever hold my heart . . . but at least here, deep in the mountains, I won't hear the constant howl of the prairie winds. It was enough to drive a person mad, to her way of thinking. She wondered how terrible it must have been for Bryan. Had he been in pain as he lay dying on the windswept prairie? She shuddered to think about him suffering at all, and prayed that his death had been swift like the ambush. Sorrow flooded her heart for what could've been.

She slipped her own mail-order-bride ad from the Bible and ran her gloved finger over the name at the bottom: Jess Gifford. That name was one of the reasons she'd answered the ad in the first place. Could it be that Jess was related to Bryan? Perhaps a distant cousin? She sighed. Probably just a coincidence . . . but there might be a slim chance. It shouldn't be too hard to find out. Now she regretted that she and Bryan hadn't talked more about his family. She smiled. The stolen moments together had been so short. Most of it had been spent kissing and planning their future, not talking about their pasts.

Greta folded the piece of paper, tucked it into the book of Psalms, and tried to read. When the conductor announced they were nearing their destination, she gathered her things together from her seat in readiness to disembark the train into this fresh, new world.

The engine puffed and ground to a screeching stop, allowing the handful of passengers to make their way toward the depot. The wiry conductor reached up and grabbed her carpetbag, set it down on the

17

depot's wooden platform, and took Greta's hand to assist her down the metal steps. "The rest of your bags will be unloaded momentarily, miss."

Feeling suddenly adrift, Greta stood numbly off to the side next to her carpetbag and scanned the platform, expecting Jess Gifford to step forward for her. Maybe he was delayed but would show up any moment. She adjusted her cape, then stepped over to a nearby bench to wait, ignoring the open stares of men about the rough-hewn depot. Mercy! The raw mining town was filled with miners, trappers, and merchants milling about. She observed the constant movement on the busy streets from where she sat.

Only moments later, she was joined by the lady who had sat across from her on the train. "May I sit here with you?" Her large brown eyes seemed kind, but she looked unsure while she waited for Greta's response.

"*Hallo. Alstublieft!* Of course!" Greta noticed the finely etched cheekbones and smooth olive complexion, framed by dark brown hair that peeked from her fashionable hat, and thought again how very pretty the woman was. As the lady bent to place her bag next to her feet, the long feather from her hat tickled Greta's cheek. Greta giggled.

"I'm sorry." The lady smiled, then took a seat on the bench and extended her hand. "I'm Cora Johnson."

"I'm Greta Olsen," she said as she took Cora's outstretched hand. "Are you waiting for someone?"

A flash of concern crossed Cora's face. "As a matter of fact, I am. And you? Are you visiting someone or moving here?" Cora folded her hands in her lap. "I'm sorry, I didn't mean to pry."

Greta smiled. "You're not. I . . . I've answered an ad for a mail-order bride." She swallowed nervously. "But I see no one has arrived to pick me up, so I thought I'd just sit here a few minutes to wait. Apparently Jess Gifford is delayed." Greta tapped her foot as she looked out over the boardwalk, hoping he would appear soon. She was tired but anxious to meet the intriguing man she'd been corresponding with.

"Did you say *Jess?*" Cora raised an eyebrow with a bewildered look.

"Yes." Greta turned sideways to face her. "Jess Gifford. Do you know him? Tell me what you know. I'm as nervous as a cat crossing a busy street —"

Cora huffed, then straightened her skirts

without looking at Greta.

"Is something wrong, Miss Johnson?"

Cora's face turned pink. Clearing her throat, she lifted her gaze and let out a deep breath, but before she could reply, a tall cowboy swaggered toward them, bowing slightly as he lifted his hat. His brown hair was matted around his head where his hat had been. He smiled broadly at them.

"I'm here to pick up Jess's mail-order brides," he said. He twirled his Stetson in his hand.

The ladies rose simultaneously. "I'm Greta Olsen, his mail-order bride. I thought Jess was to meet me. Who are you?" Greta asked, her hands on her hips. Had she heard him right? Did he say *brides?*

"Begging your pardon, *I'm* Mr. Gifford's mail-order bride." Cora whirled, glaring at Greta, her dark eyes snapping as her lady-like composure suddenly became a thing of the past.

"There must be some mistake. I thought you said *brides,* but there can be only one bride!" Greta ignored Cora's glare and faced the good-looking cowboy. He'd better have a good explanation for this. She hadn't traveled all the way here to be made a fool of.

"I'm Zach Gifford, Jess's brother, and . . .

er, you did hear me right. I did say *brides*."
He donned his hat, then reached for their
bags, lifting one in each hand.

"There must be some terrible mistake!"
Cora folded her hands across her chest. "A
man can't have two brides. Not to mention
it's illegal! This is ridiculous! And I'll not
stand for it!"

"Nor will I!" Greta reached for her bag,
but Zach held on to it. "Where is this Mr.
Gifford?"

Zach held Greta's eyes for a moment. "If
you ladies will give me a chance, I can
explain everything, but we can't stand here
squabbling in the street, now can we? I'll
take you for an early supper and we'll talk."

When the two ladies looked at each other
doubtfully, he leaned back on his boot heels
and quickly added, "Besides, that was the
last train today, so you have nowhere else to
go."

Zach's brown eyes glinted with a dash of
fire. Greta wanted to slap the silly grin right
off his face but instead mustered up the
courage to consider his plan. After all, it
was late, and what other options did she
have? She knew no one in this town. "You're
right about that, Mr. Gifford —"

"Please, everyone calls me Zach. Now let's
go rustle up a good supper over at Mabel's.

Then I'll see that you both get settled for the evening." He started walking away. With a glance over his shoulder, he nodded at them to follow.

Cora shrugged. "I suppose we have no choice until we find out what this fiasco is all about."

"*Goed.* Okay. But I'm not one bit happy about it!" Greta followed the lanky cowboy, whose boots caused puffs of dust to rise in the street.

Cora, with a sour look on her pretty face, tossed her head so that the feather in her hat bobbed. "And you think I am?"

Fifteen minutes later, after Zach had collected the rest of their luggage and loaded it into his buckboard, they were seated in a cheerful diner down the street from the train depot. His stomach growled at the smell of food, and he realized how hungry he was. He'd been so busy at the store that he'd been late meeting the train. He ordered steak and gravy for everyone, then turned his attention to the anxious ladies. Each was pretty in her own sort of way. Greta was a tall blonde with a creamy complexion and large blue eyes. Cora, a little shorter than Greta, had dark hair and exotic, deep-set brown eyes with eyebrows that arched gracefully. Two ladies who could be the devil to reckon with if crossed. Which of course, he had just done. As they awaited his explanation, he wondered where to start.

He cleared his throat and decided to plunge right in. "I know that you're both very angry with me at the moment, but I hope you'll hear me out." He set his hat on the chair next to him and looked directly across the table at the two mail-order brides. "I didn't set out to dupe you, but I wanted you to care about my brother for my own selfish reasons. You see, my brother's business took off like a steam engine when the miners descended on Central City on their way to the gold and silver deep in the mountains. I've been working right alongside him, but I have other things I'm interested in besides running a general store."

"And what has that got to do with us, pray tell?" Greta clearly was getting impatient. "Does he need two wives to help him run his store?"

Zach grinned. She really didn't mince her words, but he liked her straightforwardness. "No, but he could use more help. I'm afraid he's a bit unorganized and doesn't do well with keeping track of orders, or ordering things, for that matter. He complains but says he has no time for a wife because he's too busy, and she would need more attention than he could afford to give." He paused, watching their attentive faces. They seemed to be two totally opposite women, but that could be a good thing, couldn't it? It might make it easier for Jess to choose. "So I actually wrote those letters. I took it upon myself to correspond with you two lovely ladies seeking husbands in hopes that one of you might fit the bill as a wife for my lonely brother."

"You mean Jess doesn't know?" Greta sputtered, almost knocking over her water glass.

"We're not *things* you can just order up and amuse yourself with for your own purposes," Cora snapped. "Your letters were quite convincing — which leads me to believe you must have a wife yourself."

"Actually, I'm not married. I've courted a few nice ladies, but I'm not considering marriage right now. But this is not about me." Zach would have to tread carefully or things might not go as he planned. "I know what's good for my brother."

Greta gave Zach a hard look. "Cora's right. Now we both have arrived to marry a man who doesn't even know we exist!"

Cora looked over at Greta. "I say we leave

on the first train back to Denver tomorrow."

Greta's rosy lips pursed in an angry line. "You may be right, but I don't want to go back to Wyoming and deal with the humiliation of it all. I can't speak for you, Cora."

Zach ran his hands through his hair in exasperation. "Then you may as well stay here. Accommodations are scarce at the moment, I'm afraid. I'll put you up in a cabin for now, and you can decide how you feel tomorrow about my plan."

"And what plan is that?" Greta shot him a disparaging look.

"I'll introduce you to my brother as mail-order brides seeking husbands, who want to work in the general store. That'll give you both ample time to get to know him, and he can decide between the two of you."

Greta laughed. "Oh, I get it. He's supposed to fall in love with one of us just like that!" She snapped her fingers.

"Well . . . yes . . . as a matter of fact, I think he could. Both of you are stunning. Any man would jump at the chance." Zach leaned back in his chair.

"Just imagine that, Greta. We've been duped into falling for an imaginary love." Cora shook her head and sighed. "And I thought I'd found a man I could love. I should've known better."

The waiter appeared, placed three heaping platefuls of food before them, and refilled their water glasses. Greta looked across the table at Zach. "Well, I have no fantasy of love. I was looking for a change of scenery and maybe someone I could care about, but love . . . well, that's a different story altogether."

Cora's eyebrows shot upward, but Zach didn't question her about her hopes. Whatever they were, they were her private affair. Still, she might grow to love Jess. It could happen. Or . . . His gaze traveled to Cora. Maybe his brother would favor Cora's dark beauty.

"What do you say, ladies? Are you willing to give my plan consideration? Let's say in three weeks, if either of you hate it here or don't take a shine to Jess, then I'll pay your train fare back home." Greta groaned and Cora winced. "Or to wherever you'd like to travel."

"As far as Holland?" Greta chuckled, then took a deep breath and looked at him evenly. "Maybe it won't be all that bad. What do you think, Cora? Shall we stay here and see what develops?"

Zach held his breath. Surely one of these pretty ladies could be Jess's bride. Or had he made a huge mistake?

26

Cora dabbed her mouth with her napkin and then laid it next to her plate. "I don't relish going back to Denver, true — but you owe us an apology for toying with our hearts. I'm not sure about Greta, but I developed deep feelings for Jess through those letters, even if he didn't write them."

Zach felt the collar of his shirt tighten against his Adam's apple and the heat of embarrassment creep up his neck. "I *do* apologize, ladies. I hope you will see fit to forgive me. Either way, I think you'll like living in Central City, if you should decide to stay. If not Jess for your husband, you'd have your pick of men. The men outnumber the women five to one." He propped his elbows on the table and clasped his palms together, then leaned toward them. "Is it a deal then?" He watched as the two ladies seemed to confer through a private signal until they faced him across the table.

"Against my better judgment, I'll say yes," Cora muttered.

"*Ja*. Yes. Count me in. This should be interesting." Greta nodded her agreement. They all stood, and the ladies fell in step behind the cowboy as he walked back to his wagon.

2

Jess strode over to the glass front door of the mercantile and flipped over the sign to read CLOSED, then dragged down the shade. It had been one of those busy days when he could've used an extra set of hands, especially since Zach had slipped out, off on one of his foolish errands, no doubt. He reckoned it was time to hire another helper. He knew Zach didn't really want to work here with him.

Jess turned the key in the lock, untied his stained apron, and flung it on the nail behind the counter. Dang! He hated a dirty apron, but as usual, he'd forgotten to wash yesterday's out. He probably couldn't get the stains out anyway.

He had trouble staying organized or remembering where he put the list that he wrote each day for his customers' orders, much less remembering to wash an apron. His mind was already racing ahead, thinking of one of his biggest and most persnickety customers, Agnes Cartwright. She wasn't going to like the fact that the bolt of drapery fabric she'd ordered for her living room hadn't arrived. He chuckled. That was because, once again, he'd forgotten to add it to the order sent to Chicago.

Jess leaned back against the long wooden counter. Hours before, miners, farmers, and shop owners had flooded the store. It seemed everyone demanded something and didn't want to wait their turn. He sighed. He loved people and loved chatting with them, but it was too easy for him to get sidetracked and forget either the task at hand or the others impatiently waiting. Well, they would just have to wait their turn! He was who he was and that wasn't likely to change. Not now, not ever.

Jess decided that instead of going upstairs to his small living quarters to scratch up something for supper, he'd haul his tired legs over to Chun-Lee's. He was hungry enough to eat a bear, and his stomach was gnawing at his backbone. The morning biscuit and jerky were long gone, and not stopping for lunch today made him nearly light-headed. He intended to change his habits as soon as he could.

He snatched his jacket and hat from the

peg behind him and opened the front door. It was almost dark, and the glowing street-lights lent a comforting presence to the evening chill. He turned the key in the lock and strolled down the sidewalk.

Zach drove the ladies about three blocks to the edge of town, to a clearing dotted with a couple of cabins set among the vast expanse of rolling foothills at the base of the Bald Mountain summit. The night was clear and cloudless with a large yellow moon that gave off enough light to see. Greta's eyes adjusted to the soft darkness that enveloped them, the distant sounds of the town in the background, and her heart fell when Zach stopped in front of a rough cabin made of hewn pine chinked with mud. She could tell that it was little more than a miner's cabin and tried to hide her disappointment. She watched as he set the brake and then climbed down, turning to assist her and Cora.

"Is this your cabin?" Cora's eyes were wide as he led them to the door and pushed it open.

"No. It belongs to a trapper friend of mine who's away right now." Zach lit the kerosene lantern on the table and turned up the wick. "No electricity here, but there's another lamp between the two cots. A pump over there in the kitchen area supplies water, and the outhouse is out back."

Greta gulped and held her breath, afraid to breathe in the stale odor of tobacco and leather that clung to the air. One swift look about the cabin's one room revealed a small table with two mismatched chairs, a round hooked rug, a couple of crates that she figured must be for extra seating, and a row of pegs along one wall where a pair of pants and shirts hung. In the kitchen area, an open shelf housed blue enamel cookware, plates, and a coffeepot.

How would she ever sleep here?

"Do you mean that Cora and I are to share this cabin for three weeks?"

Zach stood with his hands resting on his hips and surveyed the one-room cabin. "I agree it's not much to look at, but it's better than sleeping out under the stars. There're two cots over there," he said, pointing toward the back of the cabin. "I'll start you a fire since it's a little drafty, then bring your baggage inside. Jeb always has a stack of firewood at the back door." He slipped out before either of them could say a word.

Greta looked over at her new companion, whose face was lined with worry.

31

"This is not acceptable at all," Cora said. "I shall be looking for other accommodations right after breakfast." She wiggled her nose at the dust.

Greta peeled off her cape and hung it on a peg, determined to make the best of the situation for at least one night. She watched as Zach quickly made a toasty fire in the grate to remove the evening chill, unloaded the rest of their belongings, and lit the other lamp. He appeared anxious to leave.

"Ladies, you can take a short walk back to town and have breakfast at the diner if you've a mind to. Just put the tab on me. Later, we'll pick up supplies that you'll be needing for cooking."

Cora's face showed wry amusement. "I doubt that I'll be doing *any* cooking in this little hovel."

Zach cocked his head in Cora's direction. "I guess if you find yourself hungry enough, you just might."

"I won't be here that long. As soon as Jess meets me, this whole thing will be settled," Cora commented through tight lips.

"At any rate, will you be taking us to meet Jess tomorrow?" Greta said, reminding him why they were here in the first place.

"Indeed." He doffed his hat at her. "Right after you have breakfast, walk on down to

Gifford's Mercantile. We open up early, and I expect I'll be there long before you rise. Get some rest. I'll be waiting for you."

Cora's eyebrows drew together in a frown. "You want us to *walk?*" She took a stance with her arms folded, expressing her displeasure at the entire episode. Greta wanted to laugh but held herself in check. Did Cora ever walk anywhere?

"We'll manage." Greta nodded at Zach, whose face showed relief. "We can take a short walk, and the morning air should be invigorating," she said, ignoring Cora's tightly pursed lips.

Zach smiled. "That's the attitude! I'd come get you, but we open at 8:00 a.m., and I thought you two might be a little tired from your travels."

"How very considerate of you," Cora said sarcastically.

"Ladies." He tipped his hat and moved toward the cabin door that still stood open. "Sleep well. I'll see you in the morning." The door banged shut behind him.

As if I could sleep here in this cramped cabin! Cora grabbed the end handle of her trunk and dragged it to the nearest cot shoved against the wall. At least it had a quilt on top. She pulled it back and found there were

33

no sheets on the lumpy mattress, which appeared to be a hundred years old. *Now why am I not surprised?* It was a miner's cabin, after all. It probably belonged to a bachelor since she saw no sign of a woman's touch anywhere. She took a deep breath and sighed loudly enough that Greta turned from the front window, where she stood watching Zach ride away.

"What's wrong?" Greta moved toward her.

Cora sat down on the edge of the cot. "Everything! No groom, two brides, a miner's drafty cabin to sleep in! What do you think?" She gave a hysterical giggle and knew that Greta thought she was losing her mind. "I don't know why I let myself get talked into this even for one evening, much less three weeks. This just won't work, I'm afraid."

Greta sat across from her on the other cot. "For now, I say we just make the best of the situation. If we feel differently at the mercantile, we could possibly find a job using other skills. You do have some other skills besides looking for a husband, don't you?" she asked.

Cora blinked, staring down at the knotty pine floor. At least it wasn't a dirt floor. Should she tell Greta that she had no real skills other than playing the piano? She certainly couldn't cook because her family had always managed to afford a cook. Her mother had insisted on it. Most of Cora's time had been occupied with reading, visiting the sick, and attending to church matters. "Well . . . I guess I can do a few things. What about yourself?"

Greta laughed. "I can always learn new things. At least I have an education. I could find something worthwhile to support me. I won't starve." She twisted sideways and pulled back the gaily colored quilt. "I see what you mean. I didn't pack sheets. But I'm dying to get these clothes off and fall into a heap, sheets or not." She kicked off her high-heeled leather shoes and proceeded to unbutton her bodice.

"I packed sheets. I can let you borrow one, and I'll take the other." Cora pulled out soft linen sheets. "These were to be for my honeymoon," she said, running her hand across the smoothness of the fabric.

"Oh, we can't use those. I'll look around. Maybe they're stored in a cupboard or one of the shelves." Greta padded around the cabin in her stocking feet.

Cora walked over to Greta and handed her a sheet. "No, really . . . take it. At least that way you can cover up with the quilt. The temperature has dipped with nightfall, and I'm sure it will only get cooler before morning."

She could see the reluctance in Greta's eyes and thought that under any other circumstances they might have become friends. "I detect an accent, and you used a word at the depot that I'd never heard."

"I'm from Holland. I arrived with my sisters a little over a year ago."

"I see. Then that accounts for your fair complexion and blonde hair. I never knew anyone from Holland."

"Well, now you do," Greta said good-naturedly with a bright smile.

Cora thought Greta was pretty and energetic, which would definitely cause competition where Jess was concerned. One look at Greta and he wouldn't be paying Cora any mind.

Cora turned and started making up her bed, suddenly very weary. She would need to visit the outhouse before bed, so she hurriedly undressed with her back to Greta and threw her robe over her nightgown. *Not that anyone would be seeing me outside for miles around!* But she clamped her mouth shut instead of grumbling out loud. She lifted the lamp off the table and pushed against the creaking back door, then traipsed quickly to where the not-so-inviting outhouse stood in the silvery moonlight.

Greta had been counting sheep, praying for sleep to take over, when she heard a loud thumping outside. Had Cora locked herself out? She had visited the outhouse more than once, and the disturbance kept Greta from sleeping. Was her stomach upset?

A scream came from behind the cabin, and the sound brought Greta bounding out of bed with a chill coursing down her spine. Frantically, she yanked open the heavy pine door and squinted into the night, her eyes trying to adjust with the aid of the moon hanging high over the timberline. She shivered with fear.

3

Greta stumbled wildly down the steps. Had Cora fallen into the hole in the outhouse? Greta had gone only a couple of steps when she felt like she'd swallowed her heart. There was something big and dark moving near the outhouse. Oh, heavens above! It was a bear! She froze momentarily, then whirled back up the steps despite the cries emanating from the privy. Back inside the cabin, aided by the light of the full moon streaming through the window, she quickly scanned each corner for a weapon. Wasn't there a gun somewhere? Sure enough, there was a rifle leaning against the wall. She grabbed it, not sure if it was loaded or not, and flew back outside.

"Help! Please, somebody!" came Cora's pitiful plea.

"Stay put, Cora!" Greta answered. The huge bear was in clear view now, prowling by the side of the privy, making deep-throated noises as it stood on hind legs and scratched at the wood door. It dropped to its feet when it saw Greta. She could smell the stench of its breath and body from where she stood nervously holding the rifle at shoulder level. With pounding heart and adrenaline coursing through her, she took aim and squeezed the trigger. The loud boom and the force of the gun sent her sprawling in the dirt.

She missed her mark and fired again into the darkness, but there were no more bullets loaded. Apparently the noise scared the bear, and its huge form lumbered off, disappearing into the dense trees. Thank God for the one shot!

She struggled to untangle her feet from her flannel nightgown and stood up. "It's all right now, Cora! You can come out," Greta said, her hands still shaking. Peter had showed them how to use a gun, but she'd never had any reason to until now. She shook the dirt from the back of her nightgown.

The door flung open wide, and Cora's white face appeared. She fell into Greta's arms. "Oh, God has mercy! Thank you for saving my life!" Cora said, then pulled away.

In truth Greta was just as shaken, but she didn't want Cora to know. "Oh, don't be so dramatic! I just scared him off. You'd do the same for me," she said, one arm around Cora and the other holding the rifle at her side. "Let's go back inside. That bear may still be lingering around."

Once inside, Cora dropped into bed and crawled under the quilt, still shivering. Whether from cold or fright, Greta wasn't sure.

"Do you feel okay? You've been up several times tonight."

Her voice low and quivering, Cora answered, "I had a little stomach upset. I'm sorry if I disturbed you. Bears were the last thing on my mind tonight." She had pulled the quilt up to her chin, and her eyes were as big as dinner plates.

Greta leaned the gun in the corner by her bed, hoping she wouldn't have need of it again. She brushed the dirt off her bare feet and hopped back into bed.

"Thanks again, Greta," Cora said. "I was scared to death. I never had to face anything like this in Boston."

"You're welcome. Now we'd better get some sleep. It's been a very long day." Greta yawned. "We'll have plenty to discuss with Zach tomorrow."

"Where in the world did you get off to

tonight, Zach? I could've used your help right about closing time. I was unusually busy," Jess said. He glanced up at the clock on the fireplace mantel when his brother stomped upstairs to their living quarters. It was after nine o'clock, and they were usually in bed early so they could be up promptly to open the store.

"Sorry. I had a little personal business to attend to," Zach answered as he removed his boots. He sighed as he wiggled his toes through his socks. "I'm gonna have to order new boots from that Montgomery Ward catalog. Either my feet have grown or I've been wearing the wrong size — not to mention my waistline is expanding!" he said, eyeing Jess.

Jess chuckled as he looked up from his easy chair, where he'd been reading the newspaper. "It's all those great Sunday dinners after church with Agnes Cartwright. You've picked up a few pounds — but I think you could stand to add a few more."

Zach put his boots neatly beside his bed, then began picking up Jess's shirt and pants strewn about the room. Jess watched as Zach followed the trail to their shared bedroom, where another shirt was flung across Zach's bed. Jess's bed was already a mess. Zach rolled the soiled pants and shirt

41

into a tight ball and placed them by the door. "How many times do I have to pick up your things off my bed?" he called over his shoulder.

Jess shrugged. "Anyone ever told you that you're starting to sound like a nagging wife?" He teased Zach but knew it was aggravating for his brother that he wasn't tidy. Jess always swore he'd get better at it.

Zach grinned in spite of his exasperation and poked his head through the doorway just as Jess threw the cushion at him. "Speaking of which — I have something to talk to you about."

Jess rose and started toward the bedroom. "Can it wait till morning? I'm going to bed now. My back is aching, and I'm not in the mood to talk about my needing a wife, if that's what's on your mind." Lately it seemed that was the focus of Zach's discussions. He slipped off his pants and shirt, leaving his long handles on, and sank into the softness of his bed, barely listening to his brother's ramblings.

Zach followed him. "It *is* on my mind. Partly. You know that I've been working on that small piece of land in my spare time, and one day I'll have me a small spread. I hate to leave you in the lurch when I'm ready to go. You need help, but more importantly, you need a wife." He pulled his shirt off, folded it, and placed it on top of the bureau for another day's wear. "I have someone I want you to meet tomorrow right after breakfast."

"What . . . ?" Jess answered sleepily, closing his eyes as soon as his head hit the pillow.

Jess sipped the strong coffee that he'd made earlier and slipped his apron on. He enjoyed the quietness of the morning hour before the town came to life. He raised the window shade and flipped the sign over, then unlocked the door. Light was just beginning to spread over the city, struggling weakly through morning clouds. Could be they'd see a brief period of rain, which normally made the day pass a little slower for him. He eased out the door and sat down on an overturned water barrel, thinking about his life thus far.

Many of the friends he'd known since childhood had married and had a passel of kids. He was still in his twenties and was in no hurry, as his brother seemed to think. He wasn't sure he wanted kids — but sometimes he found himself lonely when he took time to actually think about it, which was more frequently as of late. After his other brother died, Jess felt a part of himself missing. The three of them had been so tight. No wife was going to bring Bryan back.

He took another swig from his cup and wondered if this loneliness was from losing his younger brother or from needing a woman. Preacher Harrell always said that everyone needed a "helpmeet." But how did he know for sure?

Well, I'd better get to writing up orders before I get a tongue-lashing from Miss Agnes when she marches in today! He smiled at the thought of her. She was really a good person, and he'd seen her shooting a glance or two at him and Zach during church or when she was shopping in the store. He hadn't given her any indication lately that he was interested in her romantically, but that hadn't stopped her from trying.

He flung the last drop of his cold coffee into the street and went back inside, ready for whatever the day would hold. He enjoyed the smells that lingered in his store: leather, tobacco, liniment, and the wood-burning stove. Usually he was surrounded by a few of the old-timers jawing about the goings-on of Central City.

This was his life and he liked it well enough, but would a woman want to share it? Central City had a lot to offer in culture and had been all but declared a metropolitan city that held more influential people than Denver. But still — it was a mining town, growing fast and furious, with a lot of rough edges.

He strolled back inside, and his eye immediately landed on a large table with bolts of fabric all in a jumble after Agnes's last visit. Jess shook his head. He'd meant to straighten that *and* the pile of boots in the corner for customers to try on before ordering. He'd do it later. He slipped behind the service counter and pulled out his tablet for ordering. Best to work on that before the day became busy.

As he had the thought, the bell over the door jangled, and in piled his friends Silas and Annabelle Mead and their three young children, with Annabelle desperately trying to maintain control. The kids were already running in all directions at once.

He moved to ask if he could be of help when his good friend Cole Cartwright strode through the door behind them. Jess was glad to hear Zach finally clomp down the stairs and hurry over to assist Silas.

"Howdy, Jess." Cole extended his hand to give Jess a brief handshake. "Life treatin' you fair these days?"

"Nothing to complain about. I'm busier than ever, but that's always a good thing, I figure," Jess said. "How's things out at the Circle D?"

Cole pushed back his black Stetson, giving Jess a level gaze. "Since Pa died I'm doing my best to keep everything running on the ranch. I'll be driving in a herd to the rail soon and need to pick up supplies. Lots to get done before snow threatens, and we know that could be just about any day now." He fished in his vest pocket for his list of items and handed it to Jess.

Jess took the list and glanced over it. "I'll have this together for you in no time. Do you have something to do in the meantime?"

Cole chuckled. "Matter of fact, I do have a couple of things to do while I'm in town." He clapped Jess on the back. "Thanks, Jess," he said, strolling toward the door. "Oh, by the way, Agnes said to ask you for dinner on Sunday after church." He tipped his hat and stepped outside, causing the bell above the door to jingle loudly.

Jess stood there for a few seconds, his mind on Agnes. What excuse could he make for not having Sunday dinner? He sure was sick of his own cooking and Zach's wasn't much better, but he didn't want Agnes to get any ideas about the two of them. He

knew exactly what she had on her mind —
settling down. But he wasn't ready, and he
was certain it wouldn't be with her in the
first place.

"Jess, where in tarnation did you put those
new handsaws we just got in? Silas needs
one and I've looked everywhere." Zach
slapped his thigh in exasperation, then
glanced up at the big schoolhouse clock
hanging above the dry-goods counter.

"You watching the clock for some reason?"
Jess squinted at his brother, but Zach didn't
answer as Annabelle walked up, holding
tightly to her child's small hand. Jess turned
on his heel. "I'll go get the saw for Silas. I
think I remember where I placed the box."
Jess scooted to the back of the storage area
as Zach moved to the front of the store.

"Zach, do you think you could fit Sue with
a pair of warm boots for winter? The fur-
lined type?" Annabelle's face was serious
and her dark curls bobbed as she spoke. "I
declare she's growing up fast."

Zach leaned down to tweak Sue's cheek
affectionately. "I'm sure we can —" The
shop bell clanged, and Zach straightened
and smiled as his two protégées swept into
the store, their looks somber. He fully

expected them to ask for fare to return
home.

4

"Annabelle, would you excuse me for a moment?" Zach asked, never taking his eyes off the two ladies who stood waiting.

Annabelle nodded. She followed the direction of his gaze and studied the women as Silas joined her, his hands full of sundry items. Zach was about to head toward the ladies when Silas asked how his ranch plans were going.

Just then Jess emerged from the storage area with a shiny saw in his hand and made his way to where the group stood. He set the saw on the counter. "Here ya go. Nicest saw I could pick for you." He glanced over at the two women, who were now looking around.

"Go on and finish your shopping and we'll tally you up," Jess said. "Excuse me a moment." Silas nodded and Jess strode over to greet the women.

"Good morning, ladies. What can I help

you with this morning?"

Zach groaned. He'd wanted to reach Greta and Cora before Jess.

"We're here to see Zach," Greta said.

Zach strode quickly from the other side of the room and walked past his brother, who stared openly at the ladies.

"I'm here. How was breakfast?" Zach was thinking neither of them looked too friendly this morning.

Greta took a step closer to Zach and glared at him, her fists clenched at her side. "Maybe you should be asking how our night was." Zach stared back at her while Jess stood watching the interaction between the ladies and his brother.

Cora piped up, "It was miserable. I was scared half out of my mind!"

Zach dragged his eyes away from Greta. "Now, Cora, why in the world would you be scared out of your mind? That cabin is right cozy and well built."

Greta suddenly backed away from Zach. "What she means is we had a visit from a grizzly!"

Sue sucked in a deep breath and hugged her mama's leg tight, staring up at Greta with frightened eyes.

Greta tapped her toe on the hardwood floor. "It's a good thing there was a gun left behind by your trapper friend."

"I'd made a trip to the outhouse," Cora said, her face turning pink, "and got stuck in there when I heard this weird growling sound. I knew it wasn't a dog. Greta saved my life last night!"

Annabelle and Silas were all ears now, and Jess pressed closer with interest.

Greta smoothed down the front of her dress with her hands. "Well, Cora, I wouldn't go that far, but I think I scared him away."

"I was too scared to open the outhouse door, I can tell you that!" Cora's bottom lip trembled as she fidgeted with the buttons on her jacket.

Zach reached out a hand to Cora, but Greta pushed it away. "I'm really sorry he didn't show up while I was there, but sounds like Greta took things in hand all right." His chuckle seemed to further irritate the two.

"Cabin? What cabin? Zach, why don't you enlighten me?" Jess said, wiping his hands on his apron.

Zach's face reddened. He could feel everyone's eyes on him. "They're staying over at Jeb's cabin."

Jess looked sharply at him. "And just what

might you have to do with these two young ladies?"

Silas and Annabelle nodded their curiosity. He might as well go on and break the news to his brother now, while he was listening for once. Zach stood between the two ladies, draping an arm around each of their shoulders. "I want you to meet two very important women in your life, Miss Greta Olsen and Miss Cora Johnson. One of which will be *your* future bride."

Greta smacked at his hand and Cora took a step back.

Annabelle's eyes widened, and Silas gave his wife a warning look.

Zach sighed. Nothing like having an audience. Jess would get him for this.

"Oh my . . ." Sue said.

Jess pulled back with surprise. His gaze flew from Zach to the two women, who stood waiting. "*My* future bride?"

"Yep! Thanks to the US mail."

"Zach, what in the world are you talking about? I haven't ordered a bride! Have you been drinking or spending too much time talking to your cattle?"

"That's what I tried to talk to you about last night, but you went to sleep before I could — and you know I don't drink."

Jess's face was a thundercloud waiting to

burst. Looking over at the mail-order brides, he said, "My brother has brought you here under false pretenses. I'm very sorry if you've been inconvenienced, but he will see to it that you have fare back to where you traveled from, won't you, Zach?"

Greta pulled off her gloves and slammed them down on the counter. "I think you'd better explain to your brother what's going on, Zach." Cora opened her mouth to speak, but Greta laid a hand on her sleeve, so she pressed her lips together in a tight line.

Zach touched his brother's arm. "Can I have a word with you privately?"

Silas turned to Annabelle. "Let's go find those boots for Sue, shall we?" Before Annabelle could respond, he took hold of Sue's hand to propel her and his wife away from the brothers.

"There's nothing you could say in private that you can't say to me right here and now!" Jess's jaw clamped tight, and Zach knew if his jaw muscle twitched, he was in no mood to reason.

"Oh, I think there might be a few things I can say." Zach shifted from one foot to the other.

Greta fingered the gold locket around her neck, giving Zach a reproachful look.

"Please, go ahead. Don't stop on our account. One thing I won't be is an intrusion on such an industrious and busy mercantile owner as yourself, Mr. Gifford." She looked around with obvious disdain at the cluttered store.

Zach grinned. "Now don't go gettin' your petticoats in a tangle. We'll work this out."

"Perhaps it would be best if we left you two alone to talk," Cora said. "We can have a look around until you're through."

"I think that would be wise." Zach flashed a look at Jess. "What do you say, Brother?"

Jess threw his hands up in complete exasperation. "Let's go." He stomped toward the back of the store.

Once they were behind the curtain separating the store from supplies, Jess's tension mounted. "Zach, have you taken leave of your senses? I don't need a bride. I'm perfectly fine living alone and running the store." Jess folded his arms across his chest.

"No, you just think you are. You couldn't run this place without my help and you know it. I'd much rather be out punching cattle."

Jess caught the seriousness of his brother's true feelings in that moment. Had he unintentionally forced Zach to work with him?

"I'm sorry if you're angry with me. I tried to broach the subject last night." Zach ran his hands through his thick, wavy hair. "What you *need,* Jess, is a wife, a helper — not me! Someone to help you run the place who *wants* to, and who can rub your back at night when you've been standing all day." Zach propped his hip against the rough tabletop, letting his leg dangle. He nonchalantly picked up a knife, whacked off a hunk of cheddar cheese, and smiled at his brother, his eyes twinkling.

"I do just fine without a wife, and if you're so all-fired ready to start ranching, then go ahead, and don't let the door hit you in the back as you leave! What I do or don't do about a wife is my business, not yours." Jess drew closer and poked Zach in the chest with his finger. "Understand?"

"Would you just calm down a minute and listen to reason? I'm trying to help you. You're so distracted with running this place and making everyone happy that you don't give yourself a passing thought. I took it upon myself to help you out by placing an ad for a bride — actually, two. I thought if you had two to pick from, that would make it easy."

Jess closed his eyes briefly and shook his head. "Why didn't you just ask me about your idea?"

" 'Cause you would've said no." Zach swallowed the bite of cheese and reached for another, but Jess stopped him.

"Would you quit that while we're having a serious discussion?" Jess wanted to smack him upside the head. But then he had to admit that Zach was right — he never would take the time to find a wife. Men outnumbered the women in Central City five to one, so it was unlikely he'd ever find a single woman to his liking. Men clamored over every female as soon as they stepped foot off the train. During the winter the passes were closed, so they were basically shut off for a few months at a time.

Zach wiped his hands on his apron. "Sorry. But would you just relax? I think this will all work out, and these two ladies are eager for a husband and are willing to work in the store until you decide between the two of 'em. You can kill two birds with one stone, so to speak."

"If — and I mean *if* — I decide to go along with this nutty idea, I certainly won't be courting that outspoken one. In fact, *you* can court one of them!"

"Me?" Zach cocked an eyebrow.

Zach's look of surprise gave Jess a momentary feeling of elation. "Yes, Zach. I'm just giving you a taste of your own medicine." Jess smiled, thinking Zach's little plan had backfired. He knew that Zach wasn't interested in marriage until he got his ranch established.

"Does that mean you'll let them stay and work in the store?"

Jess scratched the stubble on his face. He hadn't taken time to shave this morning. Had he known two pretty ladies would arrive to meet him, he would've been more motivated to clean up a bit. He wondered what their first impression of him was. Against his better judgment, he found himself answering, "I'll give it a try, but not for you — for those poor ladies who traveled here on my account."

Zach slid down from the table, clapping his brother on the back. "That's more like it!"

"Don't get too excited. It'll only be for one month."

"One month?"

Jess shrugged. "Take it or leave it. This was your harebrained idea, after all."

"Oh, all right." Zach muttered something under his breath as he walked toward the front of the store, then paused. "I promise you, Jess, you won't regret it."

"We'll see about that, won't we?" Jess

watched his brother saunter back to the two waiting brides and their customers. What had he just gotten himself into?

Heaven help me!

5

Jess walked to the counter and grabbed the list he'd originally started working on before his surprise interruption. This latest shenanigan of his brother's had really been over the top.

He kept one ear cocked to Zach's exchange with the ladies while he perused Cole's list. The one called Cora was pretty with her dark hair and deep-set eyes. She seemed more soft-spoken than the other lady, Greta, who was tall with blonde hair and a flawless complexion. But what struck him besides Greta's outspokenness was the brilliance of her cornflower-blue eyes — they were searching and knowing. Just the kind of critical vision that he needed to avoid. He watched as she fingered a gold locket hanging against her bosom. Something clicked in his memory about a locket, but he couldn't remember exactly what. Many women wore fashionable lockets nowadays. He even stocked several in the broad glass case in the store. Still . . .

Jess watched as his brother escorted the women to the storage area, to give them aprons, no doubt. As they walked past him, Cora seemed nervous, but Greta looked directly at him, flashing a mischievous smile.

"You can store your things right here," Jess heard Zach inform them, then their voices faded into the background.

Silas strode over to Jess. "Jess, I think we've found all we came for this morning. Mind giving me a total?" Annabelle and little Sue were right behind him.

"Of course. I see you found the perfect pair of boots for Sue. Where did your boys get off to?" Jess said as he tallied the items.

"Annabelle sent them back outside to run off some of their energy. They would only make more of a mess than you already have here," Silas teased.

"Aw, it's not that bad. Is it?" Jess was beginning to believe Silas and his brother thought alike.

Silas only gave him a wry smile, then winked at Annabelle.

Greta emerged from the storage room. "I can see how easily that type of mess could happen, but not for long. I'll help Mr. Gifford get things more organized around here,

Mr. . . . er . . ." She stuck her hand out. "As you heard Zach say, I'm Greta Olsen."

Silas shook her hand. "I'm Silas Mead. Nice to meet you, ma'am. And this here," he indicated with a sweep of his large hand, "is my wife Annabelle and our daughter Sue."

"I've never met a mail-order bride before. You have an accent." Annabelle nodded.

"I'm from Amsterdam." Greta gave Annabelle a cordial smile. Jess couldn't help but wonder, *Is she always this happy?* Jess considered himself a cheerful person. But most women he knew were moody. Happy one minute and cantankerous the next.

"Oh my! Such a long way from home." Annabelle pursed her lips together in surprise.

Jess knew that nosy Annabelle would try to dig as much information as she could from Greta, who would probably not even notice that she'd been interrogated.

"Not really. I've been here for more than a year. I traveled from my sister's home in Wyoming."

"I see." Annabelle's eyebrows arched upward. "Welcome to Central City."

Greta leaned down to Sue. "It's nice to meet you, Sue. I see you're going to have a nice pair of sturdy snow boots for school,

61

but perhaps I can help you find something more appropriate to wear when it's nice out. What do you say?"

Sue looked at her mother, who nodded, then turned back to Greta. "I'd like that, Miss Greta."

Greta took the little girl's hand, and they traipsed off in the direction of the shoe department, such as it was, between the crowded aisles.

Annabelle turned back to Jess and Silas. "What a nice young woman you've hired, Jess. I'm sure she'll be a big help to you."

Jess didn't say a word as he wrapped their supplies in brown paper. Who did that woman think she was? One pair of boots for an elementary-school girl was sufficient! And what did she mean by "organize"? Jess was as organized as he wanted to be. He didn't need anyone to go rearranging things in his store. He could lay hands on any item desired by the clientele . . . most of the time.

Zach returned with Cora and said to Silas and Annabelle, "Greta and Cora will be working for Jess for a while."

His comment set Jess's teeth on edge as the couple stared at him. He noticed Cora's long lashes as she glanced down at her hands, saying nothing.

"You've got two right purty gals to choose

from, Jess. It might be a tough decision."
Silas counted out the money for his supplies, and Annabelle picked up the package.

"Don't you want to wait and see what Greta talks you into buying for Sue?" Jess asked.

"Oh, I plumb forgot. Annabelle, you'd better go see what she's showing Sue. Not that I'll buy it, that's for sure."

Annabelle handed him the package. "Stay put, Silas. I have a feeling you won't be able to talk Sue out of another pair of shoes. She could always use them for church or warmer weather."

Silas scratched his chin. "Way I look at it, she's growing too fast to own two pairs of shoes at a time right now. Serviceable work boots against the snow that's coming soon are good enough."

Annabelle shook her head, giving Silas a nudge on the shoulder as she walked past.

Jess chuckled. He knew that Silas had already lost that battle, but it was better for a man's ego to put up a protest. "Cora," he said, "why don't you start with wrapping up these items I've put aside for my friend Cole? I've still got a few more items to toss in the pile. He'll return soon, and I told him I'd have it all together."

Cora moved hesitantly toward the work

counter. She stared at the brown paper on the round metal holder, then began by pulling off a sheet. She glanced up at Zach, who winked at her. Jess had to admit, her smile was disarming. Just the kind that could make a man's heart flip-flop, which was what Jess's might do given half the chance.

"Don't worry about it being perfect. Cole will never even notice, I'm sure," Zach said, handing her a roll of twine.

Cora smiled back at Zach. "I have a lot to learn. I've never worked in a store before." She folded a pair of pants in half, then wrapped paper around it.

"I'll be taking you and Greta around the store today so you can familiarize yourself with how we run the place." Zach leaned one hip against the counter, propping his elbow on top. "Soon as Greta's finished with Sue."

"Did I hear you ladies say you were staying in a cabin?" Silas asked.

"Yes. Zach has put us up in his friend's cabin at the edge of town, but I hope it won't be for long."

"Not long," Zach remarked cheerfully. "Just as soon as Jess picks his bride, one of you'll be moving to the quarters upstairs."

Cora quirked an eyebrow. "Upstairs?"

Jess was just about to comment when the

chatty Greta, her arm about Sue's shoulders, walked up with a pair of Sunday-go-to-meeting shoes. If she could talk Annabelle into buying another pair of shoes, she just might be good for business.

"Greta's right. These will be perfect for church," Annabelle said, placing the shoes on the counter. " 'Course, if Joshua and Stephen see them, they'll be begging for something else too." She giggled. "But go ahead and add these to the bill, Jess."

"You got it, Annabelle." Jess took the shoes and handed them to Cora to wrap.

"And by the way, why don't you and the ladies drive over to our place for supper on Friday?" Annabelle turned to Zach. "And you too, Zach. We need to show these ladies a little Central City hospitality."

"Thanks, that's mighty kind of you. We'd love to." Jess glanced at Greta and Cora for approval. "If that's something they'd like to do."

Greta's eyes sparkled in amusement when she nodded at him. "That would be nice."

Jess's heart started thumping when he locked eyes with Greta. His hands were none too steady either as he handed Silas the wrapped shoes for Sue. What in the world was wrong with him? He'd have to avoid Greta's flirtatious eyes. She could be trouble. Cora, on the other hand, was more his type — quiet and reserved.

"Annabelle, we'd be delighted to come."

"Then it's settled —"

"What's settled?" Cole strode in, looking around at the newcomers. "My order?"

Zach laughed. "Hardly, but I'll get back to finishing the order that Jess started." He snagged the list that Jess had put aside and sauntered away.

Cole tipped his hat. "And who might your friends be, Jess?"

Jess watched as his friend surveyed the two ladies. Now just how was he supposed to announce that he had two mail-order brides? He clenched his teeth when he thought about how Zach had it all planned out. Cole liked pretty women and made no bones about it.

"Cole." Silas offered him a handshake. "We were just inviting Jess and Zach for supper Friday, as well as Greta and Cora, two mail-order brides who just arrived yesterday. You may as well come too, unless you've got plans."

Cole's eyes darted over to Greta and Cora. "Mail-order brides . . . Well, Jess, I didn't know you entertained the idea of marriage!"

Jess groaned inwardly. "I'm not sure that I

do, Cole. Meet Greta Olsen and Cora Johnson." He couldn't help but notice how both ladies stood straighter when Cole's eyes swept over them. His good looks had turned many a head in Central City. It shouldn't matter to him that Cole had their full attention, but it did.

"How do you do?" Cole took their hands in turn and bowed slightly. "Seems Jess is full of surprises."

Cora flushed, and Greta gave Cole a broad smile. Had she smiled at Jess like that? He didn't think so.

"Maybe the surprise was more from Zach," Cora murmured. There was an awkward moment of silence as she gave Cole a friendly gaze.

"We'd better go find the boys and head on back home. Like I said, you're welcome to come too, Cole," Silas said. He placed his hand on Annabelle's elbow and propelled her to the door.

"I'll consider it," Cole said, hooking his thumbs in his jean pockets.

Annabelle waved a quick goodbye, and they hurried out the door in search of their boys. A blast of cold air rushed in as the door refused to close.

"I've been meaning to work on that door frame," Jess said as he lifted the doorknob and shoved it hard so the latch plate caught.

Cole chuckled. "Jess, that door's been like that for two years now."

Jess shot him a daggerlike look, annoyed with his friend.

"I'll be happy to put that on your list of things to do, Jess," Greta said, reaching for a pencil.

"List? What list? I never make a list," Jess said. "I have it all tucked away up here." He tapped his finger against his forehead.

Greta's laughter rang out. "Well, now others will be able to see, uh, up there," she teased. "You'll have a list."

Cole placed his hand on his hip. "Miss Greta, if you get tired of wrangling with Jess or Zach, I'd be mighty happy to take you out to dinner at one of our fine restaurants. And of course you too, Miss Cora."

Cora looked from Greta to Jess without responding, but Jess thought her unhappy look said it all.

Jess humphed, giving Cole's shoulder a friendly poke. "You can't begin to handle one woman, much less two, my friend!" What in tarnation was Cole trying to do? Sweep them off their feet?

"Thank you for your invitation, Cole, and it was a pleasure to meet you, but we've barely gotten settled. Now if you will excuse us." Greta turned to Cora and said, "Come on, Cora, let's go find Zach so he can give us whatever instructions he thinks we'll need. I'll wager it won't be too much from the looks of things around here."

"I'm right behind you," Cora said as she slipped an apron over her head and tied the strings.

"I don't give up easily," Cole bellowed as they walked away.

6

Jess decided he needed some time alone. He left Zach in charge of the store, saddled his horse, Stomper, and rode off toward Black Hawk. He told Zach that he needed to check on Granny since it had been a week since either of them had dropped by. The death of his parents from influenza last year, shortly after his younger brother's death, had taken a toll on his grandmother. She seemed to age overnight far beyond her seventy years. But even though she'd slowed down, she wanted to live right where she was. Not too far from her grandsons, where she could keep an eye on them, and the graves of her son, daughter-in-law, and grandson.

Then again, it was hard to know where Black Hawk ended and Central City began these days, with the huge influx of miners and gold seekers who passed through on their way to seek their fortunes. But he wasn't complaining. Far from it. His mercantile business had increased dramatically. Maybe Greta and Cora had come at just the right time. He'd never been busier, and a helper of any sort could be useful to have around the store. He didn't fool himself with entertaining ideas of romance. Life was about work for him, and any woman he married would have to understand that.

His mind meandered just like the trail down to his grandmother's house. The August sun's warmth on his back felt good, but Jess knew it would be replaced by sharp canyon winds by the middle of September. He found himself smiling. Heavens above, he loved Colorado! Every day was like God's gift of treats served just for him. The pristine, cloudless blue sky and pine-laden scent were downright intoxicating. Much like the gleam in Greta's eyes.

Now whatever in the world made him think of that comparison? Why, he'd only just met her this morning, and Cora was right pretty as well. He was still mystified as to why Zach would do such a thing without telling him. It made Jess sharply aware that Zach preferred making his own way. He wasn't sure how that had escaped him.

He gave a gentle tug on Stomper's reins and paused at the crest of the bluff, gazing at the busy little town below. Even from this vantage point, he could see Granny's small house with its picket fence and bright trailing flowers. His heart pinched when he remembered how she'd clung to him and cried when they buried his parents — so unlike her usual tough exterior. She told him a parent is never supposed to bury her children. Jess reckoned she was right about that. Only the good Lord knew the reasons why.

Jess nudged Stomper further down the trail, suddenly anxious to see Granny and have a slice of her rhubarb pie.

Greta listened intently to Zach, who was explaining to her and Cora the particulars of running the general store.

"When we place orders, we have a checklist of supplies that we compare to the shipping paper we receive once they arrive, which is called a bill of lading." He turned the paper around so they could get a look at the sheet. "Then I just make a check mark against the bill of lading when it reaches us. I keep a labeled file right here under the counter so everything is easy to find."

"My, you're very organized," Cora said.

"I have to be because Jess isn't." He

chuckled. He pointed at some crates. "There's yesterday afternoon's orders that I checked off, but both of you can start un-crating when we're through here." Zach punched some numbers into the huge cash register. "Just put the price in on this machine, and it will total the customers' sales up for you. At the end of the day, I'll total the receipts and make sure they match what's in the drawer here. Any questions?"

"Doesn't look too complicated to me," Greta commented. "Do you decide where supplies must go, or are you up to a bit of change around here?"

Zach came over to stand next to the ladies. "You can see where sundry items go and farming implements are stored," he said with a sweep of his hand. "I'd be tickled to death if you two decide the most appropri-ate way to handle the clothing area, and maybe come up with a better way to display some of our supplies to their best advantage, if you know what I mean. I'm not good in that department, and you can tell we need some suggestions."

"I believe we can handle that, don't you, Cora?"

Cora sighed, glancing around the store. "No offense, Zach, but anything has got to be a little better than this."

Zach tapped the counter. "Good! No offense taken. Have at it, ladies."

Greta stood with her hands on her hips, making a *tsking* noise while she and Cora stared at the crates of supplies yet to be opened. They were haphazardly stacked in front of a sagging wood table laden with fabric bolts in total disarray.

"Whew! Where on earth do we start, Greta?" Cora shook her head. "I've never seen a store stocked this way, but they seem to do a very brisk business, don't they?"

Greta took a deep breath. "They do, but that doesn't mean we can't make things a little easier to find when a customer inquires." She moved toward the stack of crates. "First we need to move these, but let's not open them until we can make sense of this table and then see where the new supplies can go," she said. With Cora's help she was able to shove some of the crates to the side in order to get to the table of fabric. "Let's put the big bolts all to one side and the remnants at the other end."

Cora did as Greta suggested. "Wonder why they keep the scraps of material in the first place? Seems to me that they just take up valuable space."

Greta paused and propped her elbows on

the bolts of fabric, staring at Cora. "Don't you know that remnants are used especially for making quilts, among other things?"

Cora flushed. "I guess I did know that, but I'm afraid I'm not very acquainted with the art of sewing."

"Oh?" Greta waited for her to continue while she smoothed the wrinkled fabric and wrapped it around a bolt of blue calico.

"My mother never sewed or cooked that I can remember. We had servants to do that. About the only thing I learned was how to quilt, thanks to my church social."

"I don't mean to pry, but why would you want to be a mail-order bride? I mean," Greta hurried to explain, "domestic skills are one of the requirements." Greta watched Cora's face to see if her expression would be enlightening. Was Cora from a wealthy family? Greta had the distinct feeling there was more to Cora than met the eye. Perhaps after they knew each other better, she would open up a little.

Cora smoothed the fabric, then placed it on the pile with the others. "It's simple. I was ready to be on my own." Her tightly pursed lips and serious face made it evident that she had nothing more to add, and she kept her eyes averted from Greta.

Well, if she didn't want to talk further,

Greta wouldn't press her. Instead she said, "You know, Jess might be able to let us have a few remnants that we could use in the cabin, as long as we're staying there temporarily. I'll have to ask." Looking around the store, she started thinking ahead. "After we get this place in better order, no telling what we'll uncover." She pushed a lock of hair from her brow and wiped her hands on her apron.

Cora put her hands on her hips and nodded. "You're right about that. I know it's a general store, but it could use a woman's touch."

Greta snapped her fingers. "That's it! A little sprucing up and there'd be even more customers, especially if products are displayed in a more appealing way."

Cora agreed. "Especially with the ladies." She smiled broadly.

"You could influence Jess to purchase fashionable items that would interest the females."

Cora flashed Greta a questioning look. "Me? I hardly think he would take my advice."

"I'm not so sure . . ." Greta looked at Cora's pretty face with her dark, sultry eyes, then at her day dress, which was definitely high quality. "Your dress is the height of fashion. You know more about that sort of thing than I do."

A look of pleasure swept over Cora's face. "Well . . . maybe."

"You're being modest." Greta grabbed Cora by the hand. "Come on, my friend! Let's open up those crates. We have much to do before Jess returns."

An hour later, Zach tossed them a funny look as he stood behind the receiving counter, but they sailed right on past him, each laden with a stack of clothing they carried to tackle the clothing area. Soon they returned, and Greta approached Zach, who was unpacking a box of harnesses. He looked up. "You need something?"

"You could put it that way, I suppose." Greta glanced at Cora, who gave her a slight nod. "Cora and I decided that since we are not betrothed to either you or Jess and we'll be working alongside you, a salary should be in order."

Zach's hands stilled, and he gave them a frank stare. "That would be fair. I don't know why I didn't think of it." He picked up a pencil and did some figuring on a tablet, then turned the paper around with an amount written down. "How about this?"

Cora and Greta peered at the tablet. Fifteen dollars for each of them per week.

Greta was happy with that and nodded to Cora her agreement.

"I believe that will be agreeable," Cora replied for both of them.

"Good. I'll let Jess know. It's only fair after how hard you two are working. I really do appreciate it, and eventually Jess will too."

Greta laughed. "We're not so sure about that, but unless he stops us, we'll keep at it." Zach nodded, and Greta and Cora turned back to the clothing area.

"Granny, that's the best rhubarb pie I've had in ages," Jess said, pushing his empty plate aside and downing the hot coffee.

Granny snickered. "You mean that's the only rhubarb pie you've had since the last time you were here." She stared at him over the rim of her china cup, taking a sip. "I hear tell you've got yourself in quite a predicament!" Her blue eyes twinkled.

Jess straightened in the ladder-back chair, and it protested under his weight. "Now how did you hear about that?"

"News travels fast where the towns are like bookends, you know." Granny pulled her shawl together, waiting for his response.

"That fool grandson of yours conspired behind my back and took it upon himself to decide what's best for me. He had no right."

Granny reached across the table and patted his hand. "Now, Jess, you know he had what's best for you in mind. Might not be so bad to have another woman in the family . . . or perhaps children."

"Children? Don't go having the great-grandkids before I've even picked the bride!" Jess huffed.

Granny sat back in her chair and crossed her arms. "Let me tell you a secret, young man. The only way you're gonna know which of the gals is the right one for you is to steal a kiss!"

Jess almost dumped his hot coffee in his lap. "I mean no disrespect, but you must have lost your mind somehow during the night, Granny."

Granny chuckled. "Maybe so . . . but when it comes to women, I know what they're thinking. They want to be held, kissed, and told that there's no one like them on earth. Makes 'em feel real special. If your toes start to tingle," she said, cocking her head at him for emphasis, "then I'll guarantee she's the one!"

Jess snorted. "Whoever heard of such a rule to verify love except you, Granny? Well, don't hold your breath. It's not likely that'll happen soon, leastways not until I decide to court one of them."

"You must have a feeling toward one of them one way or the other. I heard that they're both striking beauties."

Jess swallowed hard, not meeting her gaze. "Why don't you come see for yourself this week? You can give me your opinion, 'cause I know you will anyway. Might as well get it over with," he said, shoulders sagging.

Giving him a wink, Granny shoved her chair back, picked up the cups and saucers, and carried them to the sink. "I just might do that, my boy." She walked over and gave his shoulders a hard squeeze, leaning her gray head against his. She wasn't much taller than his shoulder with him in a sitting position, and the scent of her lavender soap lingered. It reminded him of the time when he was little and she'd held him on her lap after he'd scratched his knee. Remembering that now, he felt comforted knowing that she loved him with all her heart.

"Don't look like it's the end of the world just because you have two interested women," Granny said. "Could be it's just a new beginning for a bright future. There's a whole lot of men who would love to be in your shoes, I'll wager!"

By the time Jess had returned from his time away from the store, Greta was feeling pleased with all she and Cora had accomplished. Once they'd straightened and moved things and swept the hardwood floor under the watchful eyes of Zach, the general store had taken on an entirely new look. Fresh and orderly!

Greta laughed when she saw Cora's smudged face and the hair slipping from the knot at the back of her head.

"What's that for?" Cora laughed. "You're a sight yourself!" She drew Greta over to the cheval glass between the racks of apparel so she could see for herself, and they both giggled. Greta wiped her dirty hands on her soiled apron. Her long blonde braids that had been wound tightly around her head this morning had long since slipped from the hairpins, and strands of her hair were sticking out. Somehow she'd torn her dress at the shoulder. Probably from lifting some of the wooden crates that held various supplies.

The bell clanged over the store door. Zach followed a customer to the sidewalk just as Jess returned. Greta and Cora paused in their chattering, watching as Jess stopped dead in his tracks at the front, surveying his store with wide eyes.

"What happened here?" he boomed.

Both women started to speak at once until

he held up his hand. "One at a time, please."

Cora nudged Greta forward. Greta could see that instead of him being pleased, Jess's face looked like a thundercloud. Had she taken too many liberties too soon?

"We . . . uh . . ." Greta licked her lips and spoke with trepidation. "I thought we'd tidy up a bit, so we moved a few things around here and there, and now you have more walking space to get around the store." She gave him a timid smile and waited for his response. Surely he would be pleased.

Jess stood with his hands on his hips, his face reddening. "I don't remember telling you to do that. Now I won't be able to find anything!" He flung his arms open wide.

Cora's dark brown eyes flew open in surprise or fear — Greta wasn't sure which. Greta looked at Jess's handsome face and saw his jaw muscle twitching. "On the contrary, Jess. We restacked the material by type of fabric and color and moved the clothing apparel to one spot by size and gender, so —"

Jess interrupted her. "Confound it all! I don't care if you painted the counters red, you may as well move it all back! NOW!"

Cora shrunk back with fear, but Greta stood her ground. Her hands felt damp, so she pressed her palms against her apron.

With a little convincing, he'd relent. "I can't believe you wouldn't want to improve the appearance and functionality of your store so it could possibly bring you more custom- ers! Why can't you give —"

"I said now!" Jess's brown eyes snapped. They were a warm chestnut color much like Bryan's had been. Greta shoved the memory aside.

Jess stalked past them toward the back of the store, then stomped up the back stairs to the living quarters without a backward glance. His muddy boots left a trail across the freshly swept floor.

Greta gritted her teeth. "*Ach!* I just cleaned the floor." She clenched her fists against her side, and Cora seemed dumb- founded. Greta was thankful no customer was in the store to witness the outburst.

"What an ungrateful human being!" Cora exclaimed to Greta.

Zach returned, the smile fading from his face with one look at them. "What's wrong with you two? You look as if you've just seen a ghost."

"You mean monster, don't you?"

"Huh? What are you talking about?" Zach's forehead wrinkled.

"We've just been tongue-lashed, that's what!" Cora answered, her lips tight and arms folded.

Zach scratched his scraggly beard. "What did you say? By Jess? He doesn't have a mean bone in his body."

"Unless he's crossed," Greta retorted. "After working ourselves to death in this slipshod store, your brother informed us that every bit of the merchandise must be put back exactly as it was!"

Zach's booming laughter startled her. "You must be kidding. What you've done here is an improvement, to be sure. How could he not like this?" he asked with a sweep of his hand. "I do."

Cora sniffed. "Then you'd better ask him. Guess we'll put everything back, Greta."

"No, don't do that. I'll go talk to him. You ladies can call it a day. It's getting late. Go grab some supper at Mabel's and come back in the morning. Is there anything that you need from the store before you go back to the cabin? Soap? Towels?"

Cora shook her curly brown hair, then removed her apron. "I'm not sure I'm coming back. It seems that Jess is not at all happy we're here and working for him."

Zach stepped closer to Cora, lifting her hand. "Don't give up yet. This is only the first day. It'll take some getting used to — having two women take over, I mean."

"Is that how you think of it, Zach?" Greta noticed how he stroked Cora's hand.

"I didn't mean it the way it sounded," he said, dropping Cora's hand and turning to face her. He was just as handsome as his brother, but in a more rugged sort of way, and his movements were quicker, as if he was always in a hurry or had something more important to attend to. "Neither of us is used to having a woman around, telling us how to do things, much less two women. Be patient, he'll come around."

Greta hung her apron beside Cora's and lifted her wrap off the hook behind the counter. "I wasn't trying to tell him what to do, just trying to help with the overall appearance of the store. That's all. You must admit it was untidy."

"And I for one appreciate that. This was exactly what I was hoping for — someone to whip this place into shape. You two have done more in one day than I could have in a week even if I had the time, which I don't," he said, guiding them toward the door.

Greta paused and stared into brown eyes framed with thick lashes . . . eyes that looked so familiar somehow. "Are you telling me that the real reason you brought us here in the first place was to help run the store? Funny, yesterday you said Jess needed a wife. Which is it, Zach?" She poked a finger in his chest in agitation. "Maybe I should've stayed in Cheyenne."

Zach opened the door and nearly shoved them onto the sidewalk. "I've already told you. He needs a wife. A helpmeet, just like the Bible says. Anything else you can do around here to help out is mightily appreciated," he said, his lips in a hard line. "I'll see you two in the morning, and I'll straighten everything out. All right?"

"We have little choice at this point as I see it, but he'd better have a change in his disposition by morning or you'll be buying me a train ticket back home. Is that clear?" Greta folded her arms across her chest, trying to keep from saying something she shouldn't.

"Me too!" Cora chirped.

Zach clamped his mouth shut and nodded in agreement. "Oh, don't forget — keep the gun loaded tonight." His face was serious as he hurried back inside, letting the door clatter shut.

Greta was almost certain her entire plan had been a huge mistake. Why in the world had she believed answering an ad could work for her just because it had for Catharine? Especially after Zach had written let-

86

ters to two brides. She was furious with herself for falling for this mail-order-bride ad. She flounced off toward Mabel's as Cora fell into step beside her.

7

Jess poured himself a cup of coffee, glad that Zach always kept some on the stove for when they could catch a break, then sat down in his easy chair, which held a view of Main Street below. The rest of the afternoon and evening had been a flurry of activity, and though Zach caught his eye several times, he didn't mention a word of what had transpired between him and the two women. It was just as well because he had no intention of talking about it further.

How dare those two decide how he wanted things placed! Even now he felt hot under the collar. He was happy with things just as they were. He felt sure the rearranging had all been Greta's idea. There was no need for that when he knew down to the last nail where supplies were. Zach . . . well . . . that was another thing. He could never find a thing without asking Jess of its whereabouts.

He'd caught sight of the tops of Greta's

and Cora's shiny heads beneath his window as they'd stood talking with Zach. Whatever was said, neither of them looked pleased. Then he watched as Greta strutted down the walk fast and furious when Zach went back inside. Good! He didn't care if Greta was angry. It *was* his store. But he couldn't help noticing the sway of her hips beneath her serviceable work dress and how proudly she held her shoulders. Her braids had all but fallen down her slender back. He wondered how they didn't give her a headache when bound tightly against her scalp.

Women! Who could begin to understand them? He wasn't going to waste any more time contemplating them. Yet he'd continued to watch until she and Cora crossed over to Eureka Street, disappearing into the folks on their way home as the sun began to slide behind Bald Mountain. Now a sudden weariness overcame him, and he leaned back to rest his eyes.

Jess took a long, deep breath, trying to see through the thickets, squinting against the sun's rays. In the bright light, a gold locket flashed brilliantly in view and just as quickly disappeared. Was he hallucinating? If only he could just reach his brother . . . Why wouldn't his legs move? He extended his arms to pull his brother to safety and thought he was in reach of him just a few feet ahead, but he couldn't grasp him. He felt himself slipping, slipping, and the image of his brother became fuzzy until it faded away behind the boulders . . .

The door snapped open, and Zach strode in, waking Jess. Sitting up quickly, he ran his hand through his thick hair, smoothing it. "I must've dozed off for a moment."

Zach plopped in the chair opposite him and picked up the half-full mug. "I don't know how you sleep drinking that awful, thick stuff! Why didn't you make some up fresh? That pot's been simmering for a while." He wrinkled his nose in disgust, then set the cup down. "We need to talk."

Jess started to rise. "I have nothing I want to say, so if you've come to plead the ladies' case and —"

Zach's hand stayed him. "Can you hold on just a minute without getting all het up about it?"

Jess breathed deeply. "Okay. Spit it out, little brother."

"I told them not to return everything as it was. I think they did a great job of sprucing up the place, and that was just one day!" He paused, then continued on when Jess didn't interrupt. "Be honest with yourself.

You're madder by the fact that they did everything without asking for your approval than what you think the store looks like. Am I right?"

Jess waved his hand, swishing away a fly. What had he thought? Zach was right, but Jess didn't want to admit it. "Truth is . . . I *guess* it's an improvement, but I do have my own system and ways I intend to run the store. Now I'll never find a thing."

"You couldn't ever find or keep up with anything in the first place, Jess. This will make it easier on you. In fact, it was one of the two reasons that I placed the ad in the first place." Zach leaned back in his chair, looking more relaxed now.

Jess shot him a look. "And the other reason?"

"I told you — you need a wife," he answered calmly. "Someone to look after you, 'cause you're not doing such a great job yourself. Especially now that . . ." His voice trailed off.

Jess stared back at his brother's deep brown eyes, which crinkled at the corners when he was serious. "Little brother . . . I know you worry about me, and so does Granny, but I'm really doing okay in that department. My life is busy enough without having to worry about carving out time to give attention to a woman." Besides, Jess felt no confidence that *any* woman would really want to be married to him. Why would she? He was messy, he lived in clutter, and he couldn't seem to stay focused long enough to carry out his plans or remember all of his promises to customers.

"Since the women are here, let's make the best of it. You have to admit, they're both quite attractive. And on Friday you can get to know them better when we have dinner with Silas and Annabelle." Zach grinned. "Mmm, mmm, mmm. Annabelle makes the best apple pie around these parts."

Jess walked over to the kitchen area to place his coffee mug in the sink. "And what about you? We had a bargain that you'd court one of them yourself."

Zach got up from his chair and whacked his brother on the back. "I haven't forgotten. But you have to pick first. Which one of them appeals to you more?"

"Neither!"

"Come on now . . . not even the least bit? Cora has those pretty dark eyes, and Greta's are the color of a Colorado sky — or haven't you even noticed?"

He shuffled his feet and turned to Zach. "Oh, I've noticed them all right. One is timid and mealymouthed who doesn't know sheep from chickens without someone telling her, and the other one is pushy and thinks she's just a little lower than God with her gift of knowledge," Jess said with a snicker.

Zach laughed and shook his head. "You're being too hard on them. They're just trying to get your attention. Give 'em both a chance, will ya?"

Jess wanted to change the subject. "Instead of cooking tonight, why don't we lock up and go have a steak?"

"Sounds like a good idea to me," Zach said, grabbing his jacket and following Jess out the door and down the stairs.

"Oh, I forgot to mention, Granny will probably pop in to check the ladies out for herself tomorrow."

Zach sniffed. "Now why am I not surprised?"

On the way home, Cora had insisted that they stop at Mabel's. She was certain that Mabel could pack a supper for them to take to the cabin. She was worn out — she'd never pushed and pulled or stacked anything in her life, and her arms were so tired that if she hadn't been holding the basket of food, she'd let them dangle at her sides.

"Once we have our supper, I plan to wash

up and go to bed." Cora lifted the thick cloth covering the fried chicken and bread. The smells were tantalizing, and her stomach was growling. She wasn't used to having to find her own lunch, and the small sandwich hadn't held up. Everything was completely turned upside down for her now, but she had faith that things would eventually improve for her. *If* she could tough it out.

She was beginning to wonder if she could live in the quarters above the mercantile if it came to that. Visions of her parents' home swam before her, making her heart lurch.

Greta sighed. "That chicken smells heavenly. I'm glad you thought of this. After last night's episode, maybe we can get a good night's sleep and feel refreshed by morning. Though I wonder if Jess moved everything back."

"Hmm. He did seem very insistent about it." Cora's smile faded when she glanced over at Greta. "I'm sure he's quite angry with us, don't you think?"

"Yes, but he doesn't know yet that we'll be an asset to him. He only needs to give it some thought."

They were nearly to the cabin door, and light was fading quickly as the sun dropped below the Bald Mountain peak. "Perhaps

Zach was able to make him change his mind," Cora said while Greta unlocked the cabin door. "I sure hope so."

Greta pushed open the timber door, and Cora walked in behind her and placed the basket on the table. Looking around with a critical eye, Cora said, "It's not Mabel's homey café, but it'll do for now, I suppose. I never thought I'd be staying in a miner's cabin." Would this be the kind of life she'd be forced into? What would happen if Jess didn't pick her? She would have to find some type of work. She couldn't continue to work for Jess if he tossed her over for Greta.

Suddenly her heart squeezed tight in her chest. She couldn't go home. She couldn't bear to be humiliated that way. Was she even sure she wanted to be Jess's wife?

"Me neither, Cora. But any bed looks good to me at this moment. Let's just wash our hands so we can eat, then get to bed. Then we'll both go to the outhouse and stand guard for each other." Greta giggled.

Cora wholeheartedly agreed. Though they were vying for the same man, she hoped they would still be friends. She wanted a good friend, but she needed to be careful until she knew Greta better. People were not always what they seemed.

Zach saw Granny when she drew her wagon to a stop in front of the store. She was no stranger to early rising, and he wasn't surprised that she was here before the brides had made it in this morning. He put aside the crowbar he was using to open crates so he could assist her. Jess was busy working on the books at his desk in the corner.

"Mornin', Granny! You're out and about mighty early. Here, let me help you down," Zach said as he reached for her hand.

She cocked her head sideways to glance at him and smiled. "I'm always up early, you know that. And I suppose you know why I'm here." She stepped onto the boardwalk and he released her hand.

Ignoring her last comment, Zach asked, "Did you bring me a slice of pie? Or did Jess eat every last bit?"

Granny was still spry at seventy. She was fully gray-haired and pleasingly plump but with nice skin, which she protected with a straw hat. The only thing that gave her age away were the deep lines around the blue eyes peering up at him and the stoop of her shoulders.

"Now you know I brought pie," she answered, giving him a big squeeze. "Just reach in the back there. I have a whole rhubarb pie."

Zach did as he was told. He lifted the pie from a box in the back and peeked under the linen cloth. "Mmm, my mouth tastes it already. God bless you, Granny."

When Jess saw them come in, he laid his pencil down. "I thought you'd be coming today, Granny." He walked over to kiss her cheek.

"I had to. Needed to see for myself just what's going on here." She suddenly became still and clamped her lips together while she gazed about the store. "Heavens above! What happened here?"

"See, I told you it was the wrong thing to let those two mess with our setup." Jess cast his comment toward Zach. "They're like two cleaning fanatics. Everything was just fine as it was until they came."

"Not at all — I really like it." Granny's thin lips widened to smile at her grandsons. "You said the ladies did it? I don't believe I've seen it look this orderly since your parents died. How did you talk them into that?"

"He didn't!" Zach spouted. "Greta decided to make a few changes and Cora followed her instructions."

Granny folded her hands together and pressed them into her skirt. "Then she's one smart young woman. I can't wait to meet Greta . . . and the other one —"

"Cora. They should be arriving soon." Jess strode over to the counter and reached underneath for his apron.

Granny watched Jess and Zach open another crate. One side held Country Rose dishes. The other held Blue Willow china. Zach picked up a cup and admired its delicate shape.

"Tell me then, which of you is courtin' who?" Granny asked.

"Er . . . well . . . that's for Jess to choose, and he doesn't want to do that." Zach shifted from side to side. *Here it comes. She's about to lambaste me for sending for mail-order brides in the first place.*

Granny sashayed over to look inside the crate, then clapped her hands together. "These dishes are so pretty — and I have an idea that just might work to help you boys decide. I'll offer the young ladies some tea when they arrive. Zach, you will court the one who picks the Blue Willow, and Jess, you'll court the one who picks the rose pattern."

Jess scratched his unshaven beard. "Well now, Granny, what if they both pick the same pattern? What then?"

"Hardly likely, but if that happens we'll move to plan two."

Zach laughed. "Which is?"

Granny tapped her finger on her chin. "Hmm, I don't know. But I don't have time to stand here yammering with you if I'm to make tea before they get here." She moved toward the stairs. "Jess, is that tray still in the cupboard where I left it last time?" she called over her shoulder.

"Yes, ma'am. Want me to go get it for you?" Jess started after her.

"No. I'll set the hot water to boiling. You bring me up two cups from each of the china pieces. Oh, and Zach, look for that special tea you gave me. I think they'd like it," she said, now at the top of the stairs. "And hurry up."

"Sure thing, Granny." Zach knew once Granny set her mind to something, there was no way she'd change it. "What about you, Jess? Does this sound like something you could live with?"

"Do I really have a choice?"

"Not with Granny giving orders. I don't want to cross her. No sirree." Zach reached into a tin behind the counter for the special tea. "I'll run this up to her and we'll just act normal, minding our business, when they arrive."

Jess glanced down at his pocket watch. "It's nearly eight o'clock now. Hope they didn't wind up with bear trouble again. How long do you intend for them to stay out in that cabin away from town?"

Zach paused on his way upstairs. "It won't hurt them none. Maybe toughen them up a little. It's really all we can afford now anyway."

"Hmm . . . don't seem right to me. They seem like genteel ladies."

"Are you getting tenderhearted now, Jess?" Zach teased and continued on upstairs without waiting for a response.

Jess's tough exterior belied the kindness that Zach knew was in his heart — as well as the sorrow. "Time heals all wounds," Granny always said, but Zach wasn't sure about that.

8

The Colorado sun was bright, hanging high in the sky, and puffy white clouds floated overhead as Greta and Cora walked down the busy streets of Central City.

"Goodness! We're late!" Cora grumbled. "Doesn't the mercantile open at eight o'clock?" she asked as she and Greta scurried down the sidewalk to work. "We dawdled at breakfast too long."

"I believe you're right. But I think we're only a few minutes behind. The walk takes longer than we thought. At least I had a good night's sleep. How about you?" Greta glanced sideways at Cora. There were dark circles under her eyes this morning. Was she worried about something? Like who Jess would pick as his bride?

Greta's own pulse had beat hard last night as she'd drifted off to sleep. She'd found Jess very attractive with his deep-set brown eyes and thick, dark brows. He had a pleasant-sounding voice that seemed to resonate from somewhere deep within his chest. *Better not get too attracted,* she chided herself. Cora was very cultured and pretty. What if he picked her? How would she feel? And they were fast becoming friends. Greta would step aside and be happy for her, but then what would be left for her to do?

Cora's heels rang out on the sidewalk. "To tell the truth, I fell asleep as soon as my head hit the pillow, but I kept waking up all night." She nodded at passersby.

"This wonderful morning air will get us going. It's going to be a great day! I can feel it," Greta exclaimed, and Cora eyed her. Greta felt invigorated with the dry mountain air, enjoying its crispness. Whatever the outcome, she would make the best of it.

"I can't wait to explore the town." Cora slowed her pace as they neared the store.

Jess, in the corner at his desk, barely gave them a glance when they came in, and Zach had his back turned away as he stoked the fire. A wonderful scent of apples and fragrant spices set Greta's nose to twitching.

An older lady came down the stairs, carrying a tray and greeted them with a hello. She placed the tray on the counter and walked up to them with an outstretched hand. "You must be Greta and Cora. Jess and Zach have told me about both of you. You can call me Granny."

Greta instantly liked the older lady with her broad smile and sincere eyes. She shook her hand and said, "I'm Greta and this is Cora."

"How do you do, Miss Granny," Cora said, taking her hand briefly.

Granny laughed. "No 'Miss,' dear. Just 'Granny' will do nicely. I've made us a fresh pot of tea. Won't you have some before you start whatever it is that my grandsons have laid out for you to do?"

Cora shot a look at Zach, but he didn't turn around. "Do you think that'll be okay? We've had our breakfast."

Granny waved her hand. " 'Course it will. We can chat and get to know one another," she said, then lifted the china pot to serve the steaming liquid.

As Granny poured, Greta took Cora's purse along with hers and stored them behind the counter, then grabbed two aprons. She slipped one over her head and handed the other one to Cora. She wanted to appear professional in case a customer came in. From this vantage point she could see through the glass windows that spread across the storefront and would know when someone was about to enter. She made a mental note to clean the dirty glass today. How could Jess live like that — barely being able to see out the window?

She shook her head and watched Granny pour the tea into two different cups on the tray. Immediately her eyes landed on the Blue Willow, and she felt a pang in her heart. That had been her mother's favorite china. The other cup had a pretty Country Rose pattern.

"Help yourselves, my dears." Granny gestured at the teacups as she glanced over at her grandsons. "There's sugar, cream, and lemon if you so desire."

Jess paused and turned the ledger so he could watch the three women without being seen. Greta's eyes had a luminous, soft glow. She used one slender hand to push her hair back over her shoulder. Gone were the rows of braids, and her hair fell in soft folds against her back. He felt himself staring openly at her when suddenly she sprang from behind the counter and flew out the door. He watched in horror as the stage-coach came barreling down Main Street, and it looked as though Greta was going to run directly in its path. Was the situation here so awful that she wanted to get it over with quickly? Had he been too mean to her yesterday? He felt his heart stop, but somehow his legs carried him into the street.

Greta was near the wheel of the stage as it sped by, spewing dust and debris in its wake as she bent down to retrieve something. Jess couldn't imagine what. When he reached her, she straightened and turned around to face him. A dog! She'd risked her life for a dog? What kind of woman was this?

Her face, dress, and apron were covered with flecks of mud, but she was smiling as she held up a little ball of fluff to her cheek. "Sweet little one. Don't you know you can't run at a moving stage when you're just a tiny little thing?" The puppy licked her face and wiggled in her arms.

"Greta, have you lost your good senses? You could've been killed! And all for a puppy!" Jess stood with his hands on his hips.

She lost her smile but continued to hold the squirming creature. "The little thing would have been crushed, so I had to act quickly. I could see through the window, though I don't know how because the windows are so dirty!"

Her comment grated on his nerves, but her startlingly blue eyes held him in place. For a brief second he envisioned her looking out the window, those incredible eyes searching for him or waiting for him to return from a buying trip.

Jess shook his head to clear his muddled mind. What had happened to his head since yesterday? Quickly, almost forcibly, he grabbed Greta by the elbow and steered her out of the street to the porch, where Zach and the others stood gaping at what had just happened.

"My goodness, girl!" Granny traipsed down the porch steps. "That was a close call. What in tarnation —" She stopped when she saw the puppy in Greta's arms. "Well, I declare . . ."

"I'm fine, everyone. Now we need to find out who's the owner of this sweet little puppy. Do you know, Zach?"

Zach walked over and patted the puppy. "I haven't a clue. There're plenty of strays around here, and people dump pets when they move on."

Greta's blue eyes grew wide. "How could they? That seems so cruel."

Jess let out a sigh. Could she really be that naïve? He almost laughed seeing her splattered with mud, since she seemed quite fussy about her appearance.

"Be that as it may, they still do it," Granny said.

"Greta, come on in and let's get you

cleaned up," Cora said, taking the pup and pushing it toward Zach. "Would you please see to its needs until we can find the owner?"

Seeming reluctant, Zach took the pup and looked around as if to say, "Now what?"

Jess shrugged. "You're the one with all the ideas, remember?"

The sounds of a harness and horse hooves caught the small group's attention, and they all turned to see a sleek black surrey trimmed with scarlet fringe halt at the hitching post in front of the mercantile. Jess already had Greta, a puppy, and Granny to deal with first thing this morning, and now there was Agnes in all her finery stepping onto the scene to pay a visit. No doubt to pour salt in his wounds. Zach handed the dog back to Greta and moved to assist Agnes.

Greta stared intently at the vision of beauty in the fancy carriage. She watched the lady climb down from her wagon and noticed her trim, slender ankle, briefly exposed above the delicate slipper that matched her stylish blue dress. Her head and shoulders were perfectly straight, and her broad hat was trimmed in pale blue roses. She tipped her head slightly upward to speak softly to

Zach, smiling through perfectly even teeth as they strolled toward the group.

Greta realized that she'd been openly staring when she finally heard the voice coming from the lovely vision as she drew nearer to them. Whoever she was, the very sight of her commanded a certain attention, and Greta couldn't help but notice people on the sidewalk pausing to admire her. She was sure that the lady must be aware of the attention attributed to her arrival.

That's when she noticed Jess's smile as he grasped her gloved hand and said hello. It was apparent that *he* knew her by the way he was looking at her. Greta stiffened. *More competition?* Somehow she managed to be cordial when Jess introduced her and Cora.

"Ladies, I'd like you to meet Miss Agnes Cartwright," Jess said, turning around with his hand at the small of Agnes's back.

"How do you do?" Agnes murmured with a nod of her head, then eyed Greta's mud-caked dress.

Greta mumbled a greeting, thoroughly feeling like Agnes was scrutinizing her entire ensemble. She felt like running up the stairs to hide until the beautiful lady was gone. If she thought Cora's clothing stylish, then Agnes's outfit outshined them all. Greta felt almost shabbily dressed in her homespun working dress and apron, and the mud only added to that effect.

"So nice to meet you, Agnes," Cora said. "Is there something in the store we can help you with?"

Agnes's eyes swept approvingly over Cora's dress. "Could be," she answered in a voice so rich it was like cream being poured out. No wonder men's heads turned as she continued up the steps.

"Let's all go back inside instead of looking like a committee meeting out here on the porch," Granny said. "Greta, you go on upstairs and get a fresh apron and clean that mud from your face. Jess, find an empty crate to put the puppy in for now." Granny took the puppy from Greta, plopped him into Jess's hands, and proceeded inside with the others following right behind her.

Greta hesitated, not sure she should be in a man's private quarters. They may not want her in their rooms. But Granny seemed to notice her indecision.

"Greta, quit shilly-shallying and go on upstairs and help yourself, then come back down and we'll have a nice cup of tea." She gave Greta a gentle nudge as she glanced at Jess for his approval.

"It's all right." Jess nodded. "We'll figure

something out about the puppy, but please, no more heroics." He grinned, still holding the squirming puppy, and she relaxed somewhat.

Greta bolted up the stairs. She slowly opened the door, feeling like an intruder. With a quick look about the room, she wasn't surprised to see that one side was tidy and the other side, which must have been Jess's, was in a jumble. She closed the door behind her and found the soap next to the sink, with water in a white pitcher. Looking at her reflection in the mirror above the sink, she had to laugh. No wonder Agnes was giving her strange glances. She looked a fright. Much like her sister Anna did when she returned from an afternoon out chasing butterflies or painting.

Without warning, hot tears filled Greta's eyes. She did miss her little sister. She'd try to write her sisters tonight and fill them in on things since her arrival.

After washing her face, she patted it dry and wiped off some of the mud flecks from her dress. Slowly she tiptoed over to Jess's area of the living quarters. There was a worn easy chair pulled close to the window overlooking the street. A table next to it held a Bible and a cup of coffee, and scattered on the floor were catalogs of various themes.

His bed was not made and she was tempted to do it for him, but that would be too personal. A pair of brogans and crumpled pants hung off the iron bedstead.

Zach's side was very neat for a man, she thought. His shoes were tucked under the edge of the bottom rail of the bed, and a blanket was pulled up and tucked in, with his pillow on top. He didn't appear to be in need of a woman's touch. Jess, on the other hand . . . maybe the touch he needed was Agnes's. Her countenance had certainly become brighter when she'd looked into Jess's eyes.

Greta straightened her shoulders, trying to look more confident than she felt. It was time to get back downstairs and see what the rest of the day would hold. She wanted to learn more about the beautiful Agnes.

9

"Do you live in town, Granny?" Cora was asking as Greta returned to the store area.

Granny gave a short chuckle. "Nearly. I live on Gregory Street in Black Hawk, which juts right up against the city limits of Central City. Every town just kinda grows into the next in these parts." She began preparing tea and glanced over at Jess and Zach, who stood talking near the front door and greeting customers as they arrived.

"I live with my brother on our ranch, the Circle D, but sometimes I stay in town for a couple of days at a time," Agnes declared. "I get rather lonely on the ranch and enjoy riding to town."

Greta joined the group of ladies. "I think I'll suggest to Jess to allow us a small table and a few chairs off to the side for coffee or something cool to drink for our customers," she whispered to Granny. "What do you think about that?"

"Greta, I really like that idea, but Jess may balk at the plan. He wasn't happy about the way you arranged things," she whispered back, leaning close.

"Oh, I'm not through yet, unless he throws me out."

"Don't get me wrong. I think it's a viable idea. Gives folks who've traveled to town a chance to refresh themselves. All you can do is ask him. With those blue eyes, I don't see how he could ever refuse you, my dear."

The older lady was direct, but she had a twinkle in her eye that was hard to miss.

"That's sweet of you to say. That's what I intend to do . . . but maybe another day." Greta chewed her bottom lip. "I'm afraid my mind is always thinking about new ways to improve things."

Granny looked at her closely. "You'll be very good for my grandson."

"What are you two twittering about?" Agnes interjected, sidling up to the counter next to Granny.

"If I know Greta, she's up to something," Cora responded as Greta and Granny moved apart.

"Oh, nothing important, really. Help yourself to a cup of tea, Miss Cartwright." Greta reached for a clean cup from the tray but then paused. "Then perhaps I can help you with your shopping."

"That would be heavenly, but please call me Agnes." Her voice dripped with honey, Greta thought. Agnes removed her leather gloves and set them aside with her purse, then moved toward the tea tray. Her hand hovered over the teacups. Granny stiffened, and Greta wondered what could be the matter when her smile disappeared and her forehead wrinkled.

Jess poked Zach in the ribs, motioning for him to direct his gaze to the ladies. Granny was pursing her lips together. Jess hadn't been counting on a third party choosing a cup, and he suddenly had a knot in his stomach. There were only two cups on the tray — the Country Rose and the Blue Willow. Their plan wasn't going to work.

"On second thought, I've changed my mind. I'm meeting a friend this morning for brunch, so I'll just wait," Agnes declared.

Air escaped Jess's lips as he realized he'd been holding his breath. Zach's shoulders relaxed as Agnes moved away.

Granny lifted the teapot and poured the tea into the two cups. "You two go on ahead. I'll go fetch another cup," she said, but she didn't move.

Cora reached for the rose cup. "What a

beautiful rose pattern." She carried the cup to the counter before taking a sip.

"I like the Blue Willow. My mother had a set like this in Holland," Greta said, lifting the other cup. "Mmm, quite tasty!" she said after taking a small sip. She blew gently on the liquid before bringing the cup to her lips again.

"Yes, I agree." Cora took several sips.

Jess watched as Greta's pink lips rested sensually against the teacup's rim, her luminous blue eyes looking thoughtful. Was she thinking of her family? It suddenly dawned on him that she'd chosen the Blue Willow and Zach would be courting her, not him. *Now why does it matter to me, since we move like a coyote and a hen in a chicken coop?*

He grinned at Granny, who finally poured a cup of tea for herself and sat down on a stool behind the counter, giving him a wink.

Agnes cleared her throat politely, giving the young ladies a frank gaze. "Are you two new in town? I didn't realize that Jess was hiring more help."

Cora gave Greta a floundering look. Zach and Jess scooted over before Greta could form a reply.

"To answer your question, I'm courting

Cora," Jess announced, then stood beside her.

"And I'm courting Greta." Zach winked at Greta, slipping his arm about her waist, and Greta tensed.

Greta's heart thumped, and she caught a look of surprise crossing Cora's face. When had the men decided that? It would've been nice if they'd shared the news privately. Her eyes locked with Jess's, and while she didn't know what he was thinking, she knew what *she* was thinking. She wasn't going to let them choose between her and Cora like prize steer on an auctioneer's block. Hardly! They had some explaining to do.

"Oh, that's rich. I thought mail-order brides were *brides* and there was no courting involved." Agnes snickered. "Isn't that the whole point of a mail-order bride?"

"Weddings take time to plan, but that shouldn't be a concern of yours, Agnes." Zach squeezed Greta lightly.

Uncomfortable as she was, she wanted to tell him to stop squeezing her waist, but she held her tongue. She was supposed to marry one of them anyway. Wasn't she? Greta swallowed, her mouth dry. "Well, actually, Cora and I haven't decided if we're staying or not. We've hardly been praised for all our hard work, and our accommodations have been sadly lacking."

For a moment there was uncomfortable silence, then Cora said, "That's right. We have to sort a few things out before we decide to stay or go."

Greta glanced over at Cora in surprise. Greta hadn't really meant to say what she did, but something drew her to put up a show for their sakes.

The brothers looked dumbfounded, and Granny humphed. "I think it's very kind of my grandsons to give them a chance to get acquainted. My boys have never done anything the conventional way." Her voice held a bit of a reprimand as she stared at Agnes.

Agnes's eyebrows knitted together and her hands trembled slightly, but otherwise she appeared poised. "I see . . . Well, it's none of my concern. I'm sorry if I inferred that it was my business." Agnes inhaled. She appeared to dismiss the topic and asked, "Cora, I wondered if you could help me with picking a pattern and fabric for a new gown? I couldn't help but notice the cut of your dress and the excellent detailing and quality."

Cora flushed prettily. "Thank you, Miss Cartwright."

"Please, call me Agnes, if you will. I'd like to find someone in Central City who knows how to sew a decent stitch. My last seamstress married and moved to Denver."

"Oh . . . I'm no expert with a needle. Maybe Greta?"

Greta was grateful to have a reason to pull away from Zach. Not that she didn't like him. On the contrary, but she wasn't sure she liked being put on the spot that way. "I sew a little, but Cora makes excellent choices when it comes to choosing the proper material. Maybe the two of us can help you, though I'm not sure how much time we'll have to spare to sew for you."

"Well, maybe just one dress." Agnes clearly wouldn't take no for an answer. "I can pay you well. Shall we go take a look at some material?"

"Don't let us stop you. Come on, Zach, we'd better start loading Mr. Smith's supplies." Jess's gaze darted away from Greta's. "Granny, are you going to stick around?"

"No, baby. I think I've accomplished what I set out to do this morning. I'll see you at church on Sunday," she said, rising from her stool. "Nice meetin' your two brides, and I'm sure I'll be seeing more of you two in the future. I'll have all of you down to Black Hawk for a good homemade meal.

Agnes, I'm sure our paths will cross again soon."

Agnes nodded, then Zach saw Granny to her wagon. She gave the horse a gentle whack with her whip and took off down the street into the throng of busy wagons, people, and horses. Greta decided she liked Granny's forthrightness and looked forward to seeing her again.

The next hour was spent poring over a pattern book and bolts of material and trim, as Cora and Greta tried to please Agnes with what was already in stock. Cora was extremely patient with her, but Greta was just about at her wit's end before they finally found something Agnes could agree on. To complement autumn's arrival, they decided on a plaid challis — a mixture of wool and cotton — in hues of orange and brown that would work well with Agnes's light brown hair and hazel eyes.

"Oh, that material is just perfect." Agnes clapped her hands. "I'd like to get it made into a dress for a barbecue that I'm giving after the roundup in two weeks. Would you like to come? It'll be fun, and all the folks around here look forward to my annual party."

"I would enjoy it, Agnes. Thank you," Cora said, picking up the scissors.

"Sounds like fun, and we can get to know some of the townsfolk. I'll plan on coming too," Greta replied.

Once Cora had taken Agnes's measurements, she bent over the counter to cut the amount of yardage needed to make the dress. "Greta, why don't you help Agnes pick out a complementary trim for her dress? I'll bring this over to be rung up when I'm finished."

"Oh, yes, would you help me with that, Greta?" Agnes asked. "I'm not very good at choosing colors."

Greta looked around to make certain no one else needed assistance at the moment. Jess was gathering things into a box for a customer's order, and Zach was busy hauling a sack of flour for another waiting customer. "I'd be glad to. It looks like Jess and Zach aren't in need of me now. I've just organized the ribbon and trim, so if Cora will cut me a tiny swatch, we can match something up."

"You certainly are knowledgeable about sewing, Greta, and Cora dresses with impeccable style." Agnes lowered her voice. "I can't help but wonder why she is working at all or why she wanted to become a mail-order bride. It's apparent that she's from a wealthy background. Hmm . . . something must be amiss."

Greta pretended not to hear her last comment. She knew little of Cora's past. She'd remained tight-lipped last night, so Greta didn't know any more about her than she had the day before. Except that she really liked her. *Does Agnes mean I'm a shabby dresser?* But she knew what Agnes said was true.

"You're right, Cora always looks her best. But I know a thing or two about sewing." Greta handed Agnes a small wedge of fabric, and the two of them walked over to the shelves that Greta and Cora had restacked the day before.

Greta loved the smell of material and enjoyed sewing, but she'd never sewed for anyone else before. She reached out to choose several different rolls that she thought might trim the dress and held the swatch up against the material. "I think this one contrasts nicely with that deep brown." She held a deep shade of yellow grosgrain ribbon against the swatch for Agnes to see.

"Are you sure I don't need to use satin ribbon?"

Greta drew back slightly. "For a dress for a barbecue? I wouldn't think so." She shook her head. "Wouldn't it be considered a more casual party — not formal?"

Agnes chewed her bottom lip, and Greta noticed how long her lashes were and how her brows arched naturally. She was really pretty. So why hadn't Jess courted her?

"Yes, it's casual," Agnes answered after a moment. "We'll have outdoor dancing and lots of food. It'll be great fun, and I meant it when I said you and Cora are invited. I'm sure Jess and Zach will be happy to bring you. Which reminds me, I haven't danced with Jess in a long time. Maybe Cora can spare him a dance with an old friend."

"Mmm . . . you'll have to ask her yourself," Greta responded, quickly changing the subject. "If you're happy with this, we can go tally up your order now." Agnes nodded, and they moved to where Cora stood waiting next to the cash register.

Agnes reached out her hand to stop Cora from wrapping the material and sewing notions. "No need for that. If you and Greta are willing to try your hand at sewing this frock for me, I'll let you keep it here. Then I'll come for fittings," she said, sliding her leather gloves on.

"Uh . . . as I told you, I don't know how to sew. It's best that you try to find someone else in town, unless Greta would like to try her hand at it." Cora glanced over to Greta.

"You ladies found everything Agnes

needed?" Jess asked. He directed his gaze to Greta, then glanced down at her locket. Or was he looking at something else? Either way, she pretended that his frank gaze didn't affect her.

"I believe we did." Greta tallied the items and set them aside in one pile. She wasn't sure what she should do concerning sewing for Agnes. It wasn't that she couldn't, but she was worried that Agnes might be hard to please. Should she agree to do it? It *could* help pass the time . . .

"How long before you need the dress, Agnes?" Greta knew that Jess feigned busyness at the other end of the counter, looking at the tags on some shirts that he and Zach had marked earlier. He kept one eye on the women as he counted the pile of shirts. Did he just want to be near the pretty Agnes, or didn't he trust her and Cora to add up the correct charges? He shouldn't be eyeing her while agreeing to court Cora. She bit her tongue to keep from blurting something out.

Agnes clapped her gloved hands together in excitement. "Oh, does that mean you'll do it? Wonderful!" she exclaimed, without waiting for Greta's answer. "The barbecue is in two weeks. Will that be enough time?"

Greta thought for a second. "I suppose

so, but let me remind you that I've never sewed for anyone else before."

"You'll do fine, I'm sure. Besides, my pickings are slim to none at the moment."

"Well . . . if you're sure . . ."

Cora smiled softly at Greta. "Maybe I can learn a thing or two as you make the dress."

"Who made your dress, Cora, if you don't mind me asking?" Agnes slipped her arm through her purse.

"Er . . . it was ordered from either New York or London, I believe."

Agnes's eyes narrowed. "You mean you don't know? How odd."

Greta felt uncomfortable for her friend and stepped in. "No, it's not odd at all. I'm sure Cora had better things to do than wonder when and where her dress was made." Before Agnes could inquire as to what those things were, Greta walked around to her side. "I'll walk you to the door, and we can set a date and time for you to pop back in for your fitting," she said, giving Agnes a level stare.

Cora shot Greta a grateful look as she ushered the chatty Agnes to the door, nearly nudging her down the steps to her waiting surrey. Greta wanted to have a word with Jess and Zach before another customer walked in. She thought it was only fair to ask how they'd decided about courting since she and Cora were both here because of Jess . . . or at least they thought so.

10

Zach was sweeping up a trail of flour on the floor, so Jess greeted the customers as they came in to do their shopping. A couple of them commented on how different and better the place looked. Jess hadn't been expecting anyone to notice. Had it really looked that awful before? But he just smiled and asked if there was anything in particular that he could help them with. He always enjoyed chewing the fat, so he leaned against the counter, arms folded, talking with Ed Potts and Joshua Barnes.

"Looks like we're in for some nice Indian summer weather this weekend, according to the almanac," Ed said.

"I wouldn't know, Ed," Jess said. "I never look at the almanac, so I'll have to take your word for it."

Like a father explaining to his son, Ed declared, "The almanac is usually right on target. Makes it easy to plan when to plant your garden."

Jess chuckled. "Well, I'll be sure to do that if I ever have a notion to plant one."

"Oh, you will someday when you take a missus," Joshua teased. "From the looks of it, that won't be too long now." He rolled his large, droopy eyes in the direction of Greta.

The front door slammed, nearly rattling its hinges. Greta marched up to Jess with a look of fury, and the two older men stopped jawing. Unease swept over him, and he stood erect. "Is something wrong, Greta?"

"Why didn't you tell me and Cora that you and Zach had made your choices?" Her eyes snapped with annoyance. She stopped in front of him and crossed her arms over her chest, then stood tapping her toe against the hardwood floor. The flush across her cheekbones gave color to her normally creamy complexion, and her blue eyes flashed with fire.

"We were going to tell you, but Agnes came in about that time."

"So you announce it without consulting me and Cora first? And how, pray tell, did you decide, since neither of you have so much as sat down to talk in order to get to know us!"

"We planned to get around to it in time.

If you haven't noticed, we've been a little busy today." Now he was glad his brother was going to be stuck with Greta and her hot-tamale temper! "We'll make it up to you, won't we, Zach?" he said as Zach strode over to investigate what all the fuss was about. Jess could see that Ed and Joshua had moved a step or two away, showing interest in a farming implement catalog but close enough that they could hear the conversation.

"As a matter of fact, I was just thinking that I could escort you to Silas and Annabelle's for supper tomorrow," Zach answered, setting the broom and dustpan aside. "We can talk along the way."

"But you still haven't answered my question. And where's Cora?"

Zach sidled up next to her, taking her hand in his. "She took the tray of dirty dishes upstairs. Why?"

Greta pulled her hand away. "Because she deserves to know," she said, her mouth forming a tight line. "In the first place, you wrote letters for your brother, deceiving us when we thought we would be Jess's bride. We never considered there would be competition, and Cora deserves to know."

Cora came back downstairs. "I deserve to know what?" She paused, wiping her hands on her apron.

Greta whirled around. "How they picked which one of us they will court, that's what!"

"It's really all the same to me. It's as you said, we haven't decided if we will stay or not," Cora said firmly. "So how *did* you decide?"

Jess shifted from one boot to the other. "Why don't we talk about this after hours?" He noted that off to the side, Ed and Joshua continued to browse the catalog just as their wives, Rose and Hilda, hurried over. Both had their hands full of various items but were obviously more interested in the rising voices.

"Oh no you don't. You're not getting off that easy." Greta turned to face Zach and asked, "Had you two decided this the day we arrived?"

Zach lifted his apron and wiped the dirt from his hands. "No . . . we didn't until Granny came and suggested a way to handle this."

"What did she propose?" Cora's brow furrowed.

"May as well go ahead and tell 'em." Jess knew it was the fair thing to do, but he hoped they wouldn't be angry. "Granny suggested that we make tea. Whoever picked the rose pattern would be the one I would court, and whoever picked the Blue Willow pattern would be the one Zach would court." There, he'd said it, and if they didn't like the idea, then they could leave like they'd threatened earlier. But then he remembered the way Greta had picked the Blue Willow pattern, almost caressing the cup between her slender fingers.

For a moment or two, thick silence hung in the room before Greta laughed. "*Ach!* So Granny more or less decided for you?"

"No. It was *you* who made the decision when you chose which teacup to drink from. It was just our way of solving the situation rather quickly. If you aren't happy with it, then you can get back on the train that brought you here!" Jess sounded harsher than he'd meant to, and a stricken look crossed Cora's pretty face. He didn't want to cause her to worry. He would fulfill his part of the bargain, for all the trouble Zach had put the ladies through.

"Jess!" Zach glared. "You're not gonna leave . . . are you?" Zach asked directly, meeting Greta's gaze.

She shrugged her shoulders. "I'm not certain that we're welcome."

The bell over the door jangled, bringing them back to the present as more customers entered the store, and Cora scurried over to them. Greta whirled away to help Ed and Joshua, who stood glued to the spot, joined now by their twittering wives. The men smiled and shuffled their feet, giving her a sidelong glance that lingered a little too long, Jess thought. However, he couldn't blame them for taking a second look. Greta was striking with her blonde hair and blue eyes, and charmed everyone with her Dutch accent.

Zach poked his brother on the arm. "You didn't have to sound so mean. You're gonna run 'em off with that kind of talk."

"I didn't intend to — it just came out that way. Greta's so . . . so . . . I don't know. I'm just glad you'll be the one sparkin' her, not me."

"Let's take them to dinner tonight and walk them back to the cabin. Get to know them a little better," Zach suggested.

Jess expelled air from his lungs. "All right . . . whatever you think."

"Good. I'll go tell them now." Zach grinned good-naturedly.

Jess watched his brother lumber away, his boot heels clomping loudly against the hardwood floor. His heart softened when he thought about the trouble Zach had gone to in order to make life easier for him in general. His intentions were in the right place. From now on he decided he was going to sit back and relax and see where the good Lord would lead. He strolled to the front of the store to help a miner flipping through a stack of heavy overalls, but his mind was on Greta's flashing blue eyes.

Zach was glad that Jess had calmed down. He thought Granny's plan had worked out well, even though all three of them had been worried for a few moments when Agnes had reached for a teacup. He hadn't planned on courting either of the two brides, but now he was beginning to like the idea. He'd wanted to wait until he had a few head of cattle and a small cabin before he considered taking on a wife. But he was getting tired of sleeping upstairs, sharing living quarters with Jess. He wanted to be outside under the stars when the evenings were warm enough, listening to the lowing of the cattle. It was a dream he was working and saving for. He felt cooped up in the store all day and couldn't imagine why Jess enjoyed it. It wasn't enough for him. He wanted to ride, feel the wind against his face, and have the freedom that owning a ranch could afford.

Would Greta make a good wife? He wasn't sure, but she was pleasing to the eye and liked to laugh, and Zach liked that about her. Most of all, he liked her take-charge attitude.

He watched Greta now as she talked with Ed and Joshua, and she came across as articulate, bright, and yes, maybe a little aggressive — or was that spunky? She wrapped Rose's and Hilda's items, then turned to give him a rather lopsided smile when he approached.

"Gentlemen, is Greta helping you order some new farming supplies?"

"For a fact she is, and I must say that this little lady here is quite knowledgeable," Ed said. "She knows the difference between a plow and a harrow."

"Yes, I agree. I must compliment you on hiring some help. Miss Greta, how do you know so much about farming?" Joshua asked, gazing at Greta.

"My brother-in-law is a wheat farmer in Wyoming, and I lived with him and my sister when we first came to America from Holland. One can learn all kinds of things on a farm."

"Then you'll definitely be an asset to some of our customers," Zach said. He watched her rosy lips tilt upward in a sweet smile.

"How interesting that you came to live in America. You'll have to tell us all about Holland," Hilda said, her eyes alight with genuine interest.

"So nice to meet you, Greta. I'm sure we'll be seeing a lot of you from time to time," Rose said cheerily.

Hilda nodded in agreement. "Are you responsible for the store's new organized look?"

Greta blushed. "Well . . . yes, some of it. Cora helped out too. I hope I can be of service to both of you the next time you're in the store." Greta folded her hands and rested them on her apron.

Zach was proud that the customers were already taking a liking to her. "She did a good job, didn't she, Hilda? We are appreciative of her efforts to give a bit of order to our chaos."

"We'd better be on our way now. Greta has taken our order and we'll stop by in a few weeks to pick it up." Ed clapped Zach on the back, then he and Joshua left, their wives chatting and following demurely behind.

Greta and Cora spent the rest of the day filling orders, cleaning the other side of the store, and assisting customers. Greta was grateful to be busy since it made the day pass quickly. She couldn't help but feel the watchful eyes of Zach and Jess on her and Cora's every move, as if they were expecting them to do something odd with the store's merchandise. It almost made her laugh, but when no complaints were forthcoming, she relaxed and went about doing the things that needed to be done. Ideas were already forming in her head of possible suggestions to Jess on how he could improve the display of items for customers. But she wouldn't tell him today. Enough had happened in two days to fluster him.

"I believe we're about to be escorted to dinner, and I'm looking forward to having a good, hot meal," Cora said. "We've nothing much in the cabin, and since I can't cook, well . . ."

"Cora, maybe I can help you learn some basics. We'll stock a few supplies tomorrow and figure something out to cook," Greta said cheerfully. She removed her apron and looped it across the hook behind the counter.

Cora giggled. "You may find that I'm a hopeless case, but I'd be much obliged."

"Not to worry. Experience is the key to cooking, nothing more."

Zach removed the money from the cash register to take upstairs as Jess flipped the CLOSED sign over the door.

135

"You can leave that box until tomorrow to be opened," Jess said, walking toward them. "You ladies ready for supper? You've hardly taken a break all day."

"I believe we are. I'll just get our purses and coats." Cora moved to the curtain beyond the counter that separated the store from the supply room.

When Greta and Jess were alone, Jess opened his mouth to say something to her as he stood rocking back on his boot heels.

"Is there anything else you need me to do?" Greta asked. She could hear the puppy yapping from his crate. For the time being, it was decided that the pup would stay at the store.

"No, it's not that. I . . . uh . . ." He gave a small cough, clearing his throat. "I want to apologize for sounding so harsh earlier. I shouldn't have said that. Truce?" His brown eyes reflected a seriousness that surprised her.

"Well . . . okay, apology accepted. Truce." Greta dropped her eyes under his gaze, but she sensed the tension in him. He took a step to close the distance between them and gave her a peck on the cheek, his lips soft and warm to her skin. She stumbled backward in surprise. He caught her arm to steady her as she touched her fingers to her face. "What —"

"Greta," he said, "it's only a friendly kiss — to seal a truce."

"Oh. Is that how it's done in America?" Her heart was thumping hard against her ribs as she looked up at him. His mouth twitched to thwart a smile, but before he could reply, they were interrupted by Zach's and Cora's chattering about where to dine. Zach doffed his hat, then gallantly took Greta's arm, guiding her to the door, leaving Cora to follow with Jess. As they moved to the door, they heard a loud voice, and a young man brandishing a gun quickly slipped through the unlocked door.

"Stop right where you are and hand over that bag of money lying on the counter over there!" he ordered, waving his gun around.

Cora screamed and clung to Jess's arm, and Greta's eyes flew open in fear. Zach dropped Greta's arm and stretched out his hand. "Whoa there, young man. Just take it easy." Zach took a step toward him, and the young man waved his gun again.

"Step back or I'll shoot that pretty blonde you're with." The young man's dirty black hair fell over his eyes, and his face was set in determination, leaving no doubt in Jess's mind that he was serious.

Jess glanced over at the muslin bag on the counter. Zach must have gotten distracted and forgotten to take it to the safe upstairs. He didn't want anyone to get hurt, so he'd have to hand it over to the young lad carefully. He could go off half-cocked, as foolish young men sometimes did. Jess took a few steps backward toward the counter, keeping his eye on the gun. Cora clung to Greta's arm, shaking.

The puppy yapped louder and scratched against the sides of his crate.

"Shut that dog up or he's gonna git a bullet right between the eyes! And hand me that money. NOW!"

"Please don't hurt the puppy, mister. He's harmless," Greta pleaded.

"Shut yer face, pretty girl!" His eyes slid up and down Greta's body.

Greta shrank back against Cora, turning to flash an anxious look at Zach.

Zach moved sideways to the crate to try to shush the puppy, still watching the robber. He patted the dog, which gave him a friendly lick on his fingers. Jess was hoping that Zach wouldn't do anything impulsive. He saw the fear in the lad's eyes, making him think this could be his first robbery attempt. The boy's mouth might be more dangerous than his actions. Reaching behind himself, Jess slid the muslin bag off the counter and cautiously crept forward, holding the bag within reach of the robber.

"Here, take it!" Jess thrust the bag into the man's hand as Zach yelled then lunged toward the robber, who fired a wide shot. Both women squealed and Cora covered her eyes.

The robber whirled around, flew out the door, and bounded down the stairs into the crowded streets. Jess and Zach hurried down the steps after him but, after a few minutes of chase, lost sight of him.

11

Greta was glad when she saw no harm had come to either brother as they trotted back to the store — but neither had they caught the robber. Cora wrung her handkerchief in her hands despite Greta's reassurances that everything was going to be okay. "At least no one was hurt, Cora. I think the robber was all talk."

"Maybe so, but he still got away with a lot of money!" Zach shook his head, breathing hard.

"We have to stop in and see Sheriff Mack before we have supper," Jess remarked as he reached the front steps with heaving sides. He leaned over, placing his hands on his knees to catch his breath. "I'm too old for this."

"He got away. He's just a young lad, and we're no match for someone who can run that fast," Zach said.

Cora's face reflected deep concern. "Then

we need to pray for him."

"Pray for him? He's a robber, for heaven's sake!" Zach swore under his breath. "That kid just made off with half of our earnings for the week, and you want me to pray for him?"

"That's exactly why we need to. We're to love our enemies and pray for those who persecute us," Cora said, gently touching the sleeve of Zach's coat.

Jess humphed. "Now you're sounding like Brother Abel."

Cora colored slightly. Greta quietly observed this side of her newfound friend. How odd that they could be thrown together this way and still have mutual respect. Cora had already earned it from her.

"She's right. We should," Greta agreed. "Now that you two have caught your breath, why don't we walk on over to the sheriff's office?" She started down the steps.

"Yes. Let's get going. The longer we stand here jawing about the right or wrong of it, the colder the trail will be for the sheriff." Jess reached for Cora's hand and they led the way, scurrying down the sidewalk.

During a wonderful meal of roast and potatoes at Mabel's, Greta sat next to Zach, whose leg occasionally touched hers under the small table. She wasn't sure if it was on purpose. Cora seemed pleased to be sitting next to Jess. Her upturned face glowed under the soft lighting, her rapt attention focused on Jess. She was a vision — soft and lovely — as she listened to Jess talk. Part of Greta was jealous, especially with the way Jess gazed back at Cora. But why should she care? After all, she was sitting with a good-looking and gregarious man. But there was something about Jess's mannerisms that gave her pause. Just what, she wasn't sure. Underneath his controlled exterior, he seemed to carry a certain wretchedness in his soul. Whatever it was, it could be the reason that he was unreasonable at times.

"I must say, the sheriff didn't appear to be in any hurry to track down the robber," Greta said.

Zach polished off the last of his cherry pie before answering. "I'd say you're right about that, but he had very little to go on except our description of a young man whose appearance was less than pleasant."

"I was just telling Cora that maybe we should see if we can move you two to a hotel or boardinghouse now that you've seen the robber. It might not be safe for you to be out there in that cabin alone." Jess blotted his mouth and set his napkin aside.

Cora bobbed her dark head. "So true. I never felt safe there. Could we see about doing that tonight?" she asked, dabbing the corner of her mouth with her napkin.

"The reason I don't have you in a hotel now is because there weren't any vacancies, but we could check the Teller House." Zach seemed enthusiastic about the idea as well.

Their concern made Greta feel protected, and she liked knowing that someone cared about her well-being. "The cabin is really not so bad, but whatever you decide." She looked from Zach to Jess, who narrowed his eyes and frowned.

"The Teller House is a little pricey, especially after the robber just stole half of this week's earnings," he said. "It's not too late to check again at a couple of other places when we leave here. We might get lucky." He gave Cora's hand an affectionate pat. "I know how scared you were with the bear. Let me remind you that it was Zach's idea to put you up in Jeb's cabin in the first place," Jess said, giving Zach an annoyed look.

"I did what I could on short notice. This town's been crowded ever since John Gregory discovered gold," Zach said, plunking down his coffee cup.

"Is it true that Central City is the richest square mile on earth? I overheard some customers say that," Cora said, helping herself to another cup of coffee.

Zach smiled. "That's true, Cora. Many got rich, but in the sixties and seventies the placer deposits petered out, so many miners were disillusioned and returned back East. The alternative was underground mining, and that takes money and investors."

"So how did you two wind up being mercantile owners?" Greta laid her napkin aside.

Jess shifted in his chair, turning to face her. "Our parents were stable, hardworking people who had no interest in mining, but they knew there'd always be a need for supplies for the influx of a steady, growing population. When they died from influenza, we naturally took over running the store, with Granny's help." Jess's look was sober. His sad brown eyes slid down to focus on her locket. She glimpsed the thick hair at the back of his neck curling into the collar of his blue chambray shirt, and more dark hair peeked through the top, just above his long handles.

Tearing her eyes away, she murmured, "I'm so sorry. How long ago was this, if you don't mind me asking?"

"That was a year ago . . . right after . . . er . . . well, anyway, that's all behind us now." Jess stared down at his pocket watch.

"Do you have other family or cousins?" Greta asked.

"None that we know of," Zach answered stiffly.

Jess abruptly changed the subject. "If you ladies agree, we'd like to take you to church with us on Sunday."

Cora straightened up immediately. "I'd love to. It's the best way to get involved in the community and share our common beliefs in the Almighty."

There was no mistaking the fervor in her voice, which made Greta all the more curious about Cora's background. "I'd like that as well."

"Great. Now before the evening slips away, why don't we see if we can find a hotel room," Jess said, pushing his chair back. He extended his hand to Cora.

Greta rose from the table as Zach paid the waiter for their dinner. He placed his hand at the curve of her back to escort her from the restaurant. As they walked toward the door, she felt petite against his towering form, even though she herself was tall. She appreciated his good manners and found him to be very witty and easy to talk to —

and more than once she caught his eyes lingering on her.

They were following Jess when he came to an abrupt halt, and they almost walked right into him and Cora. "What's wrong, Jess?" Zach asked.

"There's something mighty familiar about the young man over there." He tossed his head toward the corner of the dining room. Their eyes followed his to gaze upon a clean-shaven young man rising from his table, leaving a tip behind.

"You don't think —" Cora sucked in a quick breath of disbelief.

"I think it's him, just a cleaned-up version. Let's watch and follow him out," Jess whispered. Cora clung to Jess's arm, and they casually walked to the entrance not far behind the young man.

Getting a closer look, Greta believed Jess was correct in his assumption. What nerve for him to show up in a public place! But then again, no one would give him a second glance, cleaned up as he was. When he stepped out onto the porch, Jess hurried up to the man and tapped him on the shoulder. He turned around, and when he saw Jess he whirled around to make a hasty exit, but Zach was already standing in his path.

"Just what do you want?" the young man

asked. His eyes darted nervously from Jess to Zach, one hand sliding into his pocket. Without his gun to wave under their noses, he obviously wasn't in control as he had been earlier.

"I wouldn't do that if I were you. Take your hand out of your pocket, nice and slow," Zach ordered.

He did as he was told and put his hands on his hips. "Do I know you?"

"Quit the pretense, young man. You robbed us earlier this afternoon, and we're going to haul you down to the sheriff's office now that you're all nice and cleaned up." Zach grabbed the man's arm, forcing it behind his back, and he yelped.

"Wait! Please, I have your money . . . or what's left of it," he said, struggling against Zach's forceful arm. Passersby slowed down to see what the commotion was about.

The frightened look on his face made Greta almost feel sorry for him . . . almost. He couldn't be much more than sixteen, only a boy.

Jess stood legs apart, hands on his hips. "What do you mean, 'what's left of it'?"

"I spent money on a new set of trousers and a shirt, shoes, a bath, and a shave, then a meal. I hadn't had anything to eat in three days."

"So you'd rather steal than work for a living?" Jess's jaw worked in agitation. Cora made a move to say something, but Jess stayed her with his hand.

"I can't get nobody to hire me." He looked down, studying his new boots, and sighed. "I'll pay you back . . . somehow."

"Well, stealing is not the way, young man." Jess eyed him.

"I'm sure if you'd gone to one of the town's churches, they would have been more than helpful," Cora offered, smoothing the front of her dress. "Jess, maybe you could give him a part-time job sweeping or hauling orders. Something."

"Are you crazy? He just robbed us. He needs to pay for his mistakes."

"Please, mister, don't turn me in to the sheriff. I never stole a thing in my life until today. Your money's right here in my coat pocket." Perspiration beaded along his mouth and brow as he chewed the inside of his cheek, and he avoided meeting Jess's eyes.

While Zach still held his arm, the lad used his other hand to open his coat, indicating for Jess to reach in and retrieve the envelope of money. Jess opened the envelope, counting the contents. "You owe me fifty dollars," he said.

"Jess." Greta moved to touch his arm. "Cora's got a point. What if you give him a chance to make it up?"

"Yes, Jess. Think of all the good it'll do to help a young man down on his luck. We prayed for him, and now we've been given the opportunity to set it all straight," Cora pleaded.

"Are you two forgetting that he threatened to blow your brains out and shoot the puppy just hours ago?" Jess looked at Zach for support, who cocked an eyebrow.

"I don't believe he meant one word of it. It was all just talk." Greta looked back at the robber, whose face was contorted with nervousness at being caught.

Jess shook his head. "Heavens above. This goes against my better judgment *again*." Jess nodded to Zach to release the boy's arm. "Why do I let myself be persuaded by you two?" He turned and scrutinized the young man. "Boy, do you have a name?"

12

The lengthening shadows rolled rapidly over the purple peaks, and the warm day disappeared amid gathering clouds, which slid like a curtain over the sun against the western sky. Cora pulled her shawl tighter about her shoulders to ward off the chill and watched the young lad, tenderness in her heart. She mustered all her self-restraint to keep from commenting while Jess questioned him. The young man, who only an hour before had seemed so sure of himself, now stood shaking in his boots after being caught red-handed. Cora somehow felt sorry for him, but that was still no excuse for what he'd done.

"My name's Caleb — Caleb Zuckerman," the lad stuttered, raising his eyes to meet Jess's.

"How old are you, Caleb?" Zach asked, still blocking him in the event he might bolt.

"Almost eighteen." Caleb shuffled from

one foot to the other.

"Nearly a man, so it's time to start acting like one," Jess said. "Tell you what, I'll give you a chance to pay me back and make amends . . . maybe find something for you to do that's respectable. But first we have to let the sheriff know because there's a warrant out for your arrest. If you want me to call it off, then you need to come with me."

"Yes, sir, whatever you say."

"Ladies, you can stay here and wait or follow us down to the sheriff's office," Jess said. "Then we'll see about getting you a room."

Cora touched Jess's arm. "This is a good thing you're doing for this young man, and I'm sure he'll be grateful." She smiled up at him and caught a glimmer of warmth in his brown eyes as he returned her smile. *He'll make a good father. He has a soft heart.* When Jess had said grace before supper, she'd added a prayer for the man who'd robbed them, much to everyone's surprise. Now she silently thanked God for the outcome of this evening. The kid just needed a sense of direction and maybe an older man to guide him.

Jess leaned in close to Cora and quietly said, "That was a nice prayer you said at supper." Cora's face softened when she looked up at him.

"Excuse me." Greta interrupted the cozy moment. "We'll just go along with you two," she suggested, and Cora nodded her agreement. She wondered what Greta thought about the situation, but that could wait until they were alone. Perhaps tonight they wouldn't have to stay at Jeb's cabin, which would suit her just fine. She breathed deeply of the fresh night air, comforted and sure now that God had sent her here to fulfill the purpose in her heart.

Zach nudged Caleb forward with Jess flanking Caleb's side. They started down the sidewalk, and Cora and Greta followed.

An hour later, after withdrawing the charges against Caleb, the group inquired about a room at several places but were met with no vacancy. Zach decided on the Teller House on Eureka Street after all. But the women would have to share a room with the hope that another room might become available later on in the week.

"We don't have to move from the cabin, you know, now that you've found the robber," Greta said. "I'm not afraid to stay there."

"Maybe you're not, but Jess insisted on it," Zach answered.

That satisfied Greta, and she knew Cora was more than happy to eschew the cabin. Greta marveled at how everything had turned out during the course of the evening, though she had her doubts about Caleb's sincerity. Time would tell soon enough.

"I thought you said this place was out of your range," Greta commented when they entered the foyer of the hotel, which boasted 150 rooms within its five stories. It was magnificent and plush, with rich mahogany details and tapestry hangings. She could see that Cora was impressed too as she looked about with wide eyes, taking it all in.

"I think we can afford a few nights now that we've recovered most of our money," Zach said, grinning. "This hotel was built by our senator, Henry Teller, whose law practice is across the street." He strode up to the front desk, and the exuberant clerk looked up as he approached. "Bill, these are the two young ladies I told you about earlier."

Bill turned the registry around to face them. "Howdy! If you would, please sign the register and I'll give you two keys for the room that you'll be sharing." His eyes swept over the ladies with an admiring look.

Greta lifted the pen and scrawled her name on the line, then stepped aside for

Cora to do the same. From the corner of her eye, she saw Jess talking with Caleb, then the two sauntered over to Zach.

"Why don't you go to the cabin and get their belongings, Zach? Caleb will go with you. I'll meet you back at home."

Zach gave him a quizzical look. "Well . . . sure, we can do that."

The thought of anyone looking through her personal items and undergarments gave Greta pause. "I think we'll go with you, Zach. It's just a short walk, so it's not a bother."

"Good idea, Greta. My things aren't packed, and I'd rather do that myself," Cora said, giving Greta a grateful look.

Jess shrugged. "Suit yourself. In that case, Caleb, you can come back with me. I'll drag a cot out for you. I'll bid you ladies a good night and see you in the morning." They left, one tall, robust man who walked with a purpose, and one young lad, shoulders slumped, head down.

Greta watched them go, thinking Jess had seemed subdued since supper. Was it because of finding the robber, or something else?

The clerk handed one key to her and another to Cora. "Ladies, anything you need, you just let me know. We pride ourselves on taking good care of our customers. Will you be staying a week or a couple of days?"

"It hasn't been decided yet, but it could be a week or longer. Just charge it to Gifford's Mercantile," Zach replied.

"I see . . ." The clerk's eyes narrowed. "In that case, you'll need to pay in advance to secure the room for a week. We don't extend credit for such a long stay."

"Oh." Zach reached in his back pocket for his wallet. Red-faced, he looked over at Greta and Cora for help. "Could one of you loan me the money? It seems I forgot to get some of the bills from Jess," he murmured in a low voice.

The clerk gave a little cough and cleared his throat. He probably didn't believe Zach one bit, Greta thought. She dug into her purse, but Cora was quicker and handed him the necessary amount. Zach plunked it down on the counter. The clerk counted it and smiled.

Zach turned to her. "Thanks. Don't worry, I'll give it back tomorrow. Now let's go get your things. It's been a very long day."

"I couldn't agree with you more," Greta said.

"I'm so glad things turned out the way they did with Caleb. You won't regret helping that young man. You might even be able to turn him around," Cora said, walking with them out to the sidewalk. "It was the Christian thing to do."

"I'm not so sure being a Christian had anything to do with it." Zach scratched his beard absentmindedly while the ladies walked on either side of him.

"What do you mean?" Cora appeared shocked. "Don't you have a relationship with the Lord?"

Zach quirked an eyebrow. "I'm more interested in a relationship with Greta at the moment," he answered with a wink at Greta. "It's just Jess has a soft spot for young folks. Comes naturally after . . ." Zach's voice trailed off. "Anyway, he'll teach Caleb a thing or two or my name's not Zach Gifford."

"Jess has a soft spot for young folks?" Greta asked, thinking he might tell them more, but he didn't seem inclined to share for whatever reason.

It took little more than twenty minutes to retrieve their bags and return to the hotel. Greta and Cora carried their carpetbags while Zach carried their luggage in either hand. Though they trudged back uphill to the hotel, he never broke a sweat. Greta watched his broad back muscles stretch the fabric of his coat and noticed his strong forearms as he climbed the stairs and placed the luggage in front of their hotel room.

"I'll just grab my key and you can set those inside," Cora instructed him.

When the door swung open, Greta was pleasantly surprised at the nicely furnished room and the warmth of the dark wood used for the twin beds and dresser. To her delight, her feet sank into plush carpet, and a light fragrance of lemon and beeswax polish indicated that the room had been freshly cleaned. Cora walked over and lowered the shade against the darkness, and Zach placed their luggage next to their beds.

"If there's nothing else, I'll be on my way." Zach moved toward the door.

Cora lifted her suitcase to her bed, and Greta walked him to the door. "Zach, thanks for hoisting our luggage for us," she said, standing in the doorway. "Can I ask you something?"

"Of course. Anything."

Greta cast a glance over her shoulder to see if Cora was listening, then stepped into the hallway, pulling the door to. He stood close, and the scent of his aftershave tickled her nose, making her very aware of his manly physique. He was strongly built like

Bryan and was about as tall as Bryan had been, but more muscular and a couple years older, perhaps. She fixed her eyes on his and said, "I wondered why Jess appears to be so sad sometimes when he doesn't suspect anyone's watching. Is it because you brought us here? If so, then maybe I should leave . . ."

Zach reached out and took her hands in his. "Oh no. It's nothing like that at all. Jess . . . well . . . he's had his heart broken twice. Once by Agnes Cartwright, whom he courted for a while, but who stopped seeing him when a wealthy entrepreneur came to town."

"Oh. The way she acted around him, I thought she was sweet on Jess."

"She may have had a change of heart, but it's too late where Jess is concerned. I'm sure of that. He's no fool, so he's cautious."

"What was the other time?"

"I guess it's twofold, Greta. We lost our younger brother and then a couple months later, our parents." He paused, staring down at her hands in his with a distant look in his eyes, and she thought he might cry. "It's hard to lose your parents, but Jess took it really hard when our little brother died."

"I'm so sorry, Zach . . . I didn't mean to pry or make you relive old hurts." Greta gave his hand a squeeze.

He closed the gap between them. "You didn't, Greta." To her complete surprise, with a gentle tug he pulled her close, touching her mouth with his in a warm kiss. His lips felt soft, lingering for a moment until he released her. She hadn't been kissed since the day Bryan had left for Fort Bridger, and she suddenly felt an odd betrayal of sorts.

She wasn't sure what to say other than, "Good night, Zach."

His lips tilted upward in a lopsided smile, and his brown eyes twinkled. "Good night, pretty lady." He turned and headed down the stairs with a wave of his hand, and she waved back. Goodness! Two kisses in one day. Neither of them unpleasant, she thought as she closed the door, leaning back on it with a smile.

Cora was already in her nightgown, brushing her hair in front of the oval mirror that hung over the washstand. Greta admired Cora's beautiful, thick tresses, so different from her own fine and flyaway hair.

"Were you having a tête-à-tête with Zach?" She stopped her brushing in midair. "Seems as though you are both getting along *very* well."

Did Cora have eyes in the back of her

head? Surely she didn't see the kiss. "We were just talking about Jess."

"Oh?" She smiled and went back to her brush strokes, backing up to the bed to take a seat. She'd pulled the coverlets back on both beds, and Greta thought hers looked mighty inviting.

Greta pulled off her shoes and began unbuttoning the front of her bodice. "Yes. I asked Zach why Jess seemed sad sometimes."

Cora gave Greta her undivided attention and laid aside her hairbrush. Tucking her feet up under her nightgown, she wrapped her arms around her knees and leaned against the headboard. "What did he say?"

It was only fair to tell her, but she wondered why Cora hadn't asked Jess herself. Quickly Greta told Cora about the loss of their brother and parents. "I guess that's enough to make one melancholy," Greta said with a catch in her voice that seemed to surprise Cora.

"Come sit down, Greta." She patted the bed. "Is something bothering you?"

Greta sat down and faced her with a deep sigh. "It shows?"

"Only occasionally I see a faraway look in your eyes," Cora answered gently.

Greta clasped the locket around her neck.

"I was engaged to be married . . . then my fiancé, Bryan, was killed in an Indian ambush."

Cora sucked in her breath, then reached over and touched Greta's knee. "Oh, Greta! How awful! I'm truly sorry. How long has it been?"

"It was a year ago."

Cora nodded toward the chain in Greta's fingers. "Is that a locket he gave you?"

"Yes. It was for my eighteenth birthday. We were so in love." Tears streamed down her cheeks. This wasn't like her. She was used to always staying in control.

"So that's why you left Cheyenne."

Greta nodded. Cora reached into her purse, found a handkerchief, and handed it to Greta. "Here. It's clean — wipe your tears."

"It's been a long time since I cried. I'm sorry." Greta took the hanky and dabbed her eyes. "I don't know what came over me."

"Sometimes when you hear someone else say they've lost a loved one, it's like your loss is fresh again," Cora said sympathetically.

Greta blew her nose. "I suppose so. At least now you know what drives Jess."

"It makes sense to me now why he has a soft spot for Caleb. Not many men would do that."

"I believe you were instrumental in getting him to give Caleb a chance, but I have my doubts about his rehabilitation."

"I'm convinced everyone deserves a second chance in this world. With God's help, Caleb can change. It happened to me, though the Lord is still working things out. That's why I seem a bit helpless sometimes and at a loss for direction. I know I complained a lot about everything when we arrived — the cabin, being duped by Zach, and even walking instead of being driven in a carriage."

Greta laughed. "You certainly did."

Cora gave her a pouty look but continued. "As I said, I'm a work in progress. My father is a banker and all my needs were met. I wanted for nothing, but neither did I *do* anything but exist, allowing others to wait on me. It's what I knew. Not that it's a bad thing in and of itself, it's just that I had no purpose in life once I graduated from high school."

"What happened to make you change?"

"One evening a friend invited me to go hear a circuit preacher passing through Boston. It was the best thing that ever happened to me, Greta. I knew that my parents loved me, though they never told me. But that night, I heard the three little words that I long to hear — *I love you.* God spoke right then to my heart that night. I found out that all the desires of my heart were His plans for me too, but what I was looking for all along was really Him."

Greta's eyes lit up. "That's wonderful, Cora. But why did you leave home to become a mail-order bride? Surely there were eligible men of high standards whom your father knew."

"My parents disapproved of my new faith. When I began to give away my allowance to others in need and started doing charity work for the church, we argued. They wouldn't allow any of the changes that I wanted in my life." Cora's bottom lip trembled. "When I wouldn't renounce my belief in Christ, they made it so hard for me to live under their roof that I decided to answer the ad Zach placed so I could leave. It was an easy way out, I suppose." Cora looked down at the quilt and traced the pattern with her finger absentmindedly.

"Gracious! Cora, what a story. We must pray for your family to come around. It can happen, you know. Nothing is impossible with God — except maybe pitting two brides against one unsuspecting bachelor," she teased. Cora laughed with her. It was good to finally be able to talk about the situation with someone.

"I believe that God has placed me here for a purpose, Greta. I think He wanted you and me to be friends, despite the crazy situation we found ourselves in. Don't you?"

"I couldn't agree with you more. Now, to just figure out what to do about it." Greta stood and handed Cora the soiled handkerchief. "But for now, let's get to bed. At least we won't have prowling bears to worry about." Greta grinned. Cora threw a pillow at her but she dodged it, sending them into fits of laughter like two schoolgirls.

Zach whistled as he walked back to the mercantile in the soft evening light, giving a nod here and there to people on the street. It had been a strange day to say the least, but it had ended well as far as he was concerned. He hoped Caleb would be a help and not a hindrance to them. But if anyone could help him, it would be Jess, and possibly Cora with the true concern she exhibited for him.

The last few moments with Greta had been especially nice. Though she hadn't kissed him back, neither had she pulled away, and he smiled with the thought of her soft lips pressed to his. What a turn of events. This was turning out better than he ever imagined. Two beautiful, educated women.

With the way Agnes had treated Jess, he could do far worse than Cora. Zach hadn't had marriage on his own mind when he wrote those letters pretending to be Jess. But tonight he was beginning to think Greta might be someone he could enjoy coming home to. When he had his own place to come home to . . .

13

Jess woke early to the sound of rain and wind rattling the window next to his bed. He rolled onto his side and glanced over at Zach, who was still asleep, then to the kitchen area only a few feet away, where Caleb lay sleeping with his arm slung across his tanned face. The boy didn't trust him, and he felt likewise.

Jess sat up, pushing the curtain aside just as the sun peeked over the mountain, its spreading light casting hues in purple, orange, and gold as it kissed the top of Bald Mountain. Sunrise or sunset, this was a beautiful sight he never tired of, and it was a constant reminder of God's presence. Good thing too, 'cause he was going to need it. He might have bitten off more than he could chew with this unruly whippersnapper. But there was something about Caleb that reminded Jess of his younger brother. He wasn't sure why. Maybe it was the fearless adventure mirrored in Caleb's eyes.

Tears stung his eyes, but he quickly blinked them away. He slid his pants on over his long handles to ward off the morning chill and pulled on his boots as he hoofed it to the outhouse. He'd make a pot of coffee when he returned, and hopefully the others would be awake by then.

The biting rain pelted him as he hurried across the yard, his boots sinking in the soggy grass. The air carried the fresh scent of pine needles that the wind and rain had strewn about. Later, snow would blanket Central City and the townsfolk would hunker down for the oncoming winter. If Zach had his way, he would be sharing his bed with Greta before winter, but Jess wasn't too sure about Cora. It *would* be nice to have a wife to snuggle up with and make love to, but presently he had no feelings to deal with where Cora was concerned . . . at least not yet. He wasn't sure he ever would after Agnes broke his heart. He sighed and shoved the thought as far back into his mind as he could. He knew Agnes wanted another chance, but that wouldn't happen again. No sirree!

When he returned, neither man had budged, even when he swung open the door. Sometimes the rain could lull him back to sleep too, but not today. He filled the cof-feepot with water, added coffee grounds in the top of the drip pot, shoved wood into the firebox, then set the pot to boil, figuring the sounds would wake the other two.

Looking about the large room, he knew it was no place for a wife. There simply wasn't any privacy. Of course, Zach would move out if he did marry Greta, but the place wasn't much to look at, and his side of the room was always a mess. From what he could already tell about Cora, she was a refined lady and wouldn't want to live above his store. He really couldn't blame her, which made him wonder why she'd an-swered the ad for a bride. It was as plain as the nose on his face that she was used to a higher class of living — yet she seemed to have a tender heart and showed kindness toward others. It was a very admirable trait to have, and she would surely make a good wife and mother.

A noise from the corner of the kitchen proved to be Caleb yawning and stretching as he struggled to his feet. He seemed unsure as to where he was for a moment, then stumbled to where Jess stood at the stove.

"Mornin'. Do you drink coffee, son?"

"There's other things I prefer, but I'll take

a cup," Caleb said, running his hand through shaggy hair that could use a good trimming.

"There's a fresh towel and soap on the rack by the stove. The outhouse is just down the stairs and outside to the left. Help yourself while I cook us up some bacon. It's raining, so take my slicker hanging on that hook there," Jess said, motioning to the back of the door.

"You mean you care if I get wet? How do you know I won't take off?"

Jess hooked his thumbs in his pockets and stared at him. "I don't know that you won't, but I don't want you dripping on my floor. And if you want some warm food in your belly and a chance to do something with your life, you'll stay. Up to you." He shrugged and turned away, watching the boy from the corner of his eye.

Caleb's mouth went slack with surprise, then he reached for the slicker and stomped down the stairs. Jess scratched his head, watching him leave. Maybe he could get through to him and learn more about his background, but Caleb held his cards close to his chest, that was for sure.

Jess took bacon from the pantry, sliced off thick chunks, and placed them in a skillet before lighting a fire under it. Soon the bacon was sizzling and the coffee boiling, waking Zach with the sounds and smells just as Caleb returned.

"Bacon sure smells good," Caleb commented, hanging the slicker back on the hook.

"Gonna be a wet, nasty day, I think," Jess said, turning the bacon over. "I see you finally woke up, Zach." He glanced over at his brother.

Zach pulled on his pants and shuffled over to pour himself a cup of coffee. "How'd you figure I could sleep with all that racket you're makin'?"

"That's the point — you're not supposed to." Jess took a plate and lifted the bacon slices onto it. "Caleb, reach in that basket on the table there and hand me some eggs, and I'll scramble some up for us."

Caleb handed him the eggs and watched as Jess deftly cracked a half dozen into a bowl, then beat them swiftly with a fork. "Gotta whip 'em good, then they'll be light and fluffy, you know." Jess could tell by the blank look on Caleb's face that he couldn't care less as long as he got to eat, but could be he'd learn something while he was standing there.

Zach returned from his morning ablutions, washed his hands, and grabbed the plates. He plunked them on the table while Caleb filled the coffee cups. "There's a half loaf of bread in the pantry there, Caleb, if you'll get it."

After scraping the eggs onto their plates, Jess set the skillet back on the stove, and they all took a seat at the worn table. He gave thanks for the meal, but before he finished, Caleb dug his fork into the eggs.

"Whoa, son. At this table we always wait to eat until after grace is said." Jess tapped him on the arm with his fork.

"Uh, sorry." Caleb put his fork down.

Jess humphed. "You can go ahead now. I've finished. But just remember next time to mind your manners while you're here." Jess motioned for him to eat.

The men ate in silence with the sounds of wagons rumbling past, the puppy barking downstairs, and the driving rain hitting the windows in the background. "We're gonna have to feed that little puppy some table scraps when we're through." Jess watched the young man wolf down the breakfast, saying little.

Zach devoured his breakfast and took a swig of coffee. "Caleb, we have a freight order that should arrive this morning. You can come with me and help me unload it from the train to our wagon." He glanced at

Jess. "If that works for you, Jess."

Caleb nodded, scraping up the last of his eggs.

"Good idea. Then he can help uncrate the supplies. What's on this shipment?" Jess should know, but sometimes he forgot what he'd ordered from week to week. He hated details, and it seemed that Zach hadn't minded handling much of the ordering or working for the store . . . until he'd admitted the truth after Greta and Cora arrived.

"Let's see . . . lard, salt, flour, coffee, rice, sugar, molasses, vinegar, kerosene, and engine oil, mostly. I think Greta mentioned she'd like to add a couple of items on the next order."

"Is that so? I'm not surprised. Maybe I should let her do inventory next time. She'd be better at keeping track of everything and seems to like taking charge. She'll make you a good wife, Zach." Jess swallowed the last sip of coffee, trying hard to mean what he'd just said.

"We'll see. No need to rush into things."

"Since you did all the letter writin', I assume you know her and Cora better than anyone."

Zach smiled. "Maybe. Letter writin' is one thing, but actually meeting face-to-face puts a different slant on things."

"What's that supposed to mean?" Jess asked while shoving back his chair. He started clearing the dishes.

Zach shrugged, then got up and reached for his coat and jacket. "I'll have to get to know Greta better in order to find out what she's really like." He looked at Caleb. "Are you 'bout done there, boy? The train arrives at 8:15 sharp."

"Yes, sir." Caleb stood and began to move away from the table, but he came back to retrieve his dirty plate and carry it to the sink.

"Boy howdy! You're making progress already." Zach clapped Caleb's back as he met him at the door.

"But as usual I get stuck with the dishes," Jess grumbled.

"Just put some hot water over them and we'll get 'em tonight. It's almost time to open the store, and the ladies will be here momentarily."

"Wait a minute, Caleb, and you can take these scraps to the dog. When he's done eating, let him out back before you two traipse off to the train station." Jess shoved a small bowl into Caleb's hands. "I'll be down as soon as I get the dishes soaking."

Greta hurried to the store door with Cora

following behind her as a gust of wind ushered them inside, flinging the door against the wall. She tried to catch it, but the latch wouldn't hold. She must see to getting that repaired today. Feeling like a drowned rat, she looked about for something to hold the door closed. Where were Jess and Zach?

Cora closed the shared umbrella while it dripped in puddles around their feet. "Over there, Greta. A spittoon will work nicely." Cora indicated with the point of the umbrella while holding the door with her foot.

Greta pushed back the dripping lengths of her hair that had escaped her braids and propped the door with the spittoon, leaving it slightly ajar. It was doubtful many customers would brave the weather today. She straightened and looked at Cora's wet skirt, then at her own. "We're a sight for sore eyes," she said with a giggle.

"Right you are, but we will most likely dry out before anyone shows up today in this awful weather. Why, that howling wind kept me up most of the night!"

"At least we were in a nice hotel with its own restaurant and only a short walk to the store. Just think how wet we would've been if we'd had to walk from Jeb's cabin. But let's go find something to dry off with."

Greta turned when she heard Jess coming down the stairs. "Good morning. I see you met the rain coming to work. Let me grab a towel for you." He turned back to the storeroom and returned with a towel for each of them.

"I like rain, but not particularly to walk in it," Cora commented, taking the towel from him.

Jess folded his arms, observing them closely as they toweled off. Greta felt his probing eyes on her and asked, "Where's the puppy?" She looked around the room.

"He's got his tummy full, and he's fast asleep in the corner by the stove." Jess took their wet capes and draped them over a crate in front of the stove.

"He really should have a name. Don't you think?" She blotted her hair and face, giving Jess a brief glance. He hadn't taken time to shave this morning. She felt his deep-set brown eyes sweep over her, and they locked eyes briefly.

"Absolutely! So have you an idea?" Cora patted her curls back into place, donned an apron, and handed another one to Greta.

Greta walked over to the stove and bent down. "How about Rascal?" she said, kneeling down to pat him on the head as he slept.

"I like it." Cora looked down at the pup.

"It suits him. Don't you think, Jess?"

Jess strolled over. "Could be. I've never really had a dog in the store, but since he tried to warn us of the robber, if no one claims him, I could keep him as a watch-dog."

Greta's heart warmed at the thought that he would consider keeping Rascal. She stood, turning toward him. "That's sweet of you. I'll print a sign to hang in the window to see if anyone is missing him."

Jess chuckled. "I rather doubt they will be. Dogs commonly roam the streets of town, either abandoned or left behind when someone moves on."

"All the better for us then. Now, what's on our agenda today?"

Jess looped a thumb in his jeans pocket. "Zach and Caleb are at the freight station picking up our order, but in this rain it'll take awhile. When they return, we'll have a lot of new supplies to shelve. Business will be rather slow, I expect."

"Good! A slow day won't be such a bad thing." Cora hooked her arm through Jess's.

Greta watched them stroll away, a strange tug in her chest as she remembered how Jess's eyes had drilled into hers. Her mind kept going back to his kiss, however mis-placed it had been. She compared the kiss to Zach's and found Zach's lacking. Though his was sweet, Jess's unexpected kiss on her cheek had somehow touched her heart. She couldn't deny the way it made her feel and admitted that every time she was around him, something about him drew her. Of course, she could never tell Cora. It was obvious they were a perfect match.

"Jess!" Greta called out. "Do you think you could fix the latch plate on the front door? I've got it propped shut for now, but the wind is strong and the latch doesn't line up with the door."

Jess turned around, and Cora let her arm drop from his. "I'll give it a try, but I might have to order a new lock. This one's old." He ambled to the door to examine the latch. "I'll get my tools and see if I can fix it temporarily to suit your nagging." His lips twitched with a smile. "I've been meaning to do it, just never got around to it."

"That and a lot of other things," Greta said with a wink to Cora, but Cora's look was solemn.

14

The rainy day kept people indoors, but Greta was relieved. When Caleb and Zach returned with a wagonload of supplies, everyone pitched in to help. She held a tablet with orders and checked off everything on the list for inventory. She was quite pleased that Jess had asked for her help in that area. The busyness kept the day from dragging along.

"Caleb, put the kerosene next to the lanterns on the shelf to the left," Cora instructed. "How many containers are there?"

"I counted thirty, ma'am," he answered, barely pausing long enough to speak.

Greta noted the amount and watched as Jess and Zach continued bringing in other supplies. "This place will be bursting at the seams soon. Cora, we'll have to make certain every square inch is utilized," she said, tapping the pencil against her tablet.

Greta watched from the open door as Zach heaved a barrel labeled SALT with ease, carried it up the steps and inside, then plunked it down. He strode over to her, touching the tip of her nose with his finger. "You look charming when you're working intently."

Greta felt heat flood her cheeks. "Thank you," she murmured but was saved from saying anything else as Cora walked up.

"Don't forget, ladies, tonight we'll have supper with Annabelle and Silas. You'll have a home-cooked meal for a change, and Annabelle is an excellent cook," Zach said, still keeping his eyes on Greta.

"Looks like the rain is over. Maybe it'll be a nice evening, and I'm looking forward to getting to know the Meads." Cora handed Greta the bill of lading to check off once everything was unloaded.

"Let's stop for coffee," Zach suggested, and Greta was more than happy to enjoy a break. Her feet were aching from standing so much. A different pair of shoes might be needed for this job since she and Cora were on their feet all day. She began to daydream about sitting down to sew the dress for Agnes.

"I'll go fetch Caleb." Cora glanced around,

spying him between the aisles of canned goods and household supplies. She wandered toward him but hesitated, watching him for a moment. Caleb was turned away from her, but there was no mistaking that he wanted the pearl-handled pocketknife he fingered. He looked from side to side to see if anyone was watching as he put it into his trouser pocket.

"You want to take that, don't you? Is that the only way you know how to acquire something?" Cora whispered, stopping next to him.

Startled, Caleb jerked around and froze. His face spoke of youthful innocence, but his eyes told a different story. He wiped his brow with the back of his hand. "Ma'am, I've had to steal just to have food in my belly. Now that you caught me, I reckon I'll just slip out." He sighed and lowered his eyes.

"Hand it to me, please." For a moment he made no move, then he placed the knife in her outstretched palm. She put it in her apron pocket. "Thank you. Now come join us for a coffee break," she said in what she hoped was her most confident voice.

His brows furrowed. "Why would you do that for me?" he choked out.

"I'm giving you a chance to set things

right because that's what Christ would do. Now, come along so we can finish up around here."

The light in his eyes was confirmation enough that she'd just made another friend.

Jess strolled up to the counter where Greta was setting out the cups and waited for Zach to return with the coffee. "You ladies have worked hard today. The rain's about cleared out, and we'll close up soon and ride on over to Silas's for supper."

"Are we 'bout done with the unloadin'?" Caleb shuffled his feet wearily.

"Not much left on the wagon," Jess said. "Zach thinks we're in need of a coffee break. I have to agree. How 'bout you?"

Caleb shrugged. "Naw, I'm not much on drinking coffee. My ma couldn't make a decent pot."

Jess chuckled. "Well, you need to give Zach's a try," he said, clapping him on the back. "He makes a perfect cup and will win you over."

Caleb lifted a shoulder. "I guess I will then."

Zach traipsed down the stairs with the coffeepot in one hand and cookies in the other. "I brought some of Granny's sugar cookies to tide us over until supper with Annabelle and Silas." Zach glanced over at Caleb. "You're welcome to come along. Annabelle opens her home to everyone she meets." Zach strolled over to stand next to Greta.

"I don't know . . ." Caleb took the proffered cup from Zach, blowing on it gently before taking a sip.

"Annabelle must be a special lady. I think you should come with us, Caleb. Where were you raised, if you don't mind me asking?" Cora held out a cookie to him.

Jess's ears perked up as he peered over his coffee cup at Caleb, waiting for his answer.

"My father has a dairy farm in Montrose, southwest of here," he answered, looking down into his cup.

"So why did you leave your family's farm?" Greta asked.

Jess chewed his bottom lip, annoyed that once again Greta had cut right to the heart of the matter without intending to be nosy. What was it about her that drew him? The sparkle in her eyes or the quirky way she lifted an eyebrow to nearly everything she questioned? He should be concentrating on Cora, who was a nice lady with a sweet temperament and always considerate with others. It was clear that Zach was enamored of Greta, which was entirely different than what Jess knew his brother had intended.

Caleb's answer brought Jess back to the present. "Dairy farming is not for me." He set his jaw as he said it, making Jess think Caleb had left on unfavorable terms with his father.

"What do you want to do?" Jess asked. He bit into one of Granny's delicious cookies and was reminded of when he was a young boy. Granny always encouraged him to find out what life was about and pursue whatever he chose, which hadn't been hard for him. He remembered when he was just a young boy going to the store with his parents, and the mingling smells of leather products, feed supplies, dried tobacco, and the burning woodstove were forever embedded in his mind. He felt comfortable and useful then — and now. He enjoyed what he did for a living and interacting with the townsfolk.

Caleb gobbled down the last of his cookie and nodded at Jess. "Not sure — maybe go to college, but money's hard to come by for that."

Zach snickered. "Well, we already know that, after you tried to rob us."

Caleb plunked down his cup so hard the coffee splashed onto the counter. "I *said* I was sorry."

"The proof is in how you work out your

debt to us, now isn't it?" Zach narrowed his eyes at him, and Caleb shifted to one hip.

Greta touched Zach's sleeve. "Give him time, Zach."

Zach straightened. "I was only reminding him."

Jess stepped up to the counter and let Cora pour him another half cup of coffee. "That's enough about that. I'd like you to come to supper with us."

"Why? So you can keep an eye on me? I'll sit on the porch until you get back."

"No, you'll do no such thing. I thought it'd be good for you to get to know a few people . . . a little socializing. No harm in that." Jess eyed him thoughtfully.

"Say you'll come, Caleb. It's time to start over and let people help you along the way." Cora gave him a warm smile, and Caleb finally nodded okay.

Greta unbuckled her shoes and stood in her stocking feet, wiggling her toes. "I'm sorry, but I had to get these shoes off."

"Greta, *really!*" Cora gave her a shocked look.

Greta rubbed one foot over the other and sighed with relief. "I'm sorry, but standing has been hard on the balls of my feet. I'm not used to being on them all day for days in a row."

Zach grinned at her. "Aw . . . sure you weren't out dancing at parties and such in Wyoming? Though I'm glad you decided to answer my ad, I'll bet you were the main attraction for all the eligible bachelors."

Greta laughed. "Not hardly. More like helping to harvest wheat and tend to my sister's twin babies."

Jess stared down at Greta's feet, which were barely visible from under the hem of her dress. He could see the tips of her toes through her stockings. He was sure her ankles were shapely too. He dragged his eyes away.

Rascal started yapping in his crate, and Greta hurried over to him. "I'll bet you need to go outside, huh?" She reached in, lifted the lid, and scooped him up. "You poor little thing! We got so busy that we forgot all about you." Rascal wagged his tail and gave a sharp bark.

"I'll take him out. He seems to like me," Caleb said, crossing the room to where Greta stood talking to the pup.

Greta looked up. "Okay, but don't let him out of your sight. I've grown quite fond of the little ragamuffin."

"I promise to watch him. Maybe we could get a leash for him?" Caleb tucked Rascal under his arm.

"Good idea, I'll order one. I don't remember seeing one in the store," she said. "But I'll ask. Now hurry back in so we can finish up before we head off to the Meads'."

Caleb nodded and hurried out the back with the dog.

Greta walked over to where Jess and the rest were cleaning up. She slipped her shoes back on and said, "I think Caleb is trying his best, Zach."

"I hope so," he said with a wink. "Want to help me carry this back upstairs before we go to the Meads'?"

"I need to talk to Jess about something first," Greta said. She saw Jess's brow furrow.

"I'll help you, Zach. It'll only take a minute." Cora gathered the cups and empty cookie plate.

Zach gave Cora a nod. "Thanks. We'll be down in a minute," he said. Greta watched him walk toward the back stairs as Cora followed. "I've been meaning to give you back the money I borrowed," he said, handing her the bills. "Thanks."

"You're welcome, Zach." Cora tucked the money into her apron, smiling sweetly.

Jess stood with his work gloves in his hand as Greta turned to him. "What's on your mind? I need to go back outside and see what's left on the wagon."

"I . . . I had an idea I wanted to ask you about."

"I'm listening."

"What if we created an area near the stove with a small table and chairs for our customers? Then perhaps we could have some coffee or some type of refreshment." Greta held her breath until he answered.

He looked at her like she'd grown two heads. "Now why would I want to do that? That would mean more work, and who's going to have time to prepare refreshments? Everybody and his brother would be coming in for that. Besides, that takes money."

"Cora and I could . . . maybe we could just keep lemonade or tea on hand. If it got to be more than we expect, we could charge a small fee, but it'd be better if we didn't. I think serving the customers will make people satisfied." She paused, then pushed her luck a little further. "And I want to ask if you'd let me decorate the front window for fall next week."

He shook his head, locking eyes with hers. "Who do you think you are, coming in here and turning my store upside down? No table and chairs. We'll talk about the front window later." He turned back to the counter and busied himself sorting papers.

A soft answer turneth away wrath. Greta pursed her lips, reminding herself that Jess owned the store, and any new idea she might offer up would always be met with disagreement. He was so stubborn!

She stood quietly for a moment, wondering how the gentle Cora was going to be able to live with Jess's hardheadedness. Didn't he see that little things like keeping the store tidy and making it a more pleasing place to shop would only benefit him? Her mind searched for a way to convince him of her ideas. She stepped around to the other side of the counter.

"I'd appreciate it if you'd consider the idea. Just think, a man could have a seat while his wife shopped or while he waited for his supplies to be loaded. Why don't you ask Zach his opinion?" Greta risked another glance at Jess's firmly set jaw and wondered if he thought she was only a thorn in his flesh.

Caleb walked past with Rascal on his way to the dog's crate before Jess answered. "Greta, listen to me. Most customers load their own supplies, and I don't see that many women knocking the door down to shop while the menfolk are waiting."

She smiled at him. "They could be —

188

especially when I start sewing for Agnes. She seems to be a lady of influence. Maybe other ladies will consider ordering dresses through me instead of that." She pointed to the Montgomery Ward catalog on the counter in front of them. "I'm not bad with a needle, but I'll need a small area of space to sew."

He laid the papers aside, then placed his hands on his hips. "What are you going to ask for next? Wait! Don't answer. I'm sure you have something churning in that pretty little head of yours." His eyes fell on the locket she fingered absentmindedly on its chain, and his face softened. He sighed in exasperation. "You win. I'll see what Zach thinks." He called out to Caleb, "Come on, let's get the last of the supplies unloaded now that the rain has stopped."

"Sure thing," Caleb answered, pulling his gloves back on.

Greta flashed Jess a smile. "You won't regret it. *Dank U wel.*"

"Pardon?"

"It means *thank you* in Dutch."

"Hold on — I never said I agreed yet." He turned to follow Caleb outside.

"Oh, don't forget to fix that doorjamb tomorrow," she called. He paused with his hand on the doorknob and let out a huff, and she covered her mouth to stifle a giggle.

15

Zach hurried back to the carriage where everyone was waiting for him to drive over to the Meads'. His heart thumped, keeping time with his quick footsteps as he clutched the forget-me-nots he'd quickly gathered on the hillside where he liked to walk. In a short time he'd determined they should go ahead with the nuptials so life could settle back into place. He liked Greta well enough, and her beauty could set a man's blood to boil, even if she did like to be in control of things. But even that was turning out to be a good thing for the mercantile store. He intended to take her to Granny's himself even if he had to rent a horse so they could get a few moments alone. After that he'd know better how to proceed.

She was warming up to him. He was pretty sure he was ready for her. Wasn't he? Why else would his heart race and his hands get sweaty whenever he was close to her?

He almost laughed out loud at his thinking. When he was writing the letters to her and Cora, he had never considered marriage. However, the idea became very appealing once he met Greta.

"Where have you been?" Jess glared at him as he drew close to the carriage, Cora seated next to him. Caleb sat in the back and Greta across from him. "We've been waiting."

Zach swung his legs up and plopped down next to Greta. "I had something to attend to. Let's get going," he said. He turned to Greta and withdrew the flowers, still damp from the rain, from behind his back. "These are for you." He heard Jess's humph as he set the horses in a trot down the street in the direction of Silas's farm.

"Oh, how thoughtful. These are beautiful!" She held the flowers to her nose. "With such a delicate fragrance. What are they called?"

"Forget-me-nots. They're a perfect match to the blue in your eyes now that you're holding them close. They have almost no smell in the daytime, but they do late in the day and evening." His face burned, but it was worth it to have her look at him as she did now, her sky-blue eyes sparkling. His pulse quickened as he watched her arrange her full skirts and was struck once again at her slender, attractive figure. "It's not every day that a man gets a chance to sit next to a pretty lady."

A pink color tinged her cheeks, and the late afternoon breeze lifted silken strands of hair at her forehead. He couldn't help but wonder what she'd look like with her hair down, brushing her slender shoulders.

"I'm sure I'm looking a little worse for wear after all that we did today, but thank you just the same — and for the flowers." She lowered her eyes, and Zach was surprised at her modest response. She appeared to be confident most of the time, but maybe she wasn't used to receiving compliments, which he found hard to believe.

"You look as fresh as these flowers," he said, glancing over her blue homespun dress with approval. "Maybe they can be the ones you carry when we're married."

Now where had that come from? He'd sworn to himself he was going to wait until they were alone before he brought that up. He saw her back stiffen. Was that her answer? Was he rushing things? After all, that's what she'd come for. His heart sank. Had he pushed her too soon?

Caleb shifted in his seat, then stared out at the mountains as though pretending not to have heard.

"Well . . . I . . . don't know what to say." She tilted her face up to gaze at him, and his heart raced.

Zach swallowed hard. "Well, that is what you're here for, isn't it?" He took her small hand, noticing how soft it felt in his large, calloused one. "We could be married next week." They hit a bump in the road, slinging Greta against his chest, and he held her a moment, breathing in the sweetness of her hair and lavender soap smell. She pulled back and adjusted the cape around her shoulders. "Unless you need more time . . ."

"I . . . suppose we could . . . I guess I wasn't expecting it so soon." She pulled away, fingering the petals on the flowers, keeping her gaze averted.

"I'm sorry. Can you forgive me?" He glanced at Caleb, who appeared to pay them no mind. Leastways, the boy wasn't dumb. Zach was thankful that Cora and Jess were happily chatting at the front of the carriage instead of eavesdropping.

"I forgive you, Zach, but I'm a little worried since you said yourself that you weren't even considering marriage when you met us at the train depot. Are you telling me that by week's end you've had a change of heart?"

"That was before I met you and before I told Jess about the situation. Now I find myself very attracted to you. I see no reason to wait a month. I'll be a good husband to you, and one day I'll provide you with a ranch and some cattle — and children too."

One shapely brow quirked as she turned to look him squarely in the eye. "I wasn't aware that you wanted to be a rancher."

"I do. Jess is the mercantile man, not me. I need to be outdoors working with my hands. Why, does being married to a rancher not appeal to you?"

She gave a soft laugh. "No, that's not it. I've worked on a farm. I guess I can learn to be a rancher's wife."

"You don't have to sound so doggone cheerful," Zach teased. He pulled Greta close and gave her a peck on the cheek, then squeezed her waist. Caleb coughed, reminding them that they had an audience.

"Well, there seems to be a matter of where we'll live, unless you already have a ranch?" Greta sniffed the flowers again.

"I own some property not far from here and will soon start a house . . . now that I have a reason to." Zach touched the tip of her nose.

"We can talk further about our plans privately," Greta murmured. "Caleb, I forgot to thank you for walking Rascal."

Zach took the hint to close the subject, but now that he'd asked her, he was pleased that she seemed to be in agreement. Suddenly he had a hankering for Annabelle's pot roast and wondered if Greta knew how to cook.

Caleb twisted in his seat toward them. "I was glad to, Miss Greta. He was no trouble. Besides, I like animals."

"Really? Have you ever given any thought to studying animal husbandry?"

Caleb sat up taller on the seat, suddenly looking more adultlike than before. "Yes, ma'am, I have, but it takes a whole lot of money to go to school to be an animal doctor."

Greta leaned over and patted him on the knee. "Well, at least you have a job now, and that's a start."

He snorted. "Ha! I already owe my next few earnings to Jess and Zach." He looked down, clasping his hands together nervously.

"Son, if you work as hard at saving for an education as you do trying to be on the opposite side of the law, then you'll eventually do all right." Zach leaned back in his seat, folding his arms across his chest.

"I can't thank you enough for your *encouraging* words, Zach," Caleb said sarcastically.

"I don't think Zach meant to sound so harsh, Caleb." Greta flashed an annoyed looked at Zach. "You worked very hard today at the store, and if you continue, then who knows what could happen in the future." Greta's voice conveyed reassurance — how Zach knew he should have spoken. Still, he hesitated about putting too much faith in the troubled young man.

When they drove into the Meads' rain-washed yard and stopped near a cluster of aspen trees, Annabelle was waiting for them on the porch, her ample frame covered by a crisp white apron over a brown homespun dress. A couple of dogs yapped, tails wagging, and she shooed them away, while a fluffy cat scampered into the thick bushes alongside the house. A feeling of warmth flooded Cora's being. She was eager to make some new friends, and she'd felt a connection with Silas and Annabelle from their first meeting. She wagered that they were God-fearing people after observing them with their children at the mercantile.

"Land sakes!" Annabelle greeted them as she made her way down the porch steps and into the yard. "Climb down and come on inside and make yourselves comfortable." She waved to them, then paused when her eyes fell on Caleb.

Jess was quick to react and climbed down from the carriage. "Annabelle, I hope you don't mind that I brought along my new handyman, Caleb Zuckerman." Jess pulled him over to meet her, then assisted Cora out of the carriage.

Annabelle was gracious and gave Caleb a warm smile. "Jess knows everyone's welcome at our home. I hope you're hungry for pot roast. Silas!" she called out toward the barn. "Our company is here." She gave Cora and Greta a welcoming hug. "How have you ladies been? Hope Jess isn't working you to death."

"Everything's been fine with us," Greta said with a smile. "It's nice to see you again."

"Thank you for having us over," Cora chimed in. The fresh scent of rain enveloped the yard, which was edged with a lush bed of different flowers and pine straw. She thought it was charming against the backdrop of their white clapboard farmhouse.

"Did you say roast?" Zach gave Annabelle a peck on the cheek. "You know that's my favorite."

Annabelle gave him a pinch on his cheek. "That and whipped potatoes, fresh snap beans, and huckleberry cobbler with fresh cream for dessert."

Cora's stomach rumbled at the mention of the delicious fare, and Zach smacked his lips and said, "Just wait till you taste her cookin'!"

Silas scurried over from the barn as they stood in a cluster chatting. "Howdy, everyone! What are you all standing out here for? Annabelle has been waiting to dish up supper."

"You've got no argument from me. I'm starving." Zach clapped Silas on the back good-naturedly. "I want you to meet Caleb here. He's hired on to help us at the store for a while."

Silas stuck his hand out and Caleb grasped it firmly. "Good to have you, son."

Caleb nodded with a smile. "Much obliged to have supper with your family."

Silas tossed his head. "Then let's go. A young man like you needs three squares a day!"

They all laughed. Zach reached for Greta's hand, and the group followed Silas inside.

Walking into the front room of the house, Cora observed the homey atmosphere. The living room was furnished with an English cottage look, with rose-patterned pillows and subdued chintz fabric covering the couch, as if to say "come and stay awhile."

Delicate figurines graced the ornate fireplace, where burning logs snapped to ward off the early evening chill and dampness.

"Let me take your wraps, ladies, and your hats, gentlemen. You know Annabelle is strict about that sort of thing at the table." Silas chuckled as he took their belongings and disappeared.

The children tumbled down the stairs like a pile of puppies, practically on top of each other, their rosy cheeks glowing from their evening baths. "I beat both of you!" Sue yelled over her shoulder, then came to a screeching halt at Caleb's feet. She stared up at him in complete surprise, then flashed him a big smile.

Sue's brothers, Joshua and Stephen, plowed into her, propelling her forward against Caleb. He caught her with gentle hands and set her up straight. "Take it easy there, boys," he murmured.

Cora watched the little girl's face glow at Caleb's defense and decided to add to the beautiful child's moment of joy.

"Yes, gentlemen, always be kind to your little sister." She reached to stroke the girl's baby-soft cheek. "Then you'll grow up to be kind to ladies."

Annabelle grabbed Joshua by the arm. "Where are your manners?" Turning to her guests, she shook her head. "Excuse our little brood's discourteous greeting."

Sue slipped her hand into Caleb's, and he looked at her with a mixed expression of pleasure and sadness that only Cora seemed to notice. She wondered briefly if the boy had a little sister of his own somewhere.

"What's your name?" Sue asked.

"Caleb."

"Did *all* of you come to eat with us?" she asked, looking around at everyone.

They all laughed, and Silas tweaked her pigtails. "Why don't you lead the way to the dining room, little lady?"

"Come, follow me." Sue yanked on Caleb's hand. "You can sit by me."

Sue led the way, and Cora paused just inside the dining room doorway. The large, airy room was fully set with a Battenberg tablecloth beneath gleaming stemware and rose china etched in gold. The table was laden with dishes piled high with food, and the delectable smells made her mouth water. Soft candlelight created an ambience for a relaxed dining experience.

"Take any seat you like," Annabelle instructed. "I'll be back in a flash with the roast. I've been keeping it warm in the oven."

"Can I be of help, Annabelle?" Cora

paused as Jess pulled out her chair before taking a seat.

"No, dear. You're a guest. Just have a seat. Silas, will you please fill the water glasses? Greta, can I put these flowers in a vase of water for you?"

"Yes, of course." Greta extended the bouquet. "Why not let me share them as a centerpiece for your lovely table?"

"That'd be nice." Annabelle took the flowers, breathing deeply of their fragrance. She disappeared into the kitchen and was back in a flash, the flowers swimming in a cut-glass vase that she placed in the center of the table. She buzzed around the room like a butterfly at a picnic, and her cheerfulness was contagious, making everyone feel at home, Cora thought.

The children sat together at one end nearest their father, with Sue making sure that Caleb was across from her and to the left of her father. Jess sat next to Cora, and Zach and Greta sat across from them. Silas filled the glasses before taking his chair at the head of the table.

"The table looks so nice," Greta said to Annabelle, who carried in a large platter of sumptuous-looking roast.

"I wanted it to look especially nice for you ladies tonight." Annabelle's face flushed.

She set the roast down, placed her apron on the sideboard, and took her seat.

Cora noted that Caleb hardly said a word but was taking in the entire scene. She saw him stare down at all the silverware. Hadn't he ever had a nice dinner before? Perhaps his home was only a small dairy farm and not at all what she'd envisioned.

As the food was passed around after Silas said grace, Caleb caught her eye. Cora lifted her fork, indicating which utensil to use. He blinked with a weak smile, then picked up the proper fork. She felt sorry for him and was once again reminded of her own privileged life. It was her heart's desire to help people less fortunate.

She noticed that Sue kept eyeing Caleb all through dinner. As she passed him the green beans, Sue gave him another adoring look. "Mama," she said in her sweet, childish voice, "I think I've fallen in love." She stared at Caleb.

"What did you say, dear?" Her mother asked rather absentmindedly, pausing in her conversation with Jess.

"Truly I have." Sue spoke louder, eyes wide with sincerity. "With Caleb," she said with a wide grin and wide eyes.

Silas cleared his throat while Caleb nearly choked on a mouthful of food and grabbed a water glass. Cora stifled a giggle.

"Sue, just eat your dinner," her father ordered, looking somewhat flustered. It was clear that he was in no way prepared for a declaration of love from his baby girl.

"He's as handsome as your porcelain figurine on the fireplace mantel, Mama," Sue went on in a dreamy tone. Then the child looked directly at Zach, saying in a thoughtful voice, "But I would never be so foolish as to fall in love with a porcelain doll. Would you, Zach? Greta looks like a porcelain doll."

Greta blushed, and Cora wondered if the precocious child might just be speaking truths that were far beyond her age. What did the Bible say? *Out of the mouth of babes . . .* Cora glanced at Caleb, who just kept shoveling in the food under Silas's watchful eye while Zach seemed to squirm visibly in his seat.

"That will be enough, young lady." Annabelle gave her daughter a stern look to silence her.

The chattering around the table quieted a bit, though the young boys smothered laughs behind their napkins. Cora noticed a frown cross Zach's handsome features as he choked out a response to the child.

"Well . . . er . . . you're right, Greta is

beautiful and delicate like porcelain," he replied, pushing his fork nervously around his plate.

"*Ach!* Is that all you think about me — that I'm like a porcelain doll?" Greta asked. "There's much more to me than my looks, Zach." She slapped her napkin on the table.

Stephen and Joshua snickered and were met with a look from Silas that silenced them.

"I don't — I mean, I know —" Zach sputtered. "I gave you flowers," he finished lamely.

"It's going to take a lot more than that, I'm afraid," Greta said.

Sue turned her gaze on Jess. "So, what did you give Cora tonight since you're courting her, Jess?"

Cora felt Jess's body stiffen in the chair next to her. "Well, Sue . . . I guess the thought never occurred to me to, uh . . . give her something, but I wish I had."

"Mama says wishing and doing are two different things, ain't that right, Mama?"

Annabelle nodded helplessly.

Cora wondered whether it would have mattered to her if Jess *had* given her flowers.

Sue swung back to Caleb, tossing her braids. "I like you a lot," she intoned. "But

I have a question — are you a good man or a bad man?"

There was a sudden uncomfortable silence at the table. It was obvious to Cora that Sue had overheard her parents talking about the boy.

Caleb's fork clattered to his plate. "Well . . . I —" His face was scarlet.

Jess spoke up. "Sue, I don't know what you heard, but everyone deserves a second chance, and that includes Caleb. And I, for one, intend to see that he gets it."

Annabelle's face turned bright red. "Sue, your manners are sorely lacking. I'm going to ask you to leave the table if you don't close your mouth except to eat!"

"Yes, Mama." Sue cast her long lashes down at her plate.

Annabelle stood. "Anyone ready for that huckleberry cobbler now?"

Cora knew it would probably be a long while before Annabelle and Silas delivered any more dinner invitations to them. She also knew that it was bound to be a quiet ride home that night.

16

Greta had enjoyed dinner with the Meads and their children until Sue started her yammering about porcelain dolls. She was beginning to think that Zach wasn't attracted to her for her mind. The idea made her stomach churn.

Once they were back in their room, she and Cora readied for bed. Cora had propped up on pillows to read her Bible, but moments later her chin fell against her chest in sound sleep. It had been a long day, but Greta was restless, so she slid out of bed, knelt down at her trunk, and quietly lifted the lid so as not to disturb Cora.

She reached into the corner and pulled out letters tied with blue ribbon. Her heart caught in her throat as she untied the ribbon and removed a letter. Running a shaking finger across her name on the envelope, she felt tears begin to sting her eyes. *Oh, Bryan . . . how I still miss you after all this time.* She opened the letter and read his words of love and the plans he had been making for them. Catharine had told her that first loves are profound, and Greta knew it to be true. She fingered the gold locket around her neck and stifled a sob in the sleeve of her nightgown.

"Greta?" Cora struggled to sit up. "I must have dropped off to sleep. Were you crying?"

Greta got up and climbed back into bed. "I'm sorry I disturbed you," she said, sniffing. "You looked so peaceful."

"Whatever is wrong?" Cora asked as she adjusted the covers around herself. "What do you have there?"

"I was reading Bryan's last letter to me . . . It's so hard to believe even after all this time that he's gone."

"May I?" Cora asked and pointed to the envelope.

Greta handed her the envelope and waited, watching her.

Cora studied the outside of the envelope. "Greta, have you ever noticed that Bryan's handwriting is a lot like Jess's?"

Greta shook her head. "No, I haven't. So?" She gave her friend a quizzical look.

Cora handed it back to her. "Mmm . . . I'm not sure . . . It's just that I noticed after watching Jess write up orders and seeing Bryan's handwriting now. They *do* have the same last names too. Maybe they're distant cousins."

"I think it's just coincidence, Cora. Bryan lived in Wyoming, and I don't remember him mentioning Colorado." She shrugged. "Besides, I asked them at supper if they had any cousins, remember?"

"I remember. Still . . . how long did you know him before he died?"

She thought back to the spring when she'd met him. "I think it was only about four months. I guess there was a lot about him I never had a chance to learn."

"I'm so sorry it ended that way." Cora patted her on the arm. "I'm sure the Lord has plans for you. And Zach seems taken with you. Doesn't that give you something to think about with hope?"

Greta knew Cora was sincere, and maybe she was right. She should let the past go, but she would never forget how Bryan had made her feel. "Cora . . . I don't know . . . tonight after Sue's questions at supper, I felt like he only sees me as a pretty china doll. I'm not sure I want to be married at all anymore."

Cora laughed softly. "You're just getting cold feet. That Sue certainly has a gift for talking straight. I think she meant it as a compliment, but somehow she is aware at her young age that the outward appearance is not the most important. Her parents have taught her well. I don't know what Zach really thinks — only he knows."

Greta rose and wrapped the ribbon back around the stack of letters. "I'm suddenly too tired to give it any more thought."

As she placed the packet in the trunk, her hand touched a hard object. She remembered instantly what it was. It was the Blue Willow cake knife that Peter had given her for her hope chest. She carefully unwrapped the piece of muslin, and fond memories of her family in Wyoming flooded her thoughts. Suddenly she was lonely for them.

"What do you have there?" Cora peered over at her.

Greta rose, carrying the cake knife, and sat down on the edge of her bed. "It's a Blue Willow cake knife that my brother-in-law, Peter, gave me for when I marry." She held it out for Cora to see.

"My! It's very pretty," she said, admiring it. She turned it over as she inspected the design. "How very sweet."

"Yes, that's Peter. A sweet, kind man. He gave a set of Blue Willow china to my sister when he was trying to win her back." When

Cora gave her a questioning look, Greta quickly told her about Catharine and Peter's fight after they were married, the romantic resolution at the railroad depot, and how Peter described each piece of china and what they represented. Cora listened with tears in her eyes.

"She's so lucky to have found true love." Cora sniffed, then rearranged her covers, snuggling down under the heavy quilt.

"They are very happy, and now I have a niece and a nephew — twins. But it took the mighty arm of God working in their lives to get things right."

"Let's hope we won't need a knock on the head from the Lord." Cora laughed.

"Do you know the legend of the Blue Willow china?"

A crease formed between Cora's eyebrows. "I'm afraid I don't," she said.

"Legend has it that a wealthy Mandarin merchant had a lovely daughter who'd fallen in love with her father's assistant. Her father was angry because they weren't of the same social class, so he arranged for her to marry a duke. The duke arrived bearing jewels as a gift, and the wedding was supposed to take place the day the blossoms fell from the willow tree." She paused, watching Cora's growing interest, and smiled. "The night before the wedding, the assistant slipped into the palace, disguised as a servant. The lovers escaped with the jewels, running over the bridge that you see on the design here. They lived happily for many years on a secluded island. One day, the duke learned of their retreat and sent soldiers to capture the two lovers and put them to death. The gods felt sorry for them and transformed them into the pair of doves."

"What a bittersweet story," Cora whispered. "But isn't it wonderful that we have a true God who one day will transform us with a new heavenly body?"

Greta nodded. "Right you are." She wrapped the knife and placed it back in the trunk. One day, somehow she would have more Blue Willow like her mother and Catharine did.

"Why don't we shut out the light and get some rest. We'll both feel better in the morning. I think Agnes will be coming in for a dress fitting." Cora rolled her eyes, making Greta laugh.

"In that case, I need my beauty rest." Greta batted her eyes, then hopped back into bed, drawing the covers up to her chin. The room was dark save for a sliver of moonlight casting a streak across the room.

After a few minutes, she said, "Cora, thanks for being a good friend. I really wish you and Jess much happiness."

"Thank you. I wish the same for you and Zach . . ." Cora's voice trailed off, and soon Greta heard her even breathing and knew Cora was asleep.

What if Cora doesn't marry Jess for some reason? Well, could that mean . . . ? She chided herself. *Don't be foolish.* Of course Cora would marry Jess — he only had eyes for her anyway.

Jess fumed. Chen from the Chinese laundry had delivered a stack of aprons as soon as Jess opened the door for business this morning. Not that he was mad at Chen — far from it. He was a humble, hardworking man. But Jess knew he hadn't sent out aprons to be laundered, and Zach didn't care if they were even clean. So that left only one person — Greta! Just like everything else, she did things without asking him first. Like the order form she'd somehow left on the counter for his approval. The list included new fabric, thread, notions, and merchandise like toys and books for Christmas. Items Jess would never consider buying. Who needed all that stuff in the first place? He surely didn't, and he would tell her so. Things like that cost money. In a few short days, Greta almost acted as if *she* owned the mercantile!

He took a swig of his coffee, ruminating. Ever since Zach had given flowers to Greta, something about it had stuck in his craw and he'd felt slightly irritated. First, because he'd not thought of doing something similar for sweet Cora, and second, because Sue had put him on the spot last night by pointing that fact out in front of everyone.

He was kidding himself. He examined his feelings and knew the truth was that he was jealous that *he* hadn't given the flowers to Greta. She'd seemed delighted — and he had to admit they made a handsome couple. Greta with her pale skin and a dash of freckles, and those startlingly blue eyes and blonde hair. Zach with his rugged good looks and charming personality. Funny . . . he rarely compared himself with his brother, but he did always think his brother was better looking.

He sighed and braced himself as the door swung open and the two chattering ladies hastened inside. Fresh rains brought blowing wind, whipping their skirts about and silhouetting their slender forms.

"Good morning, Jess. Lovely, brisk day out, isn't it?" Cora greeted him with her usual cheerful smile.

"It is that. I rather enjoy the autumn-like weather. Just wish it'd last longer before the winter moves in to stay." He took her coat and waited while Greta removed hers.

His eyes swept over Cora's neat print dress and her hair pinned in a bun at the nape of her slender neck. She was attractive and always looked perfect, not a curl out of place, wearing a freshly ironed dress but ready to work. Then Jess looked at the strong-willed Greta in a serviceable navy dress, her usual braids pinned tightly against her scalp. *That should give anyone a head-ache,* he thought. Chuckling inwardly, he wondered if that was the reason she darted about in her no-nonsense fashion, complet-ing tasks with lightning speed that normally took him weeks. He wondered what she would look like in a sky-blue gown to match her eyes, or if, for that matter, she had any pretty dresses. Zach would need to see to it that she had one or two pretty gowns.

"I trust you slept well?" Cora asked. Her dark eyes held his.

Should he kiss her good morning? After all, she was going to be his bride, right? He leaned in and gave her a peck on the cheek. "I did, and you look as fresh as a columbine after the rain." Jess felt a little foolish, but he was determined to take his cue from his brother, who apparently knew how to woo a woman with the proper words. That's what he'd done in his infamous letters.

Cora seemed mildly surprised at his actions. Jess took Greta's coat and made a hasty retreat to hang up both coats, then returned with the starched aprons.

Greta's face was unreadable as she greeted him with a nod. "Where's Zach this morning?"

"He took an early morning ride out to his property. Seems he suddenly wants to look for a site to build a cabin. You wouldn't have anything to do with that, would you?" he teased, leaning down to lift a box.

Greta colored slightly, donning her apron over her dress. "We did talk about it last night. He wants to be married right away."

Cora stopped tying her apron strings, and Jess nearly dropped the box as he straightened. "Is that so?" His brother was wasting no time. Did he already feel real affection for Greta? Zach, the guy who once wasn't even considering marriage? *My, my, how swiftly he's changed since Greta arrived.*

"Yes. There really is no reason to wait, is there?" Greta's eyes latched on to his.

Jess stood holding the box until his arms began to cramp. Cora walked off, humming a tune to herself, while Greta straightened the fabric table.

"I . . . guess there isn't," Jess said. What else could he say? "By the way, I'd appreciate it if you'd talk to me before filling out that huge order you expect me to buy."

"What is there to talk about? Those are things necessary for customers, and I'd like to dress the front window with some fall items — you know, catch someone's eye as they walk past." She picked up the list from the counter. "Oh, and the Christmas items should be ordered now in plenty of time to arrive before December."

Jess finally set the heavy box down, feeling a crick in his neck. "Greta, that all costs a lot of money. I usually have the customer tell *me* what they want to order. It's been working out just fine."

"But don't you see — if you display some of the merchandise, you'll sell more than waiting for them to order from the catalog." She just wouldn't give up, which only increased Jess's ire. "Especially with the women. You'll make a tidy profit that will outweigh the initial spending."

"Now wait just a doggone minute," he sputtered. The bell jangled over the store's entrance, halting their conversation. Cole nodded to Cora as he strolled past her, heading straight to Greta.

"How're you folks doing this morning?" He swept off his Stetson, shooting Greta a wide grin. "I thought I'd better stop back by and see if you've decided to stay in Central City or not."

Jess watched as Greta's temperament changed instantly from efficient store clerk to blushing femininity — all soft and winsome smiles. Why did she exasperate him so much? Why couldn't she be more like Cora — quiet, unassuming, and amicable?

"Hello, Cole. I'm still here and beginning to get to know a few people. Everyone has been so nice."

"Good! Just remember, if you decide you're not going to marry one of the brothers, then I'd like a chance to be next in line."

"Don't think you'll get that chance, Cole. Seems as though Zach and Greta are planning to be married soon," Jess informed him.

Cole's flirting demeanor changed swiftly, and his expression went flat. "In that case, I'll wish you congratulations, but I still want a chance to spin you around the floor at Agnes's party."

"Thank you," Greta murmured. "I think I can spare at least one dance with you."

He smiled broadly, a twinkle in his eye.

"Well, I'll just be on my way. But I should warn you, Agnes is coming over here soon," he said with a chuckle.

"I'm ready," Greta said, turning to walk with him toward the door.

"Jess knows she can be a little tough to handle at times. I know my sister, but don't let her get away with anything." Cole paused, donning his hat. A knowing look passed between Jess and Cole.

Jess laughed. "I don't think you'll have to concern yourself with that where Greta's concerned."

She flashed him an annoyed look, then smiled up at Cole. "We're looking forward to the barbecue all the same," she said as they reached the door.

"Well . . . be seeing you around then." Cole tipped his hat, giving her a wink. He nodded to Jess. "I'll see you later, Jess. Good day."

Cole's flirting stuck in Jess's craw, but he didn't take him too seriously. They'd been friends long enough for him to know that Cole loved to flirt with a pretty girl.

As soon as he was gone, Cora announced that she was going to go visit Martha Carey, a miner's wife. "Annabelle told me Martha's husband had an injured leg from a mining accident, so I thought I'd pay her a short visit if you don't mind, Jess."

"No, I don't mind at all. The Careys haven't lived here very long. They're having a hard go of it from what I hear."

"I found some piece goods of flannel that perhaps she can use for her new baby," she said, indicating a soft blue fabric in her hand. "I'll pay for it, Jess. Oh —" She reached into her dress pocket and handed him a knife. "Would you wrap this up and add it to my bill as well?"

"Now what in the world would you be needing that for?" Jess asked, taking the knife.

"I'll explain later, but right now I need to go."

"Are you walking? Do they live outside town?" Greta wanted to know.

"Yes, I'll walk. It's just a mile or so, and it's a fine day to get some exercise. The family seems to be in need of assistance, according to Annabelle, and I'd like to help." Cora grabbed her coat and bonnet from their hook and slipped them on.

Jess opened the door for her. "You sure you want to walk that far alone? I can't leave the store right now."

Cora nodded. "I'll be fine, and the brisk air will do me good. Greta, good luck with Agnes, if she arrives before I return."

Greta giggled. "I can handle Miss High and Mighty, never fear."

Jess was sure that was an accurate statement. He watched Greta open Rascal's crate and scoop up the small dog, which licked her cheeks and hands while she nuzzled its fluffy neck. An odd thought of how it would feel to cuddle with her ran through his brain.

17

The cool morning temperature quickly warmed as the sun climbed higher in the clear, cloudless sky. Cora's back was beginning to feel warm by the time she walked past the shops and stepped off the boardwalk to follow the dirt road leading to Martha Carey's home. Clad in sensible shoes for walking, she breathed deeply of the fresh scent of surrounding juniper and pines. Soon she was aware of how labored her breathing had become on the incline to a row of houses stretched out like miniatures on the ledge above.

She paused, as much to catch her breath as to inspect the tiny yellow flowers growing on thick, shiny-leafed shrubs. They had no smell, but their delicate beauty lent a certain harmony to the landscape, which was raw from rough roads carved by miners' carts, horses, and wagons. The Colorado air certainly agreed with her constitution, and she felt invigorated by being outdoors. Yes, she mused, the Lord's handiwork touched everything in sight, from the wide-open sky to the majestic mountains to the flowers growing alongside the road.

Clutching the bundle of flannel against her chest, she struggled for balance until she finally reached the summit of her climb. It had a perfect view of Central City below. Sidestepping a puddle or two, she lifted her skirts so as not to drag them through the muck and gave a nod at those passing by who greeted her. She hoped she'd be back before Agnes arrived at the store in case Greta needed her.

She found the correct house by the description Annabelle gave her and rapped on the door. After a few moments, a young girl appeared, wearing a thin brown homespun dress. She looked to be about nine years old, with large brown eyes that gave her a gaunt appearance.

"How do you do? Is this the home of the Careys?" Cora asked.

Cora stood waiting as the girl looked over her shoulder and yelled, "Mama! We've got company." She turned back to Cora. "My mama's feeling a little poorly, but she's coming." A little boy clutched his sister's leg and looked up at her, wide-eyed. Minutes later, a weary-looking woman holding a baby stumbled to the door.

"Hello . . ." she said hesitantly, her hazel eyes staring weakly at Cora. "I'm Martha, and you are . . . ?"

"I'm Cora Johnson. Annabelle Mead told me you were new to the community, and I thought I'd stop by. I'm fairly new myself."

The lady seemed surprised momentarily, then took two steps back, nearly tripping on two more children who had crept up to see who was at the door. "So nice to meet you, Cora. Where are my manners? Please come in." She stepped aside, and the children scattered about the living room, watching their new visitor.

Cora stepped inside. Few furnishings adorned the living room, but it was neat and clean. Martha indicated a chair, and after Cora sat down, she took the other one, cradling the baby against her ample bosom. The baby looked up dreamily, then jerked as he drifted off to sleep.

"Annabelle was determined to call on you this week but was unable to, so I decided to come in her place and see if there was anything I could help you with."

Martha looked at her with dull eyes that showed she was tired. She gave Cora a weak smile. "These are my children. The oldest is

Leah, who's nine, and this is Becky, who's eight, Amos, who's six, Eddy, who's four, and the baby is Danny. He's two months today." She beamed, looking down at him.

The children smiled back, murmuring shy hellos. "Now, children, go finish your chores while Miss Cora and I visit." Martha turned to face her after the children went about their normal duties. "My husband, Horace, is lying in bed with a bad leg injury. I'm sure he'd like to meet you, but he might be napping."

"Please don't disturb him. Maybe another time," Cora said quietly, gazing at the little babe in Martha's arms. "My goodness! He's a beautiful baby with all that hair. I found this beautiful piece of blue flannel and wondered if you could use it for him. I'd have made something for him myself, but I'm not very good with a needle."

"That's so very thoughtful of you. And yes, that flannel will come in very handy. Let me put him in his cradle now that he's asleep, and I'll be right back," Martha whispered.

When she returned, Martha took the material and ran her hand over its softness. "This will be perfect for the baby's tender skin. I've been trying to teach Leah to sew." She set the fabric on the table next to the chair where her sewing basket sat. "Would you like something to drink, perhaps a cup of coffee or tea?"

"A cup of coffee would be nice, but please don't go to any trouble on my account if you don't already have something made."

"It would be my pleasure. I don't have many visitors, and between the children and the baby and waiting on Horace these days, I hardly get a chance to talk to another woman." It seemed her countenance had suddenly improved tenfold as she bustled toward the kitchen. Cora thought she might just be lonely.

"Then please let me come help you. I'm learning how not to be waited on."

Martha gave her a strange look but continued on through the kitchen door. Soon they were sitting at the kitchen table over steaming mugs of coffee laced with heavy cream amid the comings and goings of four very active but well-mannered children. Cora looked at the watch pinned to her blouse and couldn't believe a half hour had flown by.

"Oh my! I must be getting back to the store. I promised not to be long." Cora scooted her chair back.

"I've kept you too long. I'm sorry," Martha said.

"No, not at all. I promise to return another time if you'd like. Perhaps I can watch the children for you so you can have a bit of free time."

Martha's face crinkled, and Cora was afraid she might cry "You're so kind. I appreciate the offer and the material for the baby, but we'll get along. The children are a great help. Please pray for Horace's speedy recovery so that he can go back to work."

"You have my prayers, Martha. I must go now." Cora started toward the front door. "If you need anything at all, you know where I am or you can send one of the children for me."

"God bless you for being so caring. I'll stop in at the store soon to say hello." Martha squeezed her hand. Somehow she didn't look as weary as when Cora had first arrived, and she hoped their new friendship had a little to do with the light she saw reflected in Martha's eyes.

"You do that, Martha. I'd like you to meet Greta now that I've told you a little about our situation."

"I'd love to meet her. See you soon."

Cora waved goodbye and hummed to herself as she left the hilltop and headed back down to the road. She removed her cape and carried it on her arm, feeling warmer than before. Strange how the evenings and early mornings were cool but the daytime temperatures quickly soared. That was the beauty of the Rocky Mountains. Every day her love of this region grew.

Cora was glad she'd taken the time to visit the Careys. She already had a thing or two she wanted to mention to Annabelle.

Before long she heard the sound of a horse coming from behind, and she moved to the side of the road so he could pass, but instead the horse and rider drew close. She shielded her eyes from the sun and looked up to see Zach.

"Hello, little lady. Never thought I'd see you walking this far up the mountain." Zach reined his horse in next to her. "What are you doing way up here?"

"Morning, Zach." She smiled up at him. "I've been visiting the family that Annabelle told me about — the Careys. Do you always go riding in the morning?" Cora was beginning to feel the sun's heat along the nape of her neck, and she wanted to hurry on to the store before she got any warmer and stained her dress at the armpits. Not ladylike at all. Besides, they might need her help, and she'd promised not to be gone too long.

Zach pushed his hat back, crossed his wrists across the saddle horn, and gazed down at her. "I was checking on Granny this morning, and I'm 'bout to head back to town. How about a lift? You'll get back a lot quicker."

Cora contemplated his offer. Should she be seen on the back of a man's horse? It seemed so unconventional, but then she knew out West, people pretty much did what they desired, within limits. "Well . . . all right."

Zach reached down, and she held on to his arms as he lifted her into the saddle behind him. *He must be mighty strong to be able to haul me onto his horse without getting down and with nary a grunt!* She couldn't help but notice that his capable hands were calloused and not smooth like Jess's.

"You comfortable back there?" he asked over his shoulder.

"As well as I can be." Her skirts hiked up, showing part of her ankle and the edges of her pantalets sticking out from under her petticoats, but it couldn't be helped. Why, a lady shouldn't be seen this way, without the proper riding habit! She suppressed a giggle and tried to rearrange her skirts but knew they'd be sorely wrinkled by the time they reached town.

"Wrap your arms around my waist, and we'll be back at the store in a jiffy," he ordered.

"Yes, sir!" Cora slid her arms around his hard midsection, feeling the heat from his back press into her. Her face burned hot. Good thing he couldn't see her. Zach smelled of horseflesh, leather, and the outdoors — very masculine — but it didn't repel her. His muscles worked beneath his shirt as he flicked the reins, and they set off at a jog downhill in the direction of Central City.

Cora knew she liked Zach with his sometimes impulsive nature and sunny disposition, but she never allowed her mind to linger there for long. From her perch behind him, she glimpsed dark hair curling from underneath his cowboy hat, and she couldn't mistake a warm stirring in her that upset her normal balance and way of thinking. She ran her tongue around her lips to moisten her mouth — whether the dryness was caused by uneasiness, she wasn't really sure. How could she acknowledge these feelings — was it attraction? — to a man engaged to another? *And* her friend to boot! *Lord, help me! What has come over me?* She'd be glad when they got to their destination.

As all of this was going through her mind, she wasn't aware that in the last few minutes the horse had slowed to a walk.

"Well, I'll be a jumping jackrabbit!" Zach grumbled. "Stomper seems to be out of sorts for some reason. We'll have to stop and let me take a look. There's a nice spot right by Clear Creek. He can have a drink and there's a little shade there, so I'll see what's ailing him." Zach indicated the cottonwood trees alongside the creek bed and led the horse in that direction. Swinging his leg across the front of his saddle, he dismounted and turned to assist her.

With Zach's hands on either side of her waist, Cora slid from the saddle and found herself within an inch of Zach's face. She dared to tilt her chin up toward his handsome face, where she found his brown eyes locked on hers. She felt her pulse throb in her neck, and her stomach felt tiny flutters akin to a hummingbird's flight. His lips parted as he reached out and lifted a lock of hair that had fallen from its pins down her shoulder. He caressed it between his fingers as he leaned in closer, breathing in its fragrance with a languid sigh.

"I've wanted to do this since I saw you walking down the road with the sun bouncing off your shiny curls," he said huskily. His eyes swept over her.

His admission astonished her. Cora

thought surely her breathing would stop altogether as he closed the gap between them. Lowering his head, he grazed her mouth lightly, his lips full and soft, until she found herself with enough courage and desire to kiss him back. That's all it took. Zach turned and braced himself against Stomper's haunches for support, pulling her to him, and held her tightly against his chest. His broad hands stroked her hair, then slid underneath to cup her neck, gently forcing her head up again to kiss her with an intensity that she shared — and that shocked her.

When Cora finally came to her senses, she placed her palms flat against his smooth leather vest and pushed him away. What had she done? She'd betrayed her friend! Shame burned her, and she could feel her heart throbbing.

"Zach, please. We shouldn't be doing this," she cried.

"You felt it too," he rasped as he released her.

Cora took a step away and clasped her hands together to keep them from shaking, not wanting to admit how she'd felt. "It's wrong! You and Greta are going to be married," she said, releasing a shaky breath. A sudden welcoming breeze ruffled Stomper's mane, and he snorted, tossing his head, reminding them why they'd stopped in the first place. If it wasn't for the seriousness of the moment, she would've laughed.

"And what about you and Jess?" Zach gave her an exasperated look. "This is not over and done with."

"Just tend to Stomper. I'll walk back like I should have to begin with." She reached down for her cape, which had fallen to the ground. She tried to brush the bits of dirt and grass from it, but it was too warm for it anyway. She could hear the gurgling stream as it washed over the rocky creek bed, and she longed to stick her feet in its cold water.

"Think we could take a moment and enjoy a chance to dip our feet in the creek when I'm done here?"

Cora was startled. Had he just read her mind? "Maybe I can stay long enough to cool off. The stream looks inviting." She shrugged. Right now she'd rather be alone with her tangled thoughts but decided to pretend nothing had happened. It'd be easier on him, Jess, and Greta. Wouldn't it?

Zach leaned down and lifted Stomper's front hoof to examine it. He found a rock had worked its way into the shoe. He pulled out his pocketknife and was able to work the stone out. "He's gonna have a sore hoof, but he'll be okay. Looks like I'll be walking with you, though. I don't want him to bear any more weight." He held his hand out to her. "I see a nice shady spot, and I'm downright hot."

"You *are* insistent, aren't you?" Cora paused with her hands on her hips as she was about to walk back to the road. Looking up at her on the rocky slope, he noticed her finely sculpted cheekbones and olive complexion and wondered if there was Indian heritage in her background.

"Come on," he said. "The creek is calling me." He held Stomper's reins in one hand and pulled her down the slope to the creek bank with the other. He dropped the reins, allowing the horse to walk to the edge. Stomper immediately poked his muzzle in the creek.

Zach pulled off his boots and rolled his pant legs above the ankle before he turned to Cora. "Well, what are you waiting for? Come on, join me."

She stood timidly watching him, then looked at the stream, hesitating as she chewed on her bottom lip.

"I promise not to tell a single soul that you took your shoes and stockings off. It'll be our little secret," he teased with a grin.

He saw the mischievous twinkle in her bright eyes. Would she do it? After their kiss, he knew there was a fire within her, under all that outward reserve. That shocked him but pleased him at the same time.

She moved to a rock and removed her shoes and stockings, revealing attractive, slender ankles and shapely feet. He felt himself staring too long, so he waded into the stream. The shock of cold water hit him. "Hoorah! The water's cold, and I guarantee it'll cool you off!" he bellowed, then motioned for her to join him.

She stood at the water's edge, hiked up her skirts into her arms, and dipped one toe in to test the water, then finally slowly waded in. "Ahh . . . feels good on this summer day."

They stood enjoying the moment with the swirling water rushing over their toes and sunlight bouncing off the sparkling creek. After a few moments, he watched her bend down to gaze through the clear water at the pebbles beneath. She reached in to swirl the water with one hand, keeping her skirts out of the water with the other hand. She rose, splashing water at him playfully, and he splashed her back until their laughter rang out across the stillness of the day and they were both damp.

Zach enjoyed seeing this new side of her. "You're all wet now." He chuckled, and it occurred to him that she was a good-hearted woman, warm and open, maybe longing for adventure. He supposed he'd misjudged her as too prim and proper and reserved.

"Oh, it does feel delicious, but we should be getting back now." The back of her skirts had dipped into the creek. Wringing them out, she gathered them and headed back up the bank. He followed, watching the natural sway of her hips. When she sat down on the rock to don her stockings, he gazed at her again, lingering on her small foot. Tearing his eyes away, he plunked down on a boulder next to her and lifted his sock but made no move to slip it on. He suddenly felt his world spinning out of control.

"What?" she asked with a furrowed forehead.

Zach drew in a deep breath. "Oh . . . I . . . I guess I was just thinking about our kiss and how attracted I am to you. It blindsided me."

"Zach —" she began to protest.

"Cora, I think what happened earlier was so natural and not contrived. But I'm wondering what in the devil is wrong with me." He leaned over, putting his head in his hands. "I'm attracted to Greta, but somehow I feel different when I'm with you. Excited but comfortable-like. I thought I wanted to marry Greta, but lately I find myself thinking only of you." He lifted his head to gaze at her across the space between them. Her eyes softened and her face was etched with concern. He continued, "I've been trying to handle things on my own since my brother died instead of letting God direct me." He yanked on his socks and boots.

"Greta told me about your brother, and I'm so sorry. Have you tried praying about it? Maybe you're angry." Her answer surprised him, but her gaze was unwavering. His eyes traveled to the soft curve of her cheek, and he found himself wanting to stroke it.

"Could be. I'll think about that." He reached out and lifted her hand. "But I want you to know that what I feel for you is genuine." He watched the expression on her face waver somewhere between belief and unbelief, and her eyes were moist with tears.

"But it can't be, Zach. You know that. You're going to marry Greta, and you can't go back on your word." She stood, and he closed the gap between them. He bracketed her face between his hands and kissed her soundly, savoring the sweet taste of her full lips. This time she didn't pull away, and a tiny bud of hope uncurled in his heart. A sliver of sunlight through the pines caressed her face, making her appear like the angel he thought she was.

"Cora . . . I'm not sure of anything just yet. I admit I was very attracted to Greta right from the start, but it was more desire than love. I can't build a marriage on that alone. It just wouldn't be right. Greta likes living in town and working at the store. I don't think she'd like living on a ranch. I'm best outdoors and I worship in wide-open spaces. I can't be confined to that store forever."

"I already knew that about you, and I wish you well, but I'm not sure about this, Zach. Greta's been hurt once before, and I don't want to cause her any more pain. Why don't we let things go for a time and see what unfolds? And in the meantime we can each pray that God will lead us." Her voice quivered, and Zach searched her eyes.

"Does that mean I wasn't imagining your response to me?"

Cora let out a sigh and looked up at him. "No, you weren't imagining it. But we must go. I've been away far too long, and I promised Greta . . ." She whirled around, dragging the hem of her damp skirts, and climbed up the slope to wait for him.

Zach grabbed Stomper's reins and reluctantly followed, wondering how he could remedy the situation of the brides, which was all his doing in the first place. Pray? It was worth a try.

18

Shielded by a makeshift curtain that she had hung for privacy, Greta waited as Agnes stripped down to her chemise and stockings. She wasn't as tall as Greta and was a bit short-waisted but otherwise had a nice figure. This was a first for Greta to be sewing for someone other than herself, though she'd helped out her sister Anna when needed. She wanted to do her best and found she enjoyed creating something from a shapeless piece of material.

Greta sighed and tried to concentrate as she made note of the other woman's measurements while Agnes chattered away. She wanted to make certain of Agnes's size before she began to cut the fabric, and she wanted to be precise, but Agnes wouldn't hold still. Suddenly an impish thought came to Greta on just how to get the other woman to settle down.

She let out an exaggerated sound of

surprise. "Oh my . . ."

"What?" Agnes stopped in midsentence, trying to turn around to get a better look. "What is it?"

"Well . . ." Greta sighed with the ease of many years of practice teasing two sisters. "If you'd be still . . . I'm sure it's just my mistake . . ."

"What are you talking about?" Agnes froze stiff as a board, and Greta suppressed a smile.

"It's a common thing, really — you simply look smaller in the waist than what I've measured here."

"Well, land sakes — measure it again. I won't talk or move a muscle."

"All right," Greta said graciously, trying to contain her mirth. She let her thoughts drift as she measured. Cole Cartwright wasn't with Agnes this time, and Greta was thankful. Although he was good-looking and had made his intentions clear, she had all the men in her life she could handle between Zach and Jess.

She wondered what had happened to Cora. Several customers had arrived at the same time as Agnes, but between Jess, Greta, and Caleb, they'd taken care of the customers while making the impatient Agnes wait. Caleb was Johnny-on-the-spot finding items, wrapping them, and hauling them to waiting wagons. The morning passed quickly, and Greta was glad. She'd rather be busy. She was looking forward to tomorrow when they would have dinner with Granny.

"Greta, I'm sorry I'm being such a bother, but I just decided that I don't like the material we first chose and want to look at something different."

Greta held her anger in check, though the material had already been cut off the bolt. "I'll do my best to help you choose something else. Let me take your measurements one more time before we start looking, but I'm afraid that you'll have to pay for the material that I've already cut off the bolt."

"Just put it on my bill. I simply must be happy with what I'm wearing or the night will be ruined!" Agnes shifted and reached to scratch her back, then quickly clamped her hand over her mouth, bringing Greta's wandering thoughts back to the task at hand. "Oh, goodness! I didn't mean to be such a fidget. My mother used to complain that I couldn't stand still for more than two minutes," she said with a lopsided smile.

"She certainly had that right, but if you don't stand still, I promise you this dress won't be fit for wearing. But with your fair complexion and green eyes, it'll be easy to find material to complement your features and something you'll feel good in," Greta commented through tight lips. Agnes indeed had a peaches-and-cream complexion, which she protected from the sun with her broad-brimmed hats. *I bet she doesn't spend one moment outdoors,* Greta thought.

Agnes looked like she might actually blush, but Greta knew she was too proud to do that. "It's true, I don't have trouble finding fabric to enhance my fair skin. Mother used to say I'd look good in sackcloth," she said with a laugh.

"I'm sure your mother thought you were a beauty. All mothers think their daughters are the prettiest!"

"Maybe so, but Jess always told me how gorgeous I looked," she said with a smug look.

Greta turned her around. "No doubt he thought you were. Tell me, weren't you two courting at one time?"

Agnes gave her a sly look. "For a while."

"What happened? You seem to be attracted to him."

"I was foolishly interested in a businessman who was in town from Denver for a while. He turned my head but left without warning. By then Jess wouldn't have anything to do with me. I was trying to win his trust back until you and Cora arrived." Her mouth clenched as she said it. "So I suppose that's out of the question for me now. Seems he only has eyes for you, according to Annabelle." Her green eyes snapped as she looked at Greta.

Greta was taken aback. "What? Me? Hardly. But you know that Zach is courting me and Jess is seeing Cora."

"That's not the way Annabelle sees it."

Thankfully, Greta was saved from responding when she heard the door swing open, and Cora and Zach came inside, laughing. Greta finished quickly once she got Agnes to stand still, and Agnes was still subdued when Greta left her to change back into her dress. She slid past the curtain and was surprised to see a somewhat disheveled Cora followed by a bemused Zach as they paused just inside the store.

"That must've been a mighty long ride, Zach," Jess said, striding toward them as they entered the store. "Caleb and I have been busier than a one-armed horse wrangler." Jess's eyes flicked over Cora.

Greta walked over to them, noticing the wet hem of Cora's skirts where dirt had collected. Her normally tight chignon at the back of her neck was loose with trailing strands of hair. Was she imagining it, or was Cora's face flushed and her eyes brighter?

"Stomper had a stone in his hoof, and I met Cora on her way down the mountain, so we walked back together," Zach told them, his eyes swerving to give Greta a half smile. "Morning, Greta." His usual flirting seemed off a bit today.

"I see. Well, I'm glad you're back now. You and Caleb can deliver the widow Jones's order that I promised her this afternoon."

Zach seemed to want to be gone in a hurry. "I'll get right on it."

"I hadn't meant to stay so long at the Careys, but I'm glad I was missed," Cora said.

"Yes, you were missed." Jess gave Cora a sweet smile as he took her wrap from her, and his hands lingered on her shoulders for a long moment. Then he hastened away to help a customer.

Greta winced. His eyes had rested warmly on her friend, and it was obvious that he cared a lot for her. Greta longed to have him look at her that way. She glanced away, knowing she'd have to put that out of her mind — forever. Putting on her brightest smile, she said, "Cora, I've just taken Agnes's measurements and she's getting dressed."

"I shouldn't have taken so long, but I didn't think Agnes would arrive so early. Did you need my help for anything?" Cora's eyes went everywhere except Greta's face.

"No, everything is fine, but if you can help with the customers while I finish with Agnes, we'll be through soon."

"Certainly, but if you need me at all, let me know." Cora moved closer to Greta and touched her on the sleeve. "Is she being nice to you?" she whispered.

"Her usual self, but nothing that I can't handle," Greta answered softly. "How was Mrs. Carey?"

"She's very lonely and overwhelmed with a new baby and four little ones. I promised to return and see if either Annabelle or I can help out."

"Greta! Come here and button up the back of my dress now!" Agnes shrieked. Greta and Cora shared a conspiratorial look.

"Excuse me, but I believe the queen is calling," Greta whispered in Cora's ear. "We'll talk later." She scurried back behind the muslin curtain, anxious to get the dress project started. She pitied the woman who had made all of Agnes's clothes in the past. Still, while she didn't know if she could handle Agnes's bossy attitude, Greta thought it might be enjoyable to have a sewing task to keep her busy.

Cora wanted to get busy, but first she needed to see Caleb. She waited until he and Zach were on the last load of supplies for the widow Jones before she approached. "Caleb, can I speak with you a moment before you leave?"

Caleb turned to face her, his eyebrows knitted together across his forehead. "I guess . . . sure."

She pulled him near the window, reached into her dress pocket, and handed him the knife.

"What? I told you I'd put it back or pay for it." Caleb frowned, turning over the fine knife in his hands.

"It's a gift from me to you. Didn't you say you have a birthday soon? Think of it as an early present." She beamed into the young lad's face shadowed by the beginning of a beard.

"You mean you bought it for me? No one ever bought me a present before," he said. His voice deepened as he examined the knife's mother-of-pearl handle. "Thank you, Cora. It's a beauty."

Cora clasped her hands together in the folds of her skirt. "Well, it's about time someone bought you something. I'm not sure what you want to do with it, though."

Caleb shifted from one foot to the other. "I like to whittle in my free time. It sorta relaxes me."

Cora smiled. "You'd better be going — Zach's waiting for you outside."

His solemn face split into a broad smile, and to her surprise and pleasure, Caleb gave her shoulder a swift hug. He bounded out the door, taking the stairs two at a time.

She had a warm feeling in her heart as she wandered over to Greta and Agnes, who were knee-deep in bolts of material scattered across the counter. From the look on Greta's face, her friend was very perturbed.

"Have you found anything that suits you better?" Greta asked. "It looks to me like you've been through about everything we have in stock."

Cora caught Greta's eye. She knew Greta was trying hard to keep her emotions from showing. Maybe Cora could give Agnes a little nudge so she could make a decision.

Agnes looked up as she approached. "I just can't decide between the gingham and the dimity. What do you think? The pattern has an off-the-shoulder flounce blouse." She showed Cora the design.

"Hmm. I think if you choose the red-and-white gingham, you might blend right in with the tablecloths!" She laughed, then abruptly closed her mouth at the sharp look from Agnes. "But the white dimity will be cool and comfortable for a hot summer picnic."

Greta nodded. "I totally agree with you, Cora," she said, running her hand across the smooth, white fabric. "We can accentuate with your choice of ribbon and perhaps add that to a straw hat for contrast."

Agnes rested her hand on her hip and tapped her foot thoughtfully, a manicured finger against her cheek. "If you both think I won't look too washed out . . ."

"Nothing could make you look washed out, Agnes." Jess came and stood next to the ladies, a pencil behind one ear and a stack of men's work shirts filling his arms. Cora watched his warm brown eyes swerve from Agnes to Greta. His face seemed to light up — or was it wishful thinking on her part?

"You're so sweet to say so." Agnes's pink lips pouted as she watched his interest shift to Greta.

"Greta, do you think you can fold these real neat like you did the overalls? I'm afraid I'm all thumbs when it comes to presentation."

"I'll be happy to, Jess. Could you just put

them right here for now?" She cleared the end of the cutting board for him, making a place to pile the shirts. "We're nearly finished here."

"No hurry, but can you make them look like they're worth buying?" He gave her a lopsided grin as he backed away, then bumped into a sharp corner of a shelf and yelped. He rubbed his back and said, "I'll leave you ladies to finish what you're doing. I . . . uh . . . have some important matters I must attend to."

Aha! Cora thought. *I knew it! There is something about the way he watches Greta whenever she's near.* But she didn't see any reaction from Greta to indicate one way or the other that it mattered to her. Before today, Cora might've felt some jealousy, but after Zach's kisses by Clear Creek . . .

19

With just a hint of fall in the afternoon sun spreading across Granny's porch, Greta didn't think there could be a more pleasant luncheon than today's. After dinner at Annabelle and Silas's, she'd been worried about the outcome. But nothing had happened yet to upset the peace of the day. After an uplifting sermon, she and Cora were embraced by many of the churchgoers as they stood outside preparing to leave. Soon after, they'd driven over to Granny's for lunch, and none of them were disappointed as they enjoyed second helpings, which only made Granny smile wider. Greta focused on the hot corn bread, baked chicken, scalloped potatoes, and garden green beans garnished with juicy ripe tomatoes, trying to ignore the growing lump in her throat. After the meal, she helped carry Granny's famous rhubarb pie out to the porch, where everyone retired for dessert.

She cut slices while Granny plopped a dollop of cream on top, and suddenly she remembered that Bryan had loved rhubarb pie.

It was apparent in everything she said and did that Granny simply loved her grandsons, making Greta wish she had living grandparents. She wondered just how much she and her sisters had missed.

Caleb was the first to praise the dessert. "I didn't think I had room for one more bite of anything, but Granny, this is absolutely delicious!"

Granny patted his shoulder. "It's my specialty, you know!"

Cora sat next to Jess on the porch swing. Zach sat on the top step of the porch. Was it Greta's imagination, or was he avoiding her by not sitting by her? Ever since he and Cora had returned yesterday, he'd put distance between himself and Greta as they worked in the mercantile.

She watched as Granny pulled up her rocker and sat down, her round cheeks flushed with happiness. "This here's a right fine gathering of folks, but I'd rather be attending a wedding. So who's getting married and when? And Jess, I'm going to need to get into town to shop for a new hat from the milliner's. Or maybe two new hats, unless y'all are having a double ceremony, which makes more sense, after all. So, what's it gonna be?"

The creaking of Granny's rocker was the only sound that could be heard except for the slight breeze that played about the porch. Forks were frozen in midair, chewing stopped, and it seemed that a time for reckoning had come.

Caleb choked on his pie, trying to control his mirth, and Greta looked from Jess to Zach while Cora stared at her pie like it was baked rattlesnake.

Jess cleared his throat as his neck turned red. He ran a finger around the top of his starched collar, then threw a warning look at Caleb. "Granny . . . you'll be the first to know when the dates are set, which will be very soon," he said, patting Cora's arm.

"Just as long as you get on with the purpose of why Zach dragged these two fine ladies way out here to Central City. I'm not getting any younger. I'd like to see great-grandchildren before the good Lord calls me home."

Caleb clamped a hand over his mouth this time to keep from chuckling at everyone's expense. Greta was speechless and left it to Jess and Zach to respond.

"You're not going anywhere, Granny —

you're as fit as a fiddle and you know it!"
Zach remarked, taking a huge bite of pie.

"You never know, son. You never know."
She turned to Greta. "Jess told me that
you're going to sew for Agnes. I hope you're
not intending on using that old sewing
machine at the mercantile. That bobbin is a
thorn in the flesh. It never worked properly."

"Jess is right. I'm going to attempt to
make her a dress for her barbecue, but I
haven't had a chance to look at the shop's
sewing machine yet."

"I have an answer for that too! You can
borrow mine for a time. It's a gen-u-ine
Singer and runs as smooth as a top."

"Why, that would really help. Thank you,
Granny." Greta smiled back at the older
lady. Even with Granny's outspokenness,
Greta could tell her heart was in the right
place where her family was concerned. She
enjoyed being able to call the older lady
Granny, since she'd never known her own
grandmother.

"If you're finished with your pie, Jess, why
don't you go get my sewing machine from
the parlor and strap it on the wagon for
Greta?"

Jess hopped up in a hurry. "Sure thing,
Granny." He handed Cora his empty plate.
"Caleb, come give me a hand," he said as

he moved to the screen door. Caleb handed his dish to Greta, but not before taking the last bite, smacking his lips in satisfaction.

Zach shifted on the top step, laying his empty plate aside. "I'm going for a walk. Anyone want to come along?"

"I'd enjoy a walk." Cora sprang up. "Let me help carry these dishes to the kitchen."

Granny waved her off. "Greta and I'll collect them. Go on ahead. The sun will be going down soon."

Greta thought Granny had more or less pushed Cora and Zach down the porch steps and out into the yard. *Did she get the same feeling as I have?* she wondered.

After putting the dishes in the sink to soak, Greta left Granny to give instructions to Jess and Caleb on the sewing machine. She decided to take a stroll and enjoy the first free time she'd had in a while. She relished the feeling in the air and the discernible smell of autumn as she strolled underneath the towering spruce and pine, taking deep breaths. She watched a couple of chipmunks scurry away from their perch on an outcropping of rocks and heard a Steller's jay's loud squawk from atop a pine branch. Reaching the end of the trail where the forest opened up, she saw familiar faces in the clearing but paused in her tracks, not wishing to disturb the couple.

She saw Zach pull Cora close, encircling her waist, while Cora put her arms around his neck. He leaned down and kissed her long and slow, almost as if drinking an elixir that seemed to satisfy a deep thirst within him, and Cora returned his fervent kisses.

A small cry escaped Greta's lips, but she quickly covered her mouth with her hand and turned away. Once out of their hearing, she ran the opposite way of Granny's, sobbing, when suddenly she fell to her knees on the rocky, uneven ground. A sharp pain pierced her ankle. So Zach really did think of her as just a pretty face . . . but Cora? How could she? Yet in her heart she knew that it was more her pride that was wounded, not that she was jealous. And if she were honest, she was relieved. Now there would be no more pretense.

Blinking away her tears, she rubbed her ankle to ease the pain and looked around. Here the forest opened up to a summer meadow. Over the small rise, something emerged from the ground. Tombstones? Was this the Gifford family cemetery? She struggled with her tangled dress and pulled herself up, limping her way to the headstones. It was indeed the family cemetery!

The graves of Jess's parents were side by side, and behind them was Granny's husband's grave, with a plot next to it that would eventually be where Granny was laid to rest.

Then another gravestone caught her eye, more weatherworn than the others. It bore an Army insignia and was decorated with a hand-stitched American flag. Bending closer to read the name inscribed, she felt her heart slam hard against her ribs.

Sergeant Bryan Gifford
United States Army
May 1867–August 1887
Fort Bridger, Wyoming

Greta dropped beside the tombstone, stunned. Her trembling fingers ran over the stone's smooth surface and Bryan's name in reverence, her emotions running high. An ache filled her being, and she felt faint. Everything fell into place now — he was Jess and Zach's brother. That's why Jess's eyes and handwriting held an uncanny resemblance to Bryan's. Why had Bryan never mentioned he had brothers in Colorado?

So that was why the Army private had delivered the message when Bryan died. The young man had repeated it several times for her. "Ma'am, Sergeant Gifford said, 'There's only one other man worth her love . . . my brother' — and then he passed." Neither she nor the private had known he was referring to a *real* brother. Now she wondered, which brother had he meant — Jess or Zach? *Lord, help me!*

She bent over, doubled up in agony, and cried for the loss of Bryan all over again. Now that she saw his grave, it became a reality she couldn't push away any longer. She wasn't aware of the passing of time until a movement behind her cast a long shadow over the tombstone.

20

Jess made sure Granny's sewing machine was secured in the back of the wagon, then he set off to find the others. Somehow Granny had wrangled Caleb into helping her wash the dessert dishes. It'd be good for him.

Jess was proud of the way Caleb was working out at the mercantile. He'd been holding his breath, waiting for Caleb's next rascally act.

It was a perfect afternoon for either napping or enjoying a walk. Granny's front porch swing looked inviting, but he'd rather see where everyone else was. Soon he'd be taking this walk with his bride and making plans for their future.

There was a chill in the breeze, and Jess could feel it in his bones despite the warm temperature. He stepped up his pace and turned toward the family cemetery. He'd avoided it for some time now. Today was as good as any to pay his respects and see that the weeds hadn't taken over.

As the small cemetery came into view, he stopped short when he saw Greta sitting on the ground next to his brother's plot. What in tarnation was wrong with her? He cleared his throat so as not to startle her. Greta yanked her head up and turned to look at him through red-rimmed eyes, one hand resting on his brother's headstone. He walked closer, looking around, but didn't see hide nor hair of Cora and Zach.

"Greta," he murmured. He eased down beside her and rested one arm on his knee. "Why are you crying? You didn't know my brother."

Her bottom lip quivered, and she pulled a delicate handkerchief edged in lace from her dress pocket and wiped her nose. "Yes . . . I did." She hiccupped.

He knew from the tone of her voice that she was serious. He tried to comprehend what she could possibly mean but could only watch as she tenderly ran her fingers over Bryan's name.

"Bryan and I were engaged . . ." She tilted her head back up to meet his eyes.

"What? You must be kidding." Had the sun gotten to her head?

"I assure you, I am not. Bryan never

mentioned he had family in Colorado while he was in Wyoming. I answered the ad because the name Gifford was the signature . . . I guess I wondered if you were cousins, but you said you had no other extended family."

A peculiar feeling swept over him, and he remembered in one of his letters that Bryan mentioned he'd found the woman of his dreams. Now it was becoming clear. The locket . . . he said he wanted to give her a locket. The sunshine glimmered on the locket lying against Greta's dress, and he carefully lifted it, turning it over to see Bryan's initials engraved on the back. He ran his fingernail between its two sides, popping it open. The face of his brother stared back at him with the roguish grin he knew so well, and his heart lurched. Had it really been a year since his passing?

Greta stared at him, her luminous eyes searching his.

"I should've known," he murmured, reaching gentle thumbs to rub away the tears that tracked down her porcelain cheeks. "Bryan told me about this locket . . . It reminded me of something before, but I didn't remember until now," he whispered. "You asked us if we had cousins around here, and that was true — we don't. But you didn't ask if we had a sister or brother. At the time I didn't want to talk about Bryan. My mistake. I should have."

"There were similarities between him and you — your handwriting . . . even your voice." She spoke quietly and struggled to stand as she used the headstone for support, wincing. "I must confess I'm not in love with Zach. Bryan was my heart's perfect match," she said with a trembling voice. She wouldn't meet Jess's gaze, but as she tried to move, she stumbled and cried out in pain.

"You've hurt yourself?" he asked, reaching out to steady her, but she waved a hand.

"I twisted my foot, but it's not too bad . . . at least I don't think."

"Here, let me help you," he said, taking her arm while she leaned heavily on him. The sweetness of lavender water tickled his nose, and he felt a prickle of fire shoot through him. Better not to let his thoughts wander there. He could never compete with Bryan's ghost. She'd said he was her heart's perfect match. Bryan had always been the dashing one, with roguish good looks and a charismatic personality. He was the apple of their mother's eye, and though Jess adored his younger brother, he always felt he stood in the shadows.

As they moved away from the grave, Greta's face twisted in pain.

"You can't put weight on that foot." In a flash, he lifted her into his arms. "Put your arms around my neck and I'll carry you back to Granny's." He was glad when she didn't protest and did his bidding, slipping her slender arms about him. He enjoyed the silky touch of her skin against his neck as he trudged back in the direction they'd come, and though he stared straight ahead, he could feel her eyes on him. He could no more deny the strong feelings he had for her than he could the growling in his belly when he was hungry.

Carrying her now, he remembered a time the family had gathered one Easter, when he'd frantically run down this same worn path back to Granny's, carrying Bryan. Bryan had suffered a snakebite, but it was Jess's quick thinking as a young teenager that had saved his brother's life. Yet he wasn't able to save Bryan that fateful day near Fort Bridger . . .

More than once, Greta had daydreamed about being in Jess's strong arms, but now that she actually was, her thoughts were swallowed up with the fact that he and Bryan were brothers. The knowledge staggered her, and from his reaction when he examined her locket, she knew Jess felt the same. But Bryan was gone and Jess was here, holding her, caring for her. His jaw was firmly set as he looked straight ahead. Did he know that he needed her? Hadn't he seen how she'd improved the mercantile and organized things so that even his customers complimented him?

She tried to still the fluttering of her heart beating like a hummingbird's wings and finally faced the truth that she loved Jess even with his scattered way of thinking and absentmindedness. Perhaps what drew her to him was his slow and steady pace and his way of looking at life. So unlike Bryan, who was impulsive and reacted to every little thing. In hindsight, though she loved Bryan, she admitted that what she needed now was someone who was just the opposite of him. Part of that was maturing and knowing your own mind, she could hear Catharine say. She let out a sigh and hugged Jess's neck tighter.

"You hurtin' worse?" Jess looked down at her, and she noticed his nice, even teeth as he spoke his concern.

"No . . . why?"

"You're about to pinch my head off at the shoulders!"

She leaned her head back with a little smile. "Sorry. You told me to hold on." Her hand rested against the curling hair sticking out from his hat.

"Greta . . . I . . ." He stood stock-still on the worn path lined with thick trees and locked eyes with hers. "I can never be my brother, but before we get to Granny's . . ."

She could feel the thumping of his heart against her side, and the manly smell of him made her dizzy. He lowered his head and pressed his lips against hers — tenderly at first, then deepening the kiss, his hat falling to the ground. She returned his kisses with passion that coursed through her very being. He kissed her again and again until she thought her lungs would burst, stunned by her own reaction. What had just happened? He was courting Cora. She wasn't allowed to have this kind of feeling. Was she?

Through half-lidded eyes, he croaked, "Oh, Greta. I just wanted to kiss you before I let you go to my *other* brother. I must tell you, I'm not in love with Cora but with you . . . I guess I've known from the beginning, when I first argued with you. But I won't stand in the way of Zach's happiness and yours . . . You have my blessing."

Greta didn't know what to say. Maybe the truth was best. "Jess, I like Zach, but I'm afraid I don't have the kind of feelings that a woman who's about to be married should have for her future husband . . . And I can't deny how I feel about you anymore." She buried her head against his chest, feeling safe.

He jerked his head back. "You mean you care for me?" His eyes were wide with surprise.

"Yes, I do."

"I'm really surprised. But I don't believe I can stand up to the ghost of Bryan, and something tells me you're not over him yet. He was everything that I'm not."

"Why don't you let me be the judge of what I feel?" she protested.

"Doesn't matter, it's how *I* feel." He shifted her weight, reached down and slammed his hat back on his head, then started walking again, the late afternoon sun beginning to cast shadows around them. "It just won't work," he said, clamping his jaw shut.

What a mess things had turned out to be, Greta thought, but she knew he had closed the subject — kiss or no kiss. Problem was, his lips had sealed her heart.

21

Zach held Cora about the waist as they overlooked the plush valley below in comfortable silence. Variegated hues of rose and gray clouds streaked the sky, painting a picturesque blending of colors just above the horizon. He would never tire of this land. He gave Cora a squeeze and pointed with his free hand.

"This is my tiny piece of land. I've started hauling and splitting logs in that pile yonder to start a small cabin soon. I don't think Jess really thinks I'll ever settle down, but I want to . . . if I can. Losing my parents and my younger brother left me at loose ends, and I had trouble even thinking about my own future. I think it's been the same for Jess. But I really want to be out on my own." He looked at Cora, who tilted her head up at him, giving him a thoughtful expression.

"Why shouldn't you be able to? You're not as capricious as you think you are. You feel adrift when something happens in your life and you suddenly can't find your way. Which reminds me of a Bible verse that I recently came across — 'I can do all things through Christ.' "

"Cora, I'm a little thickheaded, so I need reminding occasionally. Promise me you'll do that when we're married." He chuckled, reaching to gently stroke her cheek. He felt privileged that she'd told him how she'd been treated by her parents when she became a Christian. Now he found himself wanting to love and protect her as she grew in her new faith. Maybe that would renew his fledgling trust and give him a better sense of direction. It certainly couldn't hurt as they tried to build their future based on faith in God.

"I'll be more than happy to, Zach . . . but we need to figure out the best way to work all this out." Her eyes narrowed in concern. "There's nothing I'd like more than to be your wife. I hope you understand that I have a heart to do mission work, and that might take me to town more often than you'd like. I'd also like to be able to invite less fortunate people to our home in the future."

"If that's what you feel God is calling you to do, then consider it your ministry. As long as you include me, we'll both be happy," he said with a tap on her nose.

Cora stood on tiptoes and kissed him soundly as her answer. When she started to pull back, he encircled her in a big hug. "I'm so happy I wrote those letters to you!" he said, grinning.

"I intend to take you to task for impersonating your brother with those flattering words of love!" Her eyes twinkled in amusement, and she squirmed away and turned to run back down the pathway.

"Promise? I can hardly wait," he yelled at her back as he took off after her.

"Land a' Goshen! What happened to you?" Granny popped up from her rocker, and the rest of her guests stopped chatting when Jess approached carrying Greta. Zach moved likewise to help.

"A twisted ankle. Not bad, but sore enough, I think," Greta answered, hating the sudden attention of everyone. Jess set her down and moved aside to allow Granny a closer look.

"Let's get your boot off so I can have a better look. Zach, lend me a hand," Granny said, pushing Greta's petticoats above her ankle. She shook her head. "Did you fall in a rabbit hole?"

Greta was careful to answer. "I might

have. It happened so quickly that I'm not sure."

Carefully Zach helped Granny unbutton Greta's boot and slip it off, then Granny peeled her stocking off to reveal a swollen ankle with a little blue beginning to surface.

Granny delicately probed all around her ankle and foot, and when she touched the side of her foot, Greta knew exactly where the worst pain was. "Ouch! That's the spot!"

"Is it broken?" Zach asked when Granny concluded her examinations.

"I'm an old hand at this, and I'd say it's just sprained, but not as bad as it could've been." Granny turned to Jess. "Go to the springhouse and get me a cold steak. I'm gonna wrap her leg. Zach, drag that stool from yonder and let's prop her foot up."

Jess jogged down the steps in the direction of the springhouse while Zach quickly retrieved the stool and propped Greta's foot up.

"My, I've never had so much attention. I'm all right, really," Greta insisted.

Cora walked over to kneel down and inspect Greta's foot. "Oh dear. What can I do to help, Granny?" Greta avoided Cora's eyes and leaned her head against the rocker's back, grateful that her ankle wasn't worse than it was. But how was she going to work?

"Come with me, and we'll find something to wrap Greta's foot to keep it stable. I think I have a good piece of muslin we can use." Cora followed Granny, leaving Caleb and Zach with Greta.

Caleb strolled over, his hands in his pockets. "I'm sorry you hurt your ankle, Miss Greta, but I can be your gopher," he said, his face serious.

"Caleb, that's sweet of you, and I may need your help." Greta gave him a grateful smile.

"We loaded the sewing machine in the wagon for you to take to the store," Caleb said, clearly trying to cheer her up.

"Oh, wonderful. Then I can get started sewing the frock for Agnes."

Zach pulled up a chair next to her and patted her hand. "If you'd been with me, this wouldn't have happened." He sounded so serious. It couldn't be regret, not after she saw him in an intimate embrace with Cora. Was he feeling remorseful? Did he intend to marry her and yet still spend time with Cora?

Greta modestly folded her skirt back down to hide her ankle. "It's just a small thing, Zach. Don't worry about me. I'm sure you have more important things to occupy your

271

mind than my little ol' foot."

Zach drew back. "You've been on my mind more than you know."

I'm sure I have, she thought. *Like how to tell me the truth.*

Jess strode up the porch steps, the wrapped meat in his hands, keeping her from having to respond. Maybe she should have told Zach about the headstone, but if she asked about him and Cora kissing, then he would think she'd been spying. Now she wished she'd told Jess what she'd seen.

"Here's a good cold steak," Jess said, placing the meat on the table next to Greta's chair.

Cora and Granny came bustling through the screen door. "Here we are, my little lamb," Granny said. "You just sit still while Cora and I wrap your foot tightly." She and Cora worked quietly, winding the bandage around her instep and ending right above the ankle, then tying it in place with strips of muslin. When she was satisfied it was secure, Granny nodded to Zach to place the cold steak on Greta's foot.

"Now, I hope you know, Jess, that she's not going to be able to work for a day or so. She shouldn't be hobbling around on a swollen foot," Granny said, her hands on her ample hips.

"Hmm . . . you're right, of course. But I have more than enough help." Jess leaned against the porch railing and folded his arms. Greta felt her face flush as his eyes honed in on her.

"I have a suggestion. Why don't you let Greta rest her foot here for a few days? I'll take good care of her. It'd be better than being at the hotel. What do ya say?" Granny cocked her head at Jess.

"Oh, I can't be a burden to you, Granny!" Greta protested.

"Shh, you'll be no such thing!" Granny turned back to Jess. "Well?"

"Seems logical to me." Jess scratched his chin thoughtfully.

Granny smiled at Cora. "You'll be able to have a few days alone too."

Cora shrugged her shoulders. "It doesn't matter to me. I enjoy the company, but if Greta needs to rest her foot, then this is the perfect solution." Cora snuck a glance at Zach, who up to this point had said little, but the look didn't go unnoticed by Greta.

"It's settled then. You stay here with Granny. Caleb can fetch your things and run 'em over here," Jess said.

Greta bolted up and the steak slid sideways, but Zach caught it and held it in place. "But I've got to work on Agnes's

273

dress!" she said.

"And you shall." Granny spun around to Caleb and Zach. "I hate to do this to you boys, but you're gonna have to unload that sewing machine. She can work on the dress while she's with me."

"I'll collect the material and pattern pieces and give them to Caleb to bring with a change of clothing," Cora added.

Zach and Caleb went back to unload the sewing machine while Granny fussed over Greta.

"I'm so grateful, Granny, but I hate to impose on you," Greta said.

"Ha! Impose? I've never had anyone *impose* on me, I'll tell you. If I didn't ask 'em, then they weren't invited, pure and simple!"

"Back in the parlor, Granny?" Zach asked, once he and Caleb were on the porch.

"Yes, please," Granny said, holding the screen door open for them.

"Cora, I think we all better get on back so you can pack up a few things for Greta," Jess said, then leaned down to speak to Greta. "Don't let Granny boss you around. She tends to take matters into her own hands."

Greta could feel his lips brush her hair as he spoke and was thrilled that he was so near, but outwardly she kept her composure.

Cora bent down to Greta. "You take it easy. If you want me to come over and help with the dress, I can. I know Jess can spare me."

"I'll help her cut out the dress. It'll be my pleasure to do that." Granny smiled at Cora as she saw them to the wagon, as though eager for her company to leave. Greta had to smile to herself and admire Granny's take-charge ability. This could be an interesting few days . . .

22

Caleb was whittling on the edge of the steps, his head bent as he intently studied the piece of wood, when Jess finally found him. Rascal lay curled on top of his feet. "There you are! I came to see if you wanted to join me over at Mabel's for an early supper."

Caleb glanced up in surprise and stuffed the piece of wood and knife back into his pocket. "Sure, I'm not one to refuse a good meal." He clomped down the steps, and the two of them headed down Main Street.

It was a superb day, Jess thought. Cloudless and with comfortable temperatures, but he knew it wouldn't last too long. In high country, it could all change as fast as a jackrabbit could acquire relatives. He was already missing Greta around the store, and it seemed quieter somehow. He couldn't help but notice that Cora seemed to sidestep him whenever he was near. Or was she just busier since Greta had left?

"You're walking awful fast, Jess. Something on your mind?" Caleb huffed, trying to keep up with him.

"Yep. Got a few things on my mind lately, but right now my stomach is eating my backbone, and I'm looking forward to some of Mabel's chicken-fried steak and gravy."

"Where'd Zach get off to? I noticed him leave a little while ago, but he never said where."

"He's checking out some steers that he wants to buy for his little farmette. 'Course, he has no way of keeping them enclosed on his property, so the next thing you know we'll be stretching some fence line."

"I've done a little of that back home. I could help if he'd be willing to pay me."

Jess glanced sideways at Caleb. "Well . . . that just might be a good thing for him and you, but I wouldn't expect he'll pay much. He's just getting started on this dream of his, you know."

"Everyone has dreams," Caleb muttered barely above a whisper, but Jess heard him.

"Including you, Caleb. That's what I want to talk to you about. But let's eat first. We can talk over a piece of Mabel's cheesecake." They'd reached Mabel's, and as soon as they entered her café, she greeted them cheerily.

"You boys want the specialty of the house, I take it?" Mabel beamed at them as they sat down.

"You know we do. Make sure you heap Caleb's plate high — he's got a hollow leg." Jess removed his hat and placed it next to him on the bench. He nodded to Caleb to do likewise and heard Mabel's humph.

"Coming right up then." She lumbered off, shouting orders to the cook who she insisted was her right arm, though she did most of the cooking.

Jess waited until he and Caleb were finished eating and had ordered a slice of Mabel's cheesecake before he broached the subject that was uppermost in his mind.

"Caleb, I've been impressed with how you've shown me what a hard worker you are. I know you don't want to sleep on a cot in my kitchen for too long, so I wanted to talk to you about your future." He watched as Caleb set his water glass down and shot a look at him.

"I have no place to go. I really don't mind the cot. I'm *not* going back home." Caleb's jaw was set in a stubborn clinch. "But if you want me to find someplace else to live . . ." His voice trailed off.

Jess shook his head, suddenly realizing

that Caleb wasn't a confident young man. He hoped he could change his self-esteem. "No, nothing like that. I got to thinking how you said you enjoyed being around animals and even mentioned that you might like to be a doctor one day." He paused to see if he was getting Caleb's full attention, then continued. "Perhaps you would like to go to college and learn about working with animals. A friend of mine told me about the Agricultural College of Colorado at Fort Collins. You'd have to learn animal husbandry since they don't have a veterinarian department yet, but the school is planning on offering that next year. Then you'd have all that knowledge under your belt. What do you say?"

Caleb stared at him like he'd grown two heads and wasn't sure which one to speak to first. "How do you propose that I get the tuition for that?"

Jess scratched his day-old beard. He'd forgotten to shave this morning. "We'll work on that. Do you think that your father would pay for part of it? You are still his son, after all."

Caleb snorted. "I might be his son, but he won't do it. Only if I said I'd take over the dairy farm — which I'll remind you, I won't."

Mabel plunked down two slices of cheese-cake garnished with her strawberry pre-serves and poured steaming coffee for them. When she saw they were having an intense conversation, she moved away to wait on her other customers.

"We'll figure something out. I've requested an application for the fall, just in case you were interested, and have it right here in my pocket. We'll know more about the cost once we send it back tomorrow. Meanwhile, you can continue to work for me and maybe Zach." He watched as Caleb's serious face took on a bright look, and the creases in his forehead relaxed.

"Wow! Why do you want to do this for me? Especially after I —"

Jess held up his hand. "Let's just say that I had a younger brother who was bent on getting away from Central City. He did — but now I visit his grave." Jess looked away from Caleb, astonished he'd blurted that out.

Caleb nearly choked on the cheesecake. Laying his fork aside, he said, "I'm sorry, Jess. I didn't know. Do you mind telling me what happened to him?"

"Guess there's no harm in that. It might help you understand just how short your life can be." Jess went on to relate about his brother's death, then his parents'. When he'd finished, Caleb just sat back in his chair and shook his head.

"So you see, that's part of the reason I gave you a chance to redeem yourself when you robbed us. I knew you were still wet behind the ears. I don't mind helping someone who *wants* to be helped." Jess shoved his chair back and dug in his pocket to pay for the meal.

Caleb's Adam's apple bobbed. "Gosh . . . thank you just the same. You and Miss Cora have been very kind to me. But you and Greta have been good to me too." He winked at Jess.

Now what did he mean by that? "You're welcome. But you have to promise me something." Jess laid the bills on the table and grabbed his Stetson.

"Anything." He smiled at Jess.

"I want you to write to your parents and at least tell them where you are and what you're up to. Can you do that?" Jess was standing now, and he stared down at Caleb.

Caleb wiped his mouth on the napkin and pushed back his chair. "I can try, but I'm not promising nothin'!"

"That's all I can ask. Come on, we've got customers to relieve Cora from, I'm sure." He clapped Caleb across the shoulders, and they waved to Mabel across the room as they headed back to the store. For the first time, Caleb's smile lingered.

Cora was tallying a customer's order, Caleb was sweeping and straightening shelves, and Jess was just about to go upstairs to make himself a cup of coffee when the front door jangled. Harvey walked in with mail in one hand and a package in the other. Harvey had been friends with Jess's parents and grieved right along with them when Bryan was killed, and he took it hard too.

"Howdy, Harvey! What brings you out this late? We're about to close up shop."

"I wanted to bring you this package personally, 'cause it has a return address of the US Army at Fort Bridger. Thought it might be important," Harvey said as Jess took the package. "And this here is a letter for Miss Greta Olsen."

Jess set the package on the counter, placing the letter on top. He noticed a Wyoming postmark in the upper left-hand corner. Greta's sister, maybe? "You didn't have to bring it over. I'd have made it over to the post office at some point this week. I guess I just keep forgetting."

The gray-haired man's eyes narrowed in amusement. "It's no bother. How long have

I known you?"

Jess grinned sheepishly. "I know, I know . . . me and my habits. Just the same, I appreciate it."

Cora finished with her customer and walked over.

"Well, now, is this the pretty bride I hear you're gonna marry?" Harvey asked.

"How'd you know?" Jess asked.

Harvey chuckled. "The whole town knows. News always spreads like wildfire." He turned to take Cora's hand and introduced himself. "Golly, I think you got lucky this time, Jess."

Cora blushed, tilting her head up at the older man. "It's nice to meet you, Harvey. I could be responsible for getting the mail for Jess. That is, if he'll let me." She glanced at him.

Jess shrugged. "Whatever you'd like."

"Seems only right that your wife could do that little chore for you. So when's the big day?" Harvey beamed at the two of them.

"Well, uh . . ." Jess shuffled his feet and Cora gazed down at the floor. "Not sure just yet, but we'll let you know. It'll probably be a short, simple ceremony. Maybe at the justice of the peace."

"Really? Too bad, I love wedding cake. If you need anything, anything at all, just give me a holler. I'll be going now and let you open your box." He gave a nod to Cora, then hurried out the door.

"Jess." Cora moved close to him beside the counter. "We need to talk about our wedding."

He looked into her soft brown eyes, wondering how on earth he could break her heart. "Yes . . . we will soon. I think I'll go open this package right now while I'm having coffee. You can leave and tell Caleb to lock up. We're done for the day."

"But don't you want to have dinner or something?" She gave him a dubious look.

"Not tonight, Cora. You go on and have an evening to yourself and relax in that big room without Greta." He hoped he sounded nonchalant since he wanted to be alone with the package, and he was glad that she removed her apron as he turned to take the stairs to their living quarters.

Once he set the coffee to boil, Jess pulled out a chair and laid the letter for Greta aside. He'd get Caleb to run it over to her. He stared at the box he held in his hands for a moment, then taking a deep breath, he ripped the brown paper off and lifted the shoe box lid. Inside was a letter from Major John N. Andrews on sealed Army letterhead.

Dear Mr. Gifford,

Let me express my sympathy again for the loss of your brother a year ago. Though his body was sent to you by rail for burial, his personal effects were somehow overlooked. A soldier found this box in the barracks under his cot. I'm sorry for the delay in mailing this to you, and I pray that receiving it won't bring up old wounds but will bring comfort as you read his journal.

Sergeant Bryan Gifford was an excellent sergeant and well-liked by his comrades. I pray that this will help you and your family to have some peace and comfort regarding a deserving soldier who gave his life for his company.

Kind Regards,
Major John N. Andrews
Fort Bridger, Wyoming
August 1888

Jess bowed his head as a tremendous sadness slid over him. He heard the coffeepot boil over, splattering the stovetop, so he leaped up and hurriedly grabbed a dish towel to remove the pot from the fire. He let the coffee grounds settle, all the while eyeing the box on the table. He found a clean mug and poured himself some coffee. Picking up the box, he stepped over to his easy chair next to the window, took a swig of coffee, then settled down to look at the box's contents.

There wasn't a lot inside the box, and the first thing that caught Jess's eye was the pocketknife he'd given Bryan one year for his birthday. He smiled when he saw that Bryan had kept the stripes he'd had when he was a private. A small Bible, a razor, a shaving mug, and a few loose buttons rattled around in the bottom of the box. Some letters tied with twine were nestled against what looked like a lady's delicate handkerchief. *Could this be Greta's?* He lifted it to his nose, and a delicate lavender scent filled his nostrils.

The last item was an unfinished letter in a writing tablet. Bryan must've been called to duty when he was writing it. It was addressed to Jess, and seeing it now gave him an eerie feeling, making the past feel more like the present.

With a deep sigh, Jess set the box on the floor and started reading his brother's letter.

Dear Jess,
How's my favorite brother? I hope this

letter finds you doing well. While I miss home and Mama's cooking, I'm learning to become more of a man with the duties entrusted to me, which will surely shape my life for the future. I plan to have a career in the Army.

Speaking of which, I told you about the girl I've fallen for in my last letter. We were courting frequently until I was called away to Fort Bridger. Since that time, we've become engaged! I know you, the folks, and Zach will love her too. Her name is Greta Olsen, and she's from Holland. I can't wait for you to meet her. We plan to be married soon and will make our way to Colorado when I get my next leave.

We are perfect for each other. But if I had to pick another person for her, I'd have to say you, Jess, since I hold you in such high regard. Yes, you would be a good match, but I am the lucky one this time! I intend to write Mama again, but I wanted you to be the first to know about Greta. I know you never wanted me to leave Colorado, but now I've found someone I want to share my life with. I'm sure Granny will enjoy getting to know her too. Oh, and please give my love to Granny.

We've had a few renegade Indians who have posed a threat in these parts of Wyoming, but we seem to have a handle on things in that regard . . .

Jess put the letter aside and wiped his eyes, thinking fondly of his brother. His hands curled around his coffee mug as he stared at the busy street below. Even when Bryan was knee-high to a duck, as his older brother Jess felt responsible for him. Zach was just too impulsive to think about anyone besides himself, but that was just Zach. It didn't mean he loved Bryan any less. Jess might not be able to remember to place an order or put things back in their places, and he didn't care one bit if things were organized or not, but he'd tried to set a good example for his brothers and worked hard to earn their respect as their older brother.

He could see why Greta had fallen hard for Bryan, with his dark, rugged good looks and gregarious nature. All the things Jess was not. Although he was flattered about what Bryan wrote. To think, his handsome younger brother thought enough of him to say that he was the only one worthy to love

Greta. But how to convince her of that? He just didn't know. He glanced over at her letters, tempted to open one and read of their words of love, but somehow he felt like that was betraying his younger brother. No, he'd give them to Greta.

He removed her letters and put his letters back inside the box. He'd show it to Zach tonight. Heading downstairs, Jess called out to Caleb. "You down here, Caleb?"

"Right here, Jess. What do you need?" Caleb rounded the store aisle as Jess came down the stairs. "Somethin' wrong? You don't look so chipper."

Jess ignored his question. "Could you take my horse and run this letter over to Greta? It's from her sister, and I know she'd like to have it. You can check on her and see how she's faring." He handed Caleb the packet of letters. "Tell her these came today."

Caleb frowned. "Why would she want letters that were addressed to Bryan?"

Jess heaved a sigh. "She was engaged to my brother."

Caleb stood still, holding the letters with a stunned look on his face. With an understanding expression, he said, "Jess, I'm sorry . . ."

23

Fortified by Granny's fluffy biscuits and sausage, Greta was ready to work on cutting out Agnes's dress. "My goodness, I've never tasted more delicious biscuits than yours, Granny. I need to learn how you make them."

The older lady smiled and clapped her hands with pleasure. "When you're better, you can drop by anytime for a lesson, but let me warn you there's no recipe. Just a little buttermilk, an egg, flour, and baking powder. It's all in how you stir it up. Same as with corn bread. And you'll get a taste of that for supper with my hearty stew."

Greta giggled, scooting back her chair. "I can hardly wait, but I don't see how I'll have room for another mouthful of food."

Granny started clearing the breakfast dishes. "Oh, but you will," she said with a firm nod, setting the dishes in the sudsy water. "I thought we could spread that material out on my dining room table, where it'd be easy to cut. What do you think? Are you up to it this morning?"

"Absolutely! It will take my mind off my foot." Greta smiled at the older lady. She marveled at the energy that oozed from Granny. She zipped around like a woman half her age, despite the fact that she carried a little more weight than she needed as she hurried from the kitchen. Last night, Granny had made Greta keep her foot elevated and brought her a tray for supper with broth and hot tea. Granny's attentiveness made Greta feel special, the way her mother used to dote on her daughters at the slightest cold or upset.

Granny held out a cane to her. "Here, lean on this for support till that swelling goes down. It does look somewhat better today."

"It's sore, but I agree it feels better." She took the smooth, carved cane, then followed Granny to the dining room, where she had the fabric, a big pincushion, the pattern, and scissors waiting for them. "My, you've thought of everything. I placed Agnes's measurements in with the pattern pieces, if you want to get those out. Do you have a tape measure?"

Granny reached into her apron pocket. "Right here," she said, placing the tape on the table. "I think we have everything we need. Let's get started."

Granny hummed hymns while she pinned the pattern to the fabric, and Greta did all the cutting, barely noticing the ache in her foot as the morning flew by.

"This is going to be a very pretty party dress for Agnes. She has one of these barbecues at the end of every summer — and any other time she can find a reason," Granny said. "Any reason to get my grandson to show up."

"Do you mean Jess?" Greta's heart hammered under her blouse, but she didn't look up from her cutting task.

"Yes indeed. Don't know if you and Cora were aware of it, but Jess courted Agnes for a while — that is, until a rich man came to town. She dumped Jess faster than ice melts in the middle of August. Trouble is, all of it came to naught. The smooth talker soon moved on to other adventures, but by then Jess's feelings for her had gone cold."

Greta straightened and stretched her back, which ached from leaning over the table. "But they seem like they're still good friends."

"Let's just say Jess tolerates her, and Cole is a good friend of his. But I can tell where his affections lie." Granny grinned, looking at her over the top of her spectacles.

Greta stood quietly, trying to keep the tremble in her voice at bay. "I'm glad to hear that. I . . . wasn't sure about their relationship." She lowered her eyes.

Granny looked at her with narrowed eyes, then motioned her to sit down. "You've been standing for too long."

Realizing that she'd paused from her work, Greta was grateful to oblige. The older lady took a seat next to her. "Greta, I might be old and addle-brained, but I can see the writing on the wall, even if you can't."

"Granny, what are you trying to tell me?" Deep down Greta knew exactly what she meant but thought it best not to let on.

"My dear, I see the way Jess looks at you, and he doesn't do that when Cora enters the room. You two may spar at times, but it's easy to see that my grandson is completely taken with you."

Greta felt warmth creeping into her face, but the knowledge that Granny had figured out the truth gave her hope. She stared down at her hands, trying to come up with something to say.

"Hmm . . . something tells me that I hit upon the truth. Tell me, dear," Granny said, leaning closer. "Is it true then?"

Greta chewed her bottom lip before answering. "Oh, Granny, it is true, and I think I love him too, but Cora is my friend. I know she cares for Jess, but then I saw her and Zach kissing before I fell in the cemetery. I don't understand! Zach told me he's attracted to me and wants to be married right away."

"Is that a fact, now?" When Greta nodded, Granny continued. "Well, my goodness! That changes things for sure. I guess Cora likes Jess, but if you saw her in Zach's arms, then that tells the story. There's no confusion. Pure and simple." Granny set her fabric aside. "All I can tell you is what I see . . . so take your time. Since Zach forged those mail-order bride letters, it would serve him right if he fell in love with one of you, after all his big talk of being a bachelor." Granny humphed.

"Granny, there's more to the story than meets the eye." Greta expelled air from her lungs. There, she'd said it. She would have to tell Granny about Bryan now.

Granny stood. "It sounds like the perfect timing for tea or coffee. I'll fix it while you go settle yourself in the parlor," she said, walking toward the kitchen. "I'll meet you there, and don't forget to prop your foot up."

In Granny's cozy parlor with a pot of tea and a dish of tea cakes, Greta was propped up on the settee, her foot on a cushion. Granny pulled her chair closer and spread a napkin over Greta's lap, then poured each of them tea into delicate rose china.

"Now," Granny said, settling in her wing-back chair, "you can continue with your story. Somehow I think there are a few pieces missing in my view of my grandsons' matters lately. I don't want to pry, but whatever you have to say will be held in confidence, if you wish."

Greta already knew that Granny didn't miss much when it came to observing other people, and on some level she felt comfortable telling her about Bryan. There was no other way to do it but to launch right in. "This may come as a shock, but I was engaged to your grandson Bryan before he was ambushed." She watched Granny, afraid of her reaction.

Granny clapped her hand over her bosom. Her face was solemn, losing all color, and her blue eyes flew wide open.

Greta leaned toward her. "Granny, are you all right? Oh, maybe I should have kept my mouth closed!"

Granny struggled to regain her composure, setting her teacup down on the table. "I must say that is quite a shock. I never in this world would have guessed. Have you told Jess and Zach?"

"I told Jess when I sprained my foot at the cemetery. That's when I discovered the truth myself." Greta told Granny about Jess finding her at the family cemetery, the locket, and Bryan's last request.

Granny's face softened, and her eyes filled with tears. "But how in the world did you *not* make a connection with the names?"

"How could I? Bryan never talked much about his family before he was sent to Fort Bridger. I suppose we were so consumed with each other we didn't think or talk about anything but ourselves and our future." Greta paused and sipped her tea, waiting for Granny's response.

"What did Jess have to say about it?"

"He was shocked, partly because we're so drawn to each other . . . but he told me that he can't compete with Bryan's ghost. His death was a year ago, and I believe I am ready for love, but I don't think Jess is convinced that I'm over his brother. It *was* very hard to see his headstone, and it did bring up the past and my love for him. But the tears Jess saw were my letting go of his memory, not longing for him."

"I see." Granny lifted her cup and took a little sip. "I'm not surprised at all that Bryan fell in love with you. It broke my heart when he was killed. Jess told me that he'd met someone, but that was all."

Greta fingered the heart-shaped locket around her neck and slipped it over her head. "I want you to have this now. It holds a tiny photograph of Bryan. He gave it to me for my eighteenth birthday."

"Oh, I couldn't take that. He meant it for you."

Greta reached for Granny's hand and placed the gold chain and locket in her palm. "No, it's right that you should have it now. He was your grandson, and if I'm to look to the future, I can't be bound to what could have been."

Tears spilled down Granny's cheeks as she snapped open the locket and peered at the image of Bryan. "He was so loved, Greta. He looked up to his older brothers. Thank you, I'll treasure this always. But are you sure?"

Greta gave her the warmest smile she could muster. "I'm very sure. I think he would have liked you to have it now. Perhaps he knows from heaven. Some of his last words were for me, his private said . . . that only one man was worthy of my love — his brother." She leaned back. "I'm not certain, but I think he meant Jess. Though I'll really never know, will I?"

Granny put the locket around her neck and smiled sweetly at her. "But we can pray that God will somehow reveal that to you. Would it be okay if I prayed with you about that now, Greta?"

Swallowing the lump in her throat, Greta could only nod.

Greta was sitting at the kitchen table, shelling peas, and Granny was putting the stew on to simmer on the stovetop when the doorbell chimed.

"Who could that be? I'm not expecting anyone," Granny muttered, setting aside her knife and bowl. "Let me see who it is."

Moments later, she returned with Caleb in tow. "Look who's here to see you."

Caleb shuffled in, carrying something in his hand. "I hope I'm not disturbing you ladies, but Jess asked me to run this over to you." He placed a bundle in front of Greta and handed her a letter from Catharine.

Greta exclaimed with joy as she picked up the letter. "I've been hoping to hear from Catharine." Then her eyes riveted to the small bundle tied with twine that she recognized as her letters to Bryan. "Oh . . . how did Jess get these?"

"He had a package from Fort Bridger today with some of his brother's things they'd found."

"Land sakes! After a year? My, my!" Granny said. "I wonder what else was in the box."

Caleb shrugged. "He never said, but he seemed very sad, like he'd just lost his brother last week . . ." Caleb's voice trailed off when he looked at Granny's solemn face.

Greta tried to regain her composure. "Well, thank you for bringing these, and thank Jess for me."

"I will. I need to get on back now. Are you feeling better, Greta?" he asked as he started backing out of the kitchen.

"Thank you for asking. Yes, I'm doing *goed*, thanks to Granny's felicitous attention."

"I'll see you to the door," Granny said.

"Wait! Caleb, are you in the wagon?" Greta struggled to stand and leaned on the kitchen table.

Caleb stopped at the door. "Yes. Why?"

Greta turned to Granny. "I feel like I should go to him. Seeing my letters and Bryan's things . . . I must see him." She searched Granny's face, and understanding flashed between them.

Granny took her arm. "I understand perfectly. Caleb, if you'll support Greta on the other side, we can both get her to the wagon."

"Sure thing, Granny." Caleb jumped to her side to assist her.

24

Cora strolled down the sidewalk after she left the store, glad to leave Jess in the restrained mood he was in. She wondered where Zach had taken off to, but she didn't have long to guess when she neared the hotel. He was hitching his horse to the post and turned to give her a grin.

Zach waited until she was close and said in a low voice, "I thought since you would be alone the next couple of days, we could have supper. Then I'd like to share a stroll so we can watch the millions of stars twinkling like diamonds under the canopy of the sky tonight."

"Ever the eloquent cowboy," she teased, looking into his eyes, which danced flirtatiously.

He reached for her hand and pulled her to the side of the hotel building. He pressed her gently against the brick wall and kissed her hands, then moved to her lips. His masculinity showed in the way he held her, and she felt his strong arms about her as he showered her with kisses.

"We shouldn't be doing this, Zach," Cora halfheartedly protested between kisses, spreading her hands against his chambray shirt. She could feel the pounding of his heart, which matched her own.

"You're like a drink of cold water after a dusty ride," he said huskily. "Did you miss me all afternoon?" He tilted her chin with his fingers to gaze into her eyes.

"And what if I did? What will you do about it?" Cora was enjoying this little game.

Zach put his arm about her waist and gave it a tight squeeze. "I'll kiss you all the more if you'll let me."

"I might be more inclined if we weren't in an alleyway for all passersby to see," she said, blushing. She couldn't help but notice the frank stares they were being given. "But seriously, we can't keep snatching kisses on the lurch. We have to do something about this."

Zach kissed her soundly again, then released her. "You're right, of course. I'll talk to Jess about us. You go to your room and freshen up, and I'll call for you in a half hour. How does that sound?"

She took a step back. "Are you trying to

tell me that I need cleaning up?" she said, her mouth curving into a smile.

He tapped her on the nose. "You always look lovely, but I need to get cleaned up myself. I'll be back for you, so no dallying," he ordered.

He walked her back to the front of the hotel. Cora scurried in, glad that she wouldn't have to face Greta tonight but pleased that Zach promised to talk to Jess soon.

Caleb helped Greta up the steps to the store, which he'd left unlocked until he returned. She was grateful for the cane Granny loaned her. Only one light glowed, so Jess must have gone upstairs. She turned to Caleb. "I'll go upstairs and talk to him, but wait down here for me so you can take me back home, if you don't mind. Maybe you can stay and have a bowl of Granny's stew."

"All right. Sure you don't want me to help you up the stairs?"

"I can manage fine with this cane. I'm not totally incapacitated, as Granny would have everyone believe." She gave a quiet giggle.

"If you need anything, I'll be sitting on the porch." Caleb strolled away, fishing in his pocket. Greta assumed he'd pull out his knife as he usually did when free time allowed him to whittle. She wondered what he was carving. It was sweet of Cora to buy him the knife. She was a good influence on Caleb — and all of them, for that matter, Greta thought as she continued on up the stairs. She rapped on Jess's door.

"Jess, it's me — Greta. Can I please come in?" she asked hesitantly.

The door suddenly flung open, and Jess stared down at her with a scowl. "What are you doing here?"

"I thought you might need some company, but . . ."

"Come in," he said with a sweep of his hand.

She removed her wrap and he flung it over a kitchen chair. The large room seemed dismal. He looked awful and disheveled. Had he been crying? He stood looking at her for a moment.

"Can we please sit down?" she asked.

He led the way over to the sitting area, where chairs were assembled in front of the open window. A stiff breeze blew the curtains inward. She took the chair opposite him. "Are you all right? It couldn't have been easy to receive Bryan's personal effects after all this time," she said quietly.

He looked down at the box next to his

chair, then back up at her. "No. Somehow it seemed like I'd just lost him again. Doesn't make sense, I know, but I thought I'd put most of the sadness behind me," Jess said, running his hand across his face with a deep sigh.

"No, it makes sense to me. My parents were the first ones I'd ever lost, and the wound of their deaths still haunts me from time to time."

"Like Bryan's?" His eyes bore a hole straight through to her soul, and she swallowed hard.

"I'll admit seeing his headstone brought it all back, but I think you mistook my crying as longing for him." She reached over and placed a palm on his knee. "I might have mourned what could have been, but my tears were also a release — a kind of letting go of the past, if you will. I can't live in that past anymore, Jess, and neither should you. Bryan wouldn't have wanted that for either of his brothers."

Jess sat quietly with his head in his hands for a long time. Greta was beginning to think she'd made a mistake in coming to see him when he reached down to the box and handed her a piece of paper. "Read this."

She took the paper from his hand, and

her eyes flew over the handwriting that was all too familiar. With a catch in her throat, she tried to hold back the tears that threatened to fall. She mustn't cry. Not now when Jess was hurting so much and filled with doubt. When she looked up, he held her eyes for a long moment.

"You should feel honored that he felt that way about you, Jess. Earlier your grandmother and I prayed that God would reveal an answer to me — and He did just that now."

"What do you mean?" Jess frowned.

Greta sat back in her chair. "The message I received from the private who was with Bryan when he died was that only one man was worthy of my love — his brother. I had no idea what he meant, and after a year, I guess I didn't think about it anymore. When I found out yesterday that you and Zach were Bryan's brothers, I wondered which of you he had been referring to."

"I see."

"But don't you see? If you have Bryan's approval, then nothing can stop the way we feel for each other. Not Zach, Cora, or anyone else."

A tiny smile began to form on Jess's lips. "I'll have to talk to Zach, you know."

"Yes, you will. We have to deal with this

openly." Greta started to rise but lost her balance. Jess caught her to himself and didn't let go.

"I see you have my granddad's cane, but where's your locket? You always wear it."

"It now graces Granny's neck." She gazed up at him and watched his eyes soften.

His nearness and the touch of his hands on her arms sent a shock right through her. She lifted her eyes to meet his. "Jess, I —"

He shushed her with his finger to her lips. "I need you, Greta. You've touched a chord in my being that no one ever has before."

She raised an eyebrow. "What about Agnes? I thought you were in love with her once."

"I've come to understand that what I felt for Agnes wasn't love at all. Love should be accepting each other — all our faults as well as the good parts — and wanting the best for each other. And that was definitely not what we had." He paused, still holding her. "You love me in spite of my bad habits and encourage me to do the best I can as a mercantile owner. No one's ever done that before, and as far-fetched as it seems, I love running this store. I feel like I'm offering a much-needed service. Does that make sense?"

Her arms encircled his neck. "Perfectly.

And I know I have my faults. I can be a little pushy at times." When he grinned, she continued. "I want to be by your side — day in and day out. We complement each other, don't you think?"

"That, my dear, we can do." He leaned down to brush her brow with his lips. His finger trailed down her lips to her chin, then her neck, softly caressing her skin. She breathed a deep sigh of contentment and closed her eyes, which he promptly kissed as well. "You smell so good. Have you had a chance to eat supper yet?"

She jerked back. "*Ach!* Oh, goodness. I forgot Caleb is waiting on the front porch to take me back to Granny's. I plumb forgot."

"I'll come too. Granny's never refused her grandson a meal."

Cora stepped into her dress, too nervous to work the buttons. She paused and caught her reflection in the mirror atop the bureau. She'd pulled her heavy hair up off her neck, using her favorite tortoise-shell combs, leaving a few tendrils to drift against her collarbone. The effect against the dress of yellow challis gave her a softer appeal. She smiled. Until now, she'd forgotten how much she missed dressing up, and tonight she was dressing up for the most important man in her life.

Maybe I shouldn't meet Zach. Lord, what should I do? she prayed as she leaned against the door of her room. *I don't want to hurt Jess or Greta, but I can't pretend feelings that are not there.* Her answer was swift as she recalled something the preacher had read from the book of Psalms on Sunday: "I will instruct you in the way you should choose." *Lord, I'm so grateful for the complicated and wonderful ways You brought a man like Zach to me.*

Finally, her nerves somewhat calmer, she finished the buttons, tweaked her cheeks to add a tinge of pink, and grabbed her reticule to go meet Zach. She was a little concerned that someone might say something about Zach being out to dinner with her, but Greta *was* indisposed for now . . .

Yet in her heart she felt guilty being at Zach's side until the truth was out in the open. Well, it would be settled once he talked to Jess. After all, Jess had summarily dismissed her tonight in his abrupt mood. Not very seemly for a man about to marry her, right?

She took a deep breath and started down the stairs. *Okay, Lord, I'm trusting You to work all this out.*

■ ■ ■ ■

Zach had returned with the wagon, explaining it would be far easier to take a moonlit ride after they dined at the hotel. He led the way past the mahogany desk, and Cora glimpsed the elaborate bar at the other end, complete with a brass rail where men still in their business suits stood talking or sat playing cards. They walked on until they reached the dining area and were seated at a cozy table with crisp linen. Only then did Cora notice that Zach's eyes never left her as he laid his hat aside.

"What?" she asked, spreading the napkin in her lap.

"Oh, I was just thinking what a lucky man I am to have a beautiful woman as my dinner guest," Zach answered softly, leaning across the table. "You look exquisite in that dress." His eyes traveled down to her shoulders with a pleased look.

"You're not so bad-looking yourself," Cora quipped. She loved to tease him and enjoyed their light banter as they placed their order for dinner. "I feel like a princess with her prince tonight. This hotel is beautiful. I really shouldn't be staying here and will be glad to move to a more affordable room, if you can find one for me."

Zach took a sip of his water before answering. "It is a nice hotel and pricey, that's true, but let's not worry about that for now. I want this evening to be fun for us."

"As you wish." She tried not to focus on his mouth and his warm kisses. She suddenly felt her face go warm, remembering their stolen kisses in the alley. "I must tell you, though, I was more than a little worried about us being together, even if Greta is laid up for a few days. I don't want there to be talk about us until you can talk to her and Jess."

"You're right." His voice was low. "I shouldn't act on impulse, but it's hard whenever I see you. And you, Cora, will have to speak with Jess as well, you know."

"I know that, but it seems since he's your brother, it needs to come from you first. I know the Lord will make the right opportunity for that to happen."

"I hope so. I'm not thrilled to talk to him about this." Zach sighed. "Cora, are you certain you will be happy on a ranch away from town?"

"Wherever you are is where I want to be. With faith as our centerpiece, Zach, we can accomplish a lot in our lives. I've already told you that I have a desire to do some type of missionary work locally, and it'd be nice to have an extra room in our home that can be available if someone is in need. Which reminds me — maybe I need to check on the Careys again soon."

Zach grinned. "I'll remind you, I have a better memory than Jess. I'm trying to learn to trust in what the Lord wants for us. I really have never done that before." He gave her a steady gaze, then looked up. "Here comes our dinner. I'm famished. How about you?"

They enjoyed roasted chicken, peas, and whipped potatoes, and settled on huckleberry pie for dessert. Cora was having a wonderful time. Zach covered her hand with his, and the soft candlelight added just the perfect touch to create a romantic meal and enjoyable conversation . . . until Cole and Agnes Cartwright entered the dining room.

Agnes made a beeline straight for their table. "Well, hello there. Looks like you're having an intimate dinner for two, but the players are all wrong. I don't think Greta will like this!" she said with pursed lips.

Cole came up behind her and removed his hat. "Howdy, you two. Looks like we're interrupting dessert."

Zach stood and clasped Cole's hand. "We're nearly finished. Won't you join us?"

"That would be lovely." Agnes commenced to pull out a chair, but Cole took her firmly by the elbow.

"No, we won't intrude, but give my best to Greta," Cole said.

"I'll be sure to do that. She sprained her ankle and is resting at Granny's for a few days."

"Does she know you're having dinner with Cora?" Agnes asked smugly.

"Agnes, for heaven's sake, it's none of your business." Cole swore under his breath.

Cora thought it sad that Cole had to supervise his sister's behavior. "We'll be sure to tell her later this week when she comes back to the store," she replied, hoping she and Zach appeared to have nothing to hide. She stared directly at Agnes's pinched face.

"Good! I'll drop by for a fitting then. Ta-ta." She waved when Cole murmured a goodbye and steered his sister away to the other side of the dining room.

Zach took his seat again, and Cora felt like the romantic evening had suddenly ended. But Zach seemed unaffected as he paid for their dinner, then leveled a smoldering look at her. "Don't let Agnes spoil things. Our evening is just beginning," he whispered.

25

Somewhere in the distance, an owl hooted from its perch atop a cottonwood tree, and a ball of yellow crested the top of dark mountain peaks as Zach halted the buckboard. They'd left the noisy streets of Central City behind, and he was the happiest man alive. The cool night air hadn't diminished the heat coursing furiously through his veins as he pulled Cora next to him on the seat. Niggling thoughts of Greta and Jess threatened to cloud his mind, but he pushed them aside, determined to enjoy his first date with Cora, however secret it was.

Cora snuggled against his shoulder, and they sat in comfortable silence, listening to the sounds of Clear Creek and the occasional hum of insects. She felt good in his arms, and he instinctively knew she was strong and capable enough to deal with whatever life handed her, as well as dependable.

"You feel so good next to me," he whispered, giving her shoulders a squeeze.

"Mmm . . . I could stay in your strong arms always," Cora murmured back.

He stroked her head tenderly, then played with the thick curls as they twined about his fingers as if they had a mind of their own. He leaned down to nuzzle the nape of her neck, breathing deeply of the delicate scent of her skin.

"I thought we were going to stargaze tonight," she commented. "Is that the Big Dipper over there?" She pointed upward.

"It is indeed. I marvel every time I see it," Zach replied, tilting his head back to look into the clear night sky. "My dad taught us to appreciate God's handiwork."

"The Bible says that God knows every star by name. Isn't that incredible? If He knows each star, then how much more valuable we must be to Him," she said almost reverently.

"I just thought of something else my daddy taught us. I don't know it by heart, but it goes something like this: 'When I consider the heavens and the work of Your fingers, the moon and stars — what is man that You are mindful of him? You made him a little lower than the angels and crowned him with glory and honor.' Now that's a pretty powerful statement. How really insignificant I feel sometimes," he said quietly.

Cora moved in her seat, turning to face him. "Yes, but think of God's incredible love for us. I think both of these Scriptures are from Psalms, but I'm fairly new to the Bible, so don't hold me to that."

"You could be right. I must admit I haven't regularly picked up my Bible, but what your parents teach you — you really never forget the words." His lips brushed her brow. "Cora, I think you're going to be good for me. Your fresh enthusiasm for God is contagious, you know."

"Tell that to my parents!" She laughed. "All joking aside, I do have a burning desire to learn more about the Lord. I grew up where His name was never mentioned. We celebrated Christmas for all the wrong reasons." She shook her head.

Zach stroked her hands with his thumbs. "You and I both have a lot of catching up to do, don't we?"

Granny got up from her rocking chair when her grandson, Greta, and Caleb rumbled up the drive. Jess set the brake on the buckboard and called out, "Are you up to two more guests tonight?"

"Land sakes! I'm pleased as punch to have ya!" She stepped down the porch steps, her face beaming with the delight of a much younger person.

Jess adored his grandmother, and he knew the feeling was mutual. Now it was his hope that she'd welcome Greta into the family as his wife. But just how was he going to tell her? He'd have to speak to Zach first, which was only right. With his hands around Greta's waist, he swung her down to the ground, loving the feel of her slight frame when she leaned against him for support.

"Caleb, give Stomper some fresh oats and water, then let him out to pasture until after supper."

Caleb said hello to Granny and began unharnessing Stomper.

"Be quick, Caleb. I've had my stew simmering 'cause I figured you'd all be coming back." She laughed. "Come on in."

During dinner, Caleb had two helpings of stew and corn bread, barely talking as he shoveled in his supper. Jess and Greta exchanged looks, and Jess smiled as she bit her lip to cover her laughter. He'd never be able to fill the boy up, any more than he could fill up Bryan.

Looking down the long dining room table

at Granny, Jess caught the twinkle of Greta's locket against her dress. How thoughtful and unselfish for Greta to give the locket to Granny. On the ride over, Jess had told Greta that he'd do his best to trust in what she said, and he was happy he wouldn't have to live in his brother's shadow.

Granny winked at him, making Jess smile. "Supper was great as usual, Granny."

"It sure was," Caleb added, smacking his lips. "I'd do any extra chores you have in my free time just to get to sit at your table."

"Well, thank you both. Caleb, I might be able to accommodate you. I've been wanting to paint my porch for some time now."

"I could probably get that done in two weekends." Caleb leaned back in his chair and covered a belch with his napkin.

"I might let you leave around four on Saturday, but you'd have to go to church on Sunday. You could paint after lunch," Jess remarked.

"Think you can handle the job, Caleb? I'll buy the supplies," Granny said.

"I know I can," Caleb bragged.

"Then, young man, you've got yourself an extra job and supper anytime you're hungry!" Granny rose and started clearing the table, and Greta made a move to help.

Granny tapped Greta on the shoulder.

"Oh no you don't. You just rest that foot. Jess, why don't you and Greta enjoy the porch swing before I have to take it down when the porch is painted? The weather's mighty nice now."

Greta gave the older woman a brief hug as she stood. "I told Jess you are going to spoil me rotten." She caught Caleb's eye. "Do you think you could wash the dishes for Granny?"

Caleb swallowed. "Wash dishes?"

"Don't you worry none," Granny said. "I'll wash, you dry. Fair deal?"

Caleb cocked his head at her. "You wouldn't have something sweet to nibble on, would you? Jess works me pretty hard," he answered with a grin.

Granny paused with the plates stacked in her hands. "You and I are going to get along just fine. I've been known to have a sweet tooth all my life," she answered with a laugh.

Jess tucked Greta's arm under his. "I think we can leave them alone to battle it out, don't you?" Greta nodded. He couldn't wait to be alone with her again before he and Caleb headed back to Central City. He guessed Zach had come home after he and Greta left and fixed his own supper or went to Mabel's again. At least he wouldn't have to complain about Jess's cooking tonight.

"Granny's right. It's a beautiful night and all the stars are out," Greta commented once they were settled on the swing at the end of the porch.

Jess pushed his foot against the floor to set the swing in motion, and it creaked against the rope. "I can tell that the evenings are beginning to get just a little cooler than before. But fall is my favorite time of year, and I enjoy being here on Granny's porch with you next to me. How's your foot feeling? Better, I hope?"

She looked at him, her eyes wide in the darkness with only the moon's glow for light. "It really is much better. I want to get back to the store, but Granny and I need to finish up the dress for Agnes, so could you plan on having Caleb pick me up Friday morning?"

Jess rested his arm on her shoulders. "I'll do even better than that. I'll come get you myself."

"Jess, until you talk to Zach, it'd be best to let Caleb come for me, don't you think?"

Her nearness made it hard for him to think about anything else. "I guess you're right." How in the world could he have been so against having a mail-order bride? Greta was so lovely with the moonlight bouncing off her hair, making it appear almost silvery against the pale skin of her shoulders. He lifted her hands and kissed her palms, noting her neatly filed nails. She scooted closer to lean her head against his shoulder, releasing a breathy sigh.

"Happy?" he asked.

"Contented at the moment. The motion of the swing makes my eyes heavy. Guess I'm as bad as a baby in a cradle," she said.

"Then that calls for a good-night kiss for *my* baby," he said.

She lifted her head to meet his kiss, and hers was warm, sweet, and inviting. Jess lingered there, nibbling at her lips. He could never get enough of them, and he felt his blood turn to water with every kiss she returned. At long last, he released her and closed his eyes. He leaned back against the porch swing with one arm still about her shoulders, caressing her silky hair.

She began to trace the outline of his brow, then his eyes, and continued on to touch his lips, ending with a kiss on his neck just above his collar. "And your baby thanks you."

Once Greta was ensconced in the four-poster bed under a light chenille coverlet, she finally opened Catharine's letter.

Dearest Greta,

Everyone here is doing well, and the twins are growing up fast. They keep me very busy, as you recall, so this will be a quick letter. The wheat crop looks promising for harvest soon, and Peter sends his love. Anna is doing well living with Clara, and it seems that Clara is happier having Anna as a companion.

I can't wait to hear from you about your marriage. Will you be living above the mercantile store? I hope you've made a new friend. Being away from family can be so hard.

I know this was a difficult choice for you to make after losing Bryan, but I'm glad you're ready to look forward to your future and not at what could have been. Write me all about Central City. I look forward to reading once the children are in bed.

In closing, I wanted to share some exciting news — I'm pregnant again! We are ecstatic and happy to be filling our home with children. Our blessings overflow. God has given us back the years the locusts have eaten — and I'm not speaking about the wheat crop. I can almost see the smile on your face as you read this.

I look forward to hearing from you soon. Sending you my prayers and blessings on your new life.

Love,
Catharine

Greta was lonely for her family but filled with joy for Catharine. Setting the letter aside, she made a mental note to write Catharine tomorrow. She lay back on her pillow, pulling the cover up to her chin, glad that she'd gone to see Jess when she did. Funny how they both shared grief over the same person, but until a few days ago, they hadn't known each other's pain. God worked in mysterious ways, Granny had told her when they were sewing. Greta had to agree.

Lying in the dark, she dreamily thought of her evening with Jess. The conversation at his place about his brother made it clear to her that they had connected on a deeper level than ever before. Her thoughts drifted to his lingering kisses and his hand holding hers as they cuddled. It was a nice way to end the day with the one you love. Which only made her wonder what it would be like to be his wife and be held in his arms every night. She blushed at the thought and wondered if Jess was in his bed right this minute thinking of her too.

26

Greta turned sideways in her seat to wave once again to Granny, who stood in the yard as she and Caleb drove away in the early morning light. Granny had treated her like her own daughter while Greta allowed her foot to heal for a few days. Today she had neatly wrapped it so Greta was able to get her foot back into her shoe, and although it felt snug, it felt much better. And the dress was done — with the two of them sewing, it wasn't long before they'd whipped up the dress for Agnes. Greta felt proud of the creation, which gave rein to a whole host of other possible designs in her head.

While she enjoyed her respite with Granny and her delicious meals, she realized just how much she'd missed Cora. Their friendship was special, considering how they'd met, and being outsiders automatically gave them a closer link. Like pieces of a jigsaw puzzle, their lives were being neatly pieced together with the two Gifford brothers, Granny, and their unique friendship.

"We've missed you at the store," Caleb declared, loosely holding the reins while giving Stomper his way. "Jess can't seem to get a thing straight or keep track of stuff."

Greta laughed. "I'm so glad to be missed, even if it was more for my work performance than for my amicable personality."

Caleb's face reddened. "Aw, you know what I mean."

"*Ja,* I do, Caleb. I was only teasing." Greta smiled. "What a fine morning we have. Cold in the morning, then warm by noon. I really love living in America."

"It's especially nice to be up before Black Hawk and Central City wake up and everyone gets to hustling through the streets. Kinda nice and quiet right now, just the birds and the breeze blowing the leaves around," Caleb remarked.

Greta breathed in the fresh morning air. Not much space separated the two towns, Greta thought as she took note of the brick buildings and a few weathered clapboard ones. Granny told her that most of Central City had burned in a fire back in 1874.

A movement from Caleb's left jolted her to the present, and Caleb jerked the reins, bringing the buckboard to a standstill. A horse and rider had come from behind a boulder that edged the dusty road and stopped a few feet away from them. The rider had a black kerchief around his face and nose and leaned against the saddle horn with a penetrating gaze.

"*Ach!* What's the meaning of this?" Greta exclaimed.

"Well now, you're right purty, little lady. My, my, if it ain't my cohort, Caleb. Who's your new lady friend?" The rider snickered. "Isn't she a bit outta your league?"

How did he know Caleb's name? Greta's heart began to pound against her ribs. He didn't seem to be much of a threat . . . but then again, why did he ride with a mask over his face?

"Not that it's any of your business, but she's not my lady friend! I'm not your cohort in crime either. I've left that old life behind me." Caleb stiffened. "What do you want, Jack?"

Jack's dark eyes narrowed at them. "I won't go pulling my gun on you since we're friends, but the purty lady there can toss me her reticule and her nice ear bobs I see dangling."

"I will not!" Greta blurted out, folding her arms and holding the reticule tighter. She didn't have much money, but she sure wasn't going to let him get his dirty paws on it.

"What's that you say?" Jack smirked, pulling down his kerchief. He looked only a year or two older than Caleb, ruggedly handsome, but in bad need of a shave.

Without warning, Jack slid off his horse's back and in two strides had made his way to Greta. He reached out to grab her arm, but Caleb was quicker. He lunged at Jack from the wagon and landed on top of him, forcing them both to the ground in a heap of flying arms and legs, their hats flinging in different directions.

Jack's surprise almost made Greta giggle, but this was no laughing matter. She tensed, standing up to watch the fight. Lifting bags of grain and flour and eating three square meals a day seemed to give Caleb the advantage.

Dust flew upward, choking Greta. She covered her mouth and watched as the men struggled to their feet.

"Don't let him get the best of you, Caleb!" Greta cheered him on. When Jack's fist found Caleb's side, she gasped and held her breath. And though he landed a punch in Caleb's midsection, Caleb came back with a punch to his stomach. While he was doubled over, Caleb landed another right hook to Jack's chin, knocking him to his knees. Jack wiped the blood from his jaw and lip and stared up at Caleb, swearing under his breath.

"I suggest you get back on your horse and hightail it outta here before I have to knock some more sense into you." Caleb was breathing hard, his hair hanging down in his face. He bent over to knock the dust off his hat, then slammed it back on his head, jaw clenched in a hard line. "Or maybe I should haul you off to see the sheriff."

Jack swaggered to his feet, a bright blotch of red oozing where his lip was split. "I gotta give it to you, kid, you've gotten stronger in more ways than one." He wiped his mouth on his sleeve and reached for his hat. "Sure you're happy living with that feisty blonde-haired beauty?" he asked, climbing back on his horse.

Greta could no longer keep silent. "I can guarantee he's a whole lot happier than you, so why don't you get on out of here while you still have some dignity in that bashed-in face of yours?"

Jack sneered at them. "That's too bad, honey. Me and you could've made some sweet music." He jabbed his horse's side and tore off down the road, leaving a wake of dust.

Caleb climbed back into the wagon, and Greta gasped when she saw his rapidly swelling black eye. "Caleb, you want to turn back to Granny's and let her doctor your eye?"

Caleb winced when she touched his brow. "Naw, I'll be okay. It's not the first one, and I reckon it won't be the last one either." He picked up the reins and said "giddyap" to Stomper, and they continued on their way.

She laid her hand over his. "Thanks for protecting me that way. You could've been hurt — or shot."

"Jack may be notorious, but at one time he *was* my friend when I was on the road. I knew he wouldn't really hurt us."

Greta was still reeling from the entire incident, but she smiled inwardly that Caleb seemed to have matured and changed his ways since Jess took him in.

By the time they reached the store, everyone was busy with morning customers. Cora paused from wrapping her patron's package and gasped when Caleb and Greta entered the store. "My goodness, what happened to you?"

"There was a robbery attempt, and Caleb protected me in a fistfight with the robber," Greta declared, giving the young man a quick hug. "As you can tell, he won, because we're here safe and sound."

"Fistfight?" Zach hurried over, and others gathered near to listen.

"Aw, it's nothing. I'd do it all over again." Caleb looked embarrassed. He placed the wrapped parcel that held Agnes's dress on the counter.

Cora took him by the arm. "It's exactly what one would expect of you. Now come in the back of the store and let me have a look. I see a knot forming at your temple."

"If I thought I could get all this attention from the two ladies, I'd love to have been in your shoes, Caleb." Jess winked at Caleb, his hands on his hips. His dirty apron already showed a day's work.

"I'm really fine, boss," Caleb said sheepishly

"Well, let Cora take a look." Turning to Greta, Jess said, "It's nice to have you back. I see you're not hobbling either." His eyes twinkled at her.

Zach stood next to his brother. "Let me add that we've missed you. In a short time, you've kept this place running like clockwork."

"Thank you." Greta smiled broadly at both men. "My foot is much better. It's best if I keep moving it and stretching it, or so Granny says."

"She knows best. Better listen to her expert advice. Give me your cape and I'll hang it up," Zach said. He reached for her cape and walked to the pegs in the back of the store.

"Looks like the store's busy this morning, and it's early yet," Greta said, glancing across the room.

"People like to get a head start before the midday temperatures rise," Jess said. "Oh, by the way, the table and chairs came today from Denver. I placed them near the potbellied stove. Cora said it was the perfect place for them."

Greta clapped her hands. She remembered that Jess hadn't liked the idea when she'd first approached him about it. "Oh, thank you, Jess. I can see that two customers are already taking advantage of a little respite. I knew that it would be just the thing! The customers are going to love it, I know."

Zach returned with her apron. "Here ya go, madam. Want to go check out the table and see if it's what you wanted?"

She slipped the apron over her head and was aware that both men were watching her, but she pretended not to notice. Jess regarded her a moment, then turned on his heel and walked away. She followed Zach to the table. Rose Potts and Hilda Barnes were enjoying a cup of cider and looking through the Montgomery Ward catalog. Both stopped their chatter and smiled as she walked over.

"I hear this little space by the stove was your idea, Greta," Rose said.

"And what a cozy thought. It will be most welcomed by Jess's customers, particularly on a cold winter day," Hilda added.

"Greta's been a mighty good addition to our staff," Zach said.

"Oh, I'm sure she has. But I hear you two will be tying the knot soon. After all, that's why Greta's here, isn't it?" Hilda's brows quirked.

"Right you are. I was just saying what a valuable asset she's become to both me and Jess." Zach shifted uncomfortably on his feet and gave a forced smile. "Excuse me, ladies. I have a customer."

Zach had definitely skirted around giving a wedding date, and Greta planned to do the same. "Ladies, I'm glad you're enjoying our cozy nook. Is there anything that I can help you with today?" Greta asked, hoping her voice sounded cheerful.

Rose laughed. "We're just wasting time. We've finished shopping. But I suppose now it's time to get back home." She stood, picking up her handbag. "We heard you were at

Granny's recuperating from a twisted ankle. I do hope it's improved."

Greta reached for their used mugs and cleared the table as Hilda stood. "Thank you, it's much, much better. You both have a nice rest of the day."

"See you at church then," Rose said as she and Hilda slipped out the door, chatting.

Greta continued toward the stairs to place the dirty mugs in the kitchen, but Jess stopped her.

"I'll take those upstairs. You shouldn't be running upstairs on your foot, Greta," he said softly.

She loved how her name sounded as it fell from his lips, and she tried not to focus on his mouth but dragged her eyes upward to his soft brown eyes. He appeared to want to say more when he reached for the mugs, his hands briefly brushing hers, but Cora and Caleb walked up.

"Our hero is faring well, I'd say," Cora informed them. "I cleaned his eye and put a cold compress on it for a few minutes."

Jess grinned at Caleb. "It's going to look a whole lot worse than it feels tomorrow. And by the way, Zach and I thank you for taking care of Greta."

Caleb shrugged. "It's the least I could do.

I don't want to go back to life with the likes of Jack."

"Amen!" Cora said.

Jess clapped him on his back. "Then you won't have to. Besides, you'll soon be going to school and will meet a whole passel of new friends."

"Respectable ones, I hope," Cora said.

"I can't thank you all for how good you've been to me the last few days. I don't deserve it." Caleb's eyes moistened.

"Sure you do," Jess answered. "But enough lollygagging. We've got work to do."

"I need to see Rascal. I've missed him. Where is he?" Greta asked.

"Caleb has him tied under the shade tree out back because he was underfoot this morning," Cora said. "I'm sure he's missed you so."

"Is it okay if I bring him back in now that it's not so busy?" Greta looked at Jess for an answer.

The men just rolled their eyes and watched as Greta made her way past them to the back door in search of her precious puppy.

Rascal barked when he saw her coming and pulled against the rope, obviously happy to see her. She bent down to kiss his furry head, then picked him up. "You missed me. I missed you too, Rascal." He licked her face and hands with his warm tongue, making her giggle. She unclipped the rope from his neck and entered the back door and hallway. She had a clear view of the counter through the doorway, and what she saw made her heart sink.

27

Jess was looking for a catalog item for a customer when he saw a folded page with a circle around Blue Willow dishes. Now who was ordering those? He couldn't remember anyone asking about them, but maybe Cora or Greta knew.

It had taken all the self-control he had not to kiss Greta soundly when she walked in today. His ardent feelings for her more than surprised him, since taking on a bride hadn't even been in his realm of thought several weeks ago. But now he didn't know how he could do without her. He loved her laughter, her exuberance for life . . . and though he hated to admit it, she'd kept him organized and on track with the store. On the porch swing with her, he'd felt comfortable and contented, as if he'd known her all his life. A smile formed as he stared out the front windows.

Cora finished with a customer and walked

over to where he stood gazing into space. "Jess . . . Jess," she said, clearing her throat. "Should I go make a fresh pot of coffee for our customers, or perhaps cider?"

"Hmm?" Jess sprang back to the present, feeling guilty for daydreaming. "Oh . . . yes . . . sure thing." *What am I going to do, Lord? How do I tell sweet, gentle Cora that I can't marry her?*

She looked down at the page he pretended to peruse. "I guess you saw where I circled the Blue Willow china. I'm thinking I'd like to order that for Greta as a wedding gift. They are a bit pricey, though. What do you think?"

Jess swallowed hard. "That's a nice present, but I think there may be some of those dishes of my mother's in Granny's attic. Dishes all look the same to me, though, to tell you the truth. If you'd care to go through a bunch of stored boxes up there, you can take what you want."

"Really? Oh, Jess, do you think you could take me to Granny's and let me see if I can find them?"

"Sure. We can do it later this afternoon."

She flung her arms around his neck and kissed him with joy on the cheek. "You're so sweet to me. This is going to be the perfect wedding gift for my dear friend. She will love them," Cora whispered. "Now don't tell."

Jess saw the sparkle of excitement in her eyes, and it was clear in his mind just how quickly the two ladies had become friends. He smiled back, then gently peeled her arms from around his neck. It flustered him for her to show her affection, and he knew she expected a kiss in return, but he just couldn't give it, so he said, "I don't mind at all, Cora." He took a step back and saw Greta holding Rascal as she entered the hallway. Had she seen the kiss? He hoped not. Her face showed no emotion to indicate that she had.

"I'm going upstairs to make coffee, and I'll return in a flash, Greta," Cora told her friend.

Greta stood like a statue, observing the flush on Cora's cheeks. A tiny piece of her heart had died in that moment when she witnessed her and Jess's kiss. Was he playing them both? She was a fool for thinking he loved her in such a short time. But she hadn't wanted to be like all the other mail-order brides she'd heard about who got married as soon as they stepped off the train. Some of those marriages of convenience worked, and others had turned out disastrously. She wanted her marriage to mean something. As Cora had said, she wanted to hear "I love you." There was little chance of that now.

And what about Cora? First Greta had seen her in Zach's arms, and now Jess's. What was going on? She'd have to find out, even if it meant confronting Cora directly.

With heavy steps, she went on past Jess. When he touched her on the sleeve, she didn't stop, using the dog in her arms as her excuse. Her bright day had turned to gray, she thought as she settled Rascal in his crate, leaving the crate door open just a bit. "Now you be a good boy and mind your manners today," she told him, wagging her finger at him. When his sad brown eyes blinked at her, she brushed away the tears in her own eyes and paused to give him a reassuring squeeze.

She heard the bell over the door jangle, and from the chatter of voices, she knew that it was Agnes and Cole. Just what she needed to make her day even worse — a dress fitting with insufferable Agnes. She straightened, lifting her shoulders back, then plastered on a smile and hurried over to greet them. At least she found Cole to be much nicer than his sister.

Agnes peeled off her gloves, and with a

disapproving glance at Greta's feet, she humphed. "I see your foot must be better."

"Yes, Agnes. A lot better," Greta said.

"Then I hope it didn't keep you from making my dress for the party." She stuffed her gloves into her handbag and snapped it shut.

Agnes's indifference to her suffering didn't surprise Greta. "Not at all. It's completed. If you'll just step behind the curtain, I'll go get it." Greta waited until she walked away, then turned to Cole, who stood patiently with a smile. "And you, Cole — are you doing well?"

Cole observed her with interest through long, thick lashes before answering. "Good as ever, Miss Greta," he said, removing his hat. "She talked me into accompanying her today, but I'm glad because it gave me a chance to see you again." He held up his hand. "Yes, I know you're marrying Zach, but a fella can still feast his eyes on a lady of beauty."

In spite of herself, she found herself blushing. "You're too kind. I'd better hurry and get her dress. I don't want to keep her waiting. Make yourself at home."

"I'll go get Jess and bend his ear while I wait." Cole turned toward the counter where Jess was.

"He's assisting Silas and Annabelle."

"No problem. I'll just wait." He smiled back at her.

"Then have a seat by the stove. We have a table and chairs now. Cora should be back down soon with fresh-brewed coffee."

"You don't say? Now that's what I call customer service." He grinned and strode over to sit at the new table to wait on his sister.

Greta quickly retrieved the box that Granny had placed the dress in and slipped behind the curtain, where Agnes stood waiting with an impatient glare. "Here we are. I think it turned out lovely."

Agnes's eyes lit up when Greta removed the dress from the box. "Ooh, I can hardly wait to try it on." Agnes snatched the dress from Greta's fingers, pulled it over her head, and whirled around to gaze at herself in the mirror. "Will you button up the back for me?" she asked.

"Certainly. You'll be the hit at your party —" Greta frowned, trying to pull the back of the dress together at the waist until her fingers hurt. "Hmm . . ." The two pieces of fabric were about an inch from closing. *Now how did that happen?* she wondered, biting her lip. *I know Granny and I went over the measurements more than once before we sewed the whole thing up and added buttons.*

"Is something wrong?" Agnes looked at the mirror that reflected Greta behind her.

"Agnes . . . are you standing up straight? Could you suck in your stomach just a wee bit?"

"Of course I'm standing up straight! Didn't you make the dress according to my measurements?"

Greta took the tape measure from her apron pocket and carefully measured Agnes's waist again, then glanced at the numbers she'd jotted down last week. Agnes was not going to like her answer. Not at all!

"I'm sorry, Agnes, but the dress is an inch away from closing at the back, near your waist." She walked around to face Agnes and her displeasure.

"How on earth can that be? Really! Don't you even know how to take accurate measurements?" Her annoyance was obvious. "Why did I trust you in the first place?"

Greta blinked, biting her lip to keep from saying something she'd only come to regret. She thrust the paper with her measurements in front of Agnes's nose. "See for yourself. It appears that you've gained a pound or two at your waist since we took these. The dress matches my numbers."

She watched as Agnes stared down at the

paper, all color draining from her face. "No!" Agnes shrieked, letting the paper flutter to the floor.

Jess and Zach were talking with Cole and the Meads when they all heard Agnes scream.

"Whatever is wrong with Agnes?" Cora asked, hurrying over to set the coffeepot and mugs down.

Cole laughed heartily. "Agnes!" he called out loud enough for the entire store to hear. "I think you've been eating too many of Mabel's biscuits while staying in town." He turned to the group. "She'll let me have it later, but I just couldn't resist. I've been telling her that she can't sit all day and let people wait on her, but do you think she'll listen?"

"I'd better go see what I can do to help Greta out then," Cora said, shaking her head as she scurried over to the curtained area.

"You do that, Cora. I'll see you later. I'm taking Caleb out for a few hours to help me clear a path to my cabin site. See you later, Cole." Zach winked at her, then went in search of Caleb.

"Do you need some help, Greta?" Cora

asked as she stepped inside the curtained-off area. "Is everything okay? Can I help?"

"You tell that brother of mine he'll pay for blurting that out for the world to hear!" Agnes sputtered, her hands on her hips. Greta glanced at Cora, who stood helpless, and gave her an "I told you so" look. She almost felt sorry for Agnes.

"*Nee.* No, it appears that this dress will have to be let out a good half inch on either side, if there's enough fabric to let out. If so, it won't take me long," Greta mumbled through the pins sticking out of her mouth. "I can probably have the dress ready late tomorrow afternoon, but not before since I'll have to reset the buttons," she said with a hint of irritation. She turned her attention to marking the dress with the pins rather than let Cora read her eyes. Of course, Cora couldn't know that Greta had seen her and Jess together earlier. Greta must have time to think this through later.

"Oh dear . . . I see. Then I'll just let you work." Cora turned to leave. "Just let me know if there's anything either of you need."

"There. I've pinned where it needs to be," Greta said, standing back to look up at Agnes on the upturned crate.

Agnes took the dress off and handed it to Greta. With trembling lips she muttered,

"I'm sorry, Greta, for talking to you that way. I shouldn't have. Cole loves to tease me, but . . . unfortunately, he's right. I've been eating far more than I've been doing anything productive." She pursed her lips into a tight line.

"It's all right. I never had brothers, and you're lucky to have one to tease you. We'll get this taken care of, and you'll be the prettiest one at your barbecue." Greta choked out the words, but she did mean it. Agnes was very pretty, even if she'd put on a few pounds. "I'm glad that you gave me a chance to make the dress for you. It's generated a greater interest for me in sewing."

Agnes stepped off the crate and donned her dress. She pulled on her gloves, picked up her handbag, and turned to leave, then paused. With a somber face she sighed, twisting her purse strings with agitation. "I do want to be your friend since you're new here. We've gotten off to a bad start, but I meant no harm, truly." Her eyes misted. "I guess I was just jealous of you and Jess."

"Well . . . you're badly mistaken about me and Jess. I thought I told you that he and Cora were getting married."

"Maybe you did, but it was Cora whom Zach took to dinner at the Teller House while you were indisposed at Granny's . . .

so naturally I assumed —"

"You assumed wrong. They're just friends." *If only she'd seen what I saw earlier.*

Agnes's trim eyebrows elevated. "It didn't look that way to me, but whatever you want to believe. I'll be back for the dress tomorrow. Better watch out for these men. They're not always truthful, you know."

Greta was beginning to get a glimpse of that fact.

28

Cora grabbed her coat and ran out to meet Jess, who was waiting to take her to Granny's. She stopped long enough to tell Caleb to let Zach and Greta know not to wait for her for supper. She was pleased with herself for having thought of the Blue Willow for Greta's wedding present . . . but not for a wedding to Zach. She wondered if Greta could come to care for Jess or perhaps someone like Cole. Cole did seem to have an eye for her.

The night Greta had shown Cora the Blue Willow cake server and told her the legend of Blue Willow, she'd gotten the idea of the dishes for her friend. Now if she could just find them in Granny's attic . . . *if* there were any Blue Willow dishes there.

Jess assisted her into the wagon, and soon they were making their way through the crowded Main Street toward Black Hawk. Maybe this would be a good time to talk, but she'd promised Zach that she'd let him talk to Jess the first chance he got. The chance hadn't revealed itself yet, to her knowledge.

"I guess I could've borrowed a horse from you." Cora tried small talk.

"It's no trouble, honestly. I can drop you off and come back after supper. If you find the dishes, then we can put 'em in the wagon. You couldn't very well carry them that far," Jess remarked, watching the crowded road and weaving his way among wagons, people, and horses. "But I have to warn you. You might not be able to locate them right away. Granny's been hoarding stuff for years. She might know where she placed my mother's dishes, though. Hard to tell."

Cora glanced at Jess. Why didn't he try to hold her hand? Or talk to her about their wedding? He had no idea about her feelings for Zach and could've used this as an opportunity while he and Cora were alone. Not that she wanted him to, but she was curious that he hadn't so much as tried. Strange man.

"She won't mind that I'm showing up unannounced, will she?"

Jess laughed. "Granny? Never. That woman was born to boss — er, talk."

Cora chuckled at his comment. "Yet everyone seems to adore her, don't they?"

"You're right. They do, and there's not a more sincere heart in all of Colorado."

Cora nodded in agreement.

The remainder of the ride was pleasant, with the slant of late afternoon sun between the crowded shops and housetops and a cool wind that hinted at the promise of fall. Cora breathed in the freshness of juniper and the heavy fragrance of pine, enjoying the chance to be outdoors again, which made her think about embarking on an exciting life with Zach on his ranch once they were married. There would be many opportunities to relish the outdoors. She could hardly wait for that day.

Jess dropped her off at the front porch, and Cora waved him on as Granny opened the door.

"I hope you don't mind that I dropped by."

Granny pulled her inside. "I'm always glad to have company, but why did Jess bring you and leave? There must be something on your mind. Please come on in." She had a crocheted shawl about her shoulders, covering a pretty black dress dotted with dainty white flowers and a lace collar.

"Yes, Granny, there is, and I think maybe

you could help us out."

Granny raised an eyebrow and listened intently while Cora told her of her mission. "My dear, you are welcome to search the attic for that box, but I don't recollect that Jess put that box of his mother's dishes in the attic. That doesn't mean he didn't, either." She sighed, and sadness showed on her wrinkled face. "It was all I could do to get through those first few months after losing them." Her blue eyes grew glassy.

Cora leaned over and put her arm about Granny's shoulders. "I'm so sorry. Won't it be wonderful that in heaven, God will wipe away all our tears?"

"Yes, it will." Granny sniffed into her hankie. "Thank you for reminding me, Cora. I'll try to remember that. Now let me show you the attic. I have supper simmering on the stove to attend to, but you can look to your heart's content." She moved spryly up the creaking attic stairs at the back of the hallway, and Cora followed.

Granny opened the attic door. "There should be enough light for another thirty minutes, which could give you a small start. As you can see, nothing is really labeled or organized."

"Hmm, I see what you mean," Cora commented as her eyes scanned the musky attic chock-full of stuff. "I'd better get started then."

"I'll be in the kitchen, and if you'd like you can stay and have a bite to eat with me," Granny said over her shoulder as she headed back down the stairs.

"I'd like that very much. I'll be down directly," Cora said.

Now, where to begin? Cora decided that it was logical that a more recently stored box would be placed nearest the front, so she started there. The attic creaked with every step she took. Since it was stuffy, she tried to open the window for some air, but it was stuck tight. She pounded at the edges with her hands, and finally it unstuck from its sash so she was able to shove the window up. She sucked in the fresh air.

Looking down below, she smiled when she saw a pretty backyard full of a variety of flowers and an old wooden park bench under a tree. Ahh . . . she'd love to be sitting there reading. Maybe another day — today she had work to do.

Dust flew from the top of the first box she reached for, and she sneezed heartily. This box held mostly mementos and scraps of newspaper clippings. She couldn't help but take a closer look.

She found a faded clipping of John Gregory, who hailed from Georgia, discovered the Gregory Gulch mine, and started the gold rush of Central City. Another article was related to a fire that destroyed most of Central City in 1874, and one was about William Gilpin, Colorado's first territorial governor. It was interesting to learn more about the town she would be living in.

Cora dragged over a box to sit on and opened another box. She laughed when she saw assorted children's toys. She wondered if they'd belonged to Zach and Jess. Most likely they had.

She was beginning to feel warm and was delighted when a stiff breeze blew in, rattling the window. The attic moaned as the elm tree branches swayed against the eaves. It was a cooler night than they'd had so far, and she was glad that she'd picked up her coat at the last minute. She was beginning to get used to the erratic temperatures of Colorado — the weather changed as quickly as a woman changed her mind.

Another box held scraps of material, probably for quilt making. She made a mental note to ask Granny if she was planning on using the bits and pieces. Cora could turn them into a beautiful quilt for her and Zach. She enjoyed the solitude quilting afforded her.

It wasn't long before Granny called out from the bottom of the attic stairs for her to come down. Cora peered at the watch fob hanging from her blouse and was surprised to find nearly an hour had elapsed. She hadn't noticed the waning sunlight with its speckled effect on the attic room until now, and soon it would be dark.

"I'm coming down now," she answered, shaking the dust from her dress. She'd have to come back tomorrow and plow through a few more boxes. But what if Granny was right and there were no dishes?

I'll just have to get an order out for the Blue Willow right away, that's what I'll do.

Greta sat near the sewing machine, grateful that Granny had loaned it to her, and ripped out the seam at the waist where the skirt attached to the bodice of Agnes's party dress. At least she wouldn't have to sew this by hand. She glanced up to see Cora get in the wagon with Jess. The seam ripper in her hand stilled as she watched the two of them laughing and in apparent good spirits. Tears sprang to her eyes and she looked down, but she couldn't see the threads to rip out. She wiped her eyes and tried to focus on letting out the dress. It wouldn't do for her fingers to slip and slice a gap in the pretty material. Not after she'd spent so much time trying to create the perfect dress for Agnes.

In her heart she truly wanted Cora to be happy . . . but did it have to be with Jess? Somehow she must have misread the looks that Cora had given Jess as just friendship. *Cora doesn't have an unkind bone in her body, and she definitely has more compassion in her little finger than I have in my entire body. Maybe she's even more godly than I.* Perhaps that was what Jess saw in Cora.

When Jess kissed Greta, he never said he loved her, did he? She tried desperately to recall what he'd said that day at the cemetery and the day he'd received the box of Bryan's personal effects. Her thoughts were all in a jumble.

She would have to resign herself to the fact that Jess and Cora would soon be wed. She heaved a deep sigh. Life would continue . . . somehow. But oh, how her heart ached, and it seemed much worse this time than when Bryan had died.

Another idea came to her as she finished tearing out the waistband. She would go tell Zach that they should go ahead with their ceremony or wedding — whatever it was to be — as planned in the beginning, right after he and Jess had had the women choose the china cups. Then maybe he could take her to his ranch and she wouldn't have to face seeing Jess with Cora.

29

Jess was just pulling up in front of the mercantile when he saw Greta leaving. She was talking to Caleb, who was leaning back in a chair against the wall, whittling. Jess stood there watching her. She was as pretty as the most delicate hummingbird that drank from the columbines, but that image belied the strength he knew she held inside. He needed someone like her who loved him unconditionally. But today she'd been exceptionally cool, not stopping to have lunch and burying her head in the sewing machine, determined to get Agnes's dress ready by tomorrow. That's when he decided to give her a wide berth. She was upset about something, and when she was ready to talk, he'd be there. Could it be she was miffed that he hadn't talked to Zach yet? He kept getting mixed signals from everyone to the point that he wasn't sure about anything.

He tried to recollect their talk the night he'd received the package from Fort Bridger. If memory served him correctly, as he was wont to forget so many things, he thought she'd said she had put Bryan in her past. So what went wrong? Had he said or done something to offend her?

Jess stepped up to the porch. "Howdy," he said, shoving his hat back in order to get a closer look at Greta's face. "You about to go to the hotel for the night?"

"No, I'm just taking a break, but I'll be back to finish working on Agnes's dress." Her voice sounded dull and flat, and she didn't meet his gaze.

"Oh . . . I was going to see if you wanted to have supper." He looked over at Caleb. "I see you made it back. Where's Zach?"

"He took off for the lumber store. He's figuring how much he'll need for a barn," Caleb answered, pausing from his hobby.

"I see." Jess scratched his chin, still unshaven from this morning. "What are you whittling there?" he asked, still keeping an eye on Greta. She was standing so close to him that he could smell the delicate lavender that she used to wash her hair.

Caleb held his creation up for them to see. "I was just telling Greta it's an angel, or at least I hope it resembles one. I want to give it to Cora. Think she'll like it?"

"Why, it's lovely, Caleb! Of course she will. What a talent you have." Greta admired the wood figurine. "How sweet of you to do that."

"Greta's right, it's nice." Jess ventured a glance at Greta. Her veiled blue eyes held his for a moment, then looked away, and she seemed to shrink back into the folds of her coat. "Caleb, do you mind giving Stomper his oats? Don't put him in the barn yet. I have another trip to Granny's to make soon."

"Sure thing, Jess." Caleb hopped up, put his knife back in one pocket and the figurine in the other, and tromped down to where Jess had left Stomper hitched to the wagon.

"See you both later," Greta said, sounding a little stilted. She continued down the porch steps.

Jess watched the gentle sway of her hips as she strolled down the sidewalk, head held high, with all the aplomb of a princess. All she needed was a crown. He wanted to be the one to treat her like a princess, but for some reason she was giving him the cold shoulder. Maybe he'd get a chance to find out what was wrong when she returned to finish Agnes's dress. Since it was a nice, cool day, he felt in need of a short nap to clear the clutter in his head after locking up the store for the day.

Greta resisted the urge to peek over her shoulder to see if Jess was still standing there. No matter, she didn't want to make him think she cared that he was or not, so she looked straight ahead with her mind on Zach and her ceremony. Further down the street, she saw a weathered sign with letters in bright red that read SUZANNE'S MILLINERY. She'd been meaning to stop in there for some time now and decided there was no time like the present. Quite possibly she might find something to lift her spirits and be useful as well.

The storefront boasted delicate collars, hats, gloves, and a pair of fashionable shoes the color of chestnut. The latter interested her the most. Hoping to browse before the store closed for the day, she pushed open the door, and a lovely smell of lilac toilet water and pungent herbs filled the room, which she immediately found relaxing. Several ladies milled about oohing and aahing over a table that held delicate lingerie.

"May I be of assistance?" A pretty lady with a warm smile approached her.

"I'm not sure . . . I kept seeing your sign

and decided to pop in before you closed today."

"When I have customers, unless it's excessively late, I stay open to accommodate their needs." She stuck her hand out. "I'm Suzanne Marshall, but please call me Suzy."

Greta shook her hand. "Greta Olsen. Nice to meet you, Suzanne . . . Suzy."

"You go ahead and look around if you care to, unless there was something in particular . . ."

Greta laughed. "There wasn't until I saw the pretty shoes in the window. They'd be perfect for fall weather."

"Oh, those. Yes, indeed they would. Shall I see if we have your size while you have a look around?"

"I'd like that. Thank you." Greta gave her the size, and Suzy disappeared to the back of the shop. Greta perused the store, finding much to delight her. There was an array of pretty hats and bonnets, so she started trying them on. The fancier ones would have to wait until she could afford them, but she'd love to have a hat for Agnes's barbecue. After trying several, she picked up a huge straw hat with wide floppy sides, the crown decorated with spring flowers, and decided this one suited her. Would Jess even notice? Hardly. His eyes would be on Cora.

"I like that one on you, Greta," Suzy said as she came back holding the box of shoes. "The blue ribbon is a perfect match to your eyes."

"And it will shade my entire face." Greta giggled. The price was reasonable. She decided she had to have it.

"Why don't you come over and have a seat and try on the shoes?" Suzy led her over to a seating area with a velvet settee in rose with two matching chairs.

"You have a beautiful shop," Greta remarked, taking a seat and slipping off her left shoe. Her right foot was still swollen — more so now, at the end of the day.

Suzy knelt down, her skirts billowing about her like a mushroom as she removed the shoes from the box. She slipped the left one on Greta's foot.

"Ohh, I really like these." She stuck her foot up and admired how the shoe looked on it.

"Shall we try the right one on as well? You should walk around in them to be certain."

"Yes, I should, but I sprained my foot and it's still a little swollen. I expect it would be tight."

"I'm sure that in another week or two,

you'll be able to wear these, and they'll complement any dress you wear into the fall and winter." Suzy stood up, allowing Greta to get up and walk around the room. "There's a full-length mirror on the wall by the dresses if you'd like to see how they look. I'll be back in a moment after I attend to my other customers."

Greta walked over to the mirror and gazed at her feet, liking what she saw — except when her eyes traveled up to look at her face. There were circles under her swollen eyes from crying all afternoon, and red streaks in her eyes from squinting to rip out the tiny threads in the dress seam. Luckily, she'd been in her little sewing area, away from the customers, letting Jess and Cora manage them.

She chided herself for spending so much time in Suzanne's shop. She thought she should hurry on and have a light supper, then get back to finishing Agnes's dress. She didn't want to disappoint her first customer.

When Suzy returned, Greta handed her the hat and the shoes. "I've decided to take both."

Suzy smiled. "Good choices. Do you want to wear the hat?"

"Could you wrap it? I want to keep it for a barbecue later." Greta handed her some bills to pay for her things, then waited as Suzy took care to place the hat in a nice hatbox. She noticed no ring on Suzy's left hand.

"Suzy, you don't have to give me one of your nice hatboxes. Paper will be just fine."

"I insist," Suzy said. "I want you to be a returning customer, and I hope I've met a friend. I'm fairly new here."

Greta returned her smile. "You can count on it, Suzy. I work at Gifford's Mercantile, but I have to say, entering your shop is an altogether enjoyable experience for me. I've only been here a couple weeks myself." Greta wasn't about to tell her about the mail-order-bride mix-up, even though they were the only two left in the shop. "I'm sorry if I held you open."

"Not at all." She handed Greta the packages. "Please come back soon . . . and bring a friend."

Greta nodded and scurried out the door. The wind had picked up considerably, so she thought a cup of hot chicken soup at Mabel's would be just the thing.

The supper crowd was in full swing as Greta gazed about for an empty table. A tall, familiar gentleman stood up and motioned to her. She hardly recognized Cole without his hat. He was wearing his normal cowboy attire, and as usual his clothing was neat. He grinned as she approached, weaving between the tables to his.

"Are you alone?" she asked. She really didn't want to try to play dinner guest with Agnes. She'd rather find another place to eat.

"I am. Please join me." He pulled out a chair for her, then placed her packages on an empty seat.

"Thank you, Cole." She took a seat and he handed her the menu. "I believe I'll just have a cup of soup tonight. Where's Agnes?"

Cole gave her a sober look. "Seems she's skipping supper tonight after my rude comment this afternoon." His jaw tightened. "I shouldn't have said anything. At least not where everyone could hear. I apologized, but now she thinks she's fat and is ashamed of herself."

"Oh dear! She'll get over it once she sees how fetching she'll look in the new dress. I guarantee she'll turn heads." Greta gave her order to the waiter, and Cole did likewise.

"I hope you're right. So where's your fiancé?"

"You mean Zach?"

"Who else would I be talking about?" He grinned, displaying a nice set of even teeth.

Greta flushed. "Of course. Well, he was at the lumberyard last I heard. He's been working on getting his ranch started whenever he gets a chance and the store's not too busy." She hoped he wouldn't ask her any more questions.

"Is that so? Pretty woman like you shouldn't be left to find her own dinner when she has no home to go to." His gaze was so intent that she looked away, flustered.

He was right. She should be with her future husband. But was it Zach? She was starting to get a headache by the time their soup arrived, so she avoided his question, spreading her napkin in her lap.

But Cole wasn't through. "Greta, I want you to know, if things don't turn out as you'd hoped, I'd like the chance to court you proper."

What should she say? Cole was nice enough, handsome, and owned a ranch. But there was no attraction to him at all. "Cole, I truly am flattered and honored that you think that highly of me without really knowing me."

He leaned back in his chair. "I know a lot about you just from observation. So if you change your mind . . ."

"Cole, have you met Suzanne Marshall, who owns the millinery?" she asked, trying to change the subject.

"I don't believe I have." He chuckled. "I'm not a regular at that kind of shop, you know."

Greta laughed. "I'm sure. Anyway, she's new to town and single and, I must add, quite pretty. Maybe I could introduce the two of you."

"Playing matchmaker now, like my sister tries to do?" He quirked an eyebrow.

"No. It's just that I met her myself a little while ago, and the thought occurred to me that you might want to meet her. She's a very nice-looking woman, and an entrepreneur too." She laid her spoon aside and finished her roll, letting that bit of information sink in.

"A lady of means, perhaps? Sounds interesting . . . very interesting."

The remainder of the meal was pleasant. Cole made her laugh and put her at ease. As he escorted her to the door, handing her the packages, they parted ways — she in the direction of the hotel and he on his way back to the boardinghouse where he stayed when in town. Greta watched him go, wondering why life couldn't be simple when it came to love.

On her walk back to the store, she had a wonderful idea. She would make Cora a gown suitable for her wedding once she finished with Agnes's alterations. And she knew just the material she would use! She could stay late and work in the evenings after work. That'd be easier than having Cora see the confusion on her face, and it could be a peace offering for the friend she'd come to care about.

30

Refreshed after his fifteen-minute nap, his stomach growling, Jess figured he'd go get a bite to eat since there wasn't much in his kitchen to cook. Caleb was off somewhere on his own, and Zach hadn't returned from the lumber store. Plucking his leather vest off the back of a kitchen chair, he ran his hand through his hair and locked the door, then took off in search of supper.

Dusk was settling over the busy town as shopkeepers closed for the day. He was considering a roast beef sandwich with some of Mabel's homemade pickles. He could almost taste it now. When he neared the café, lights inside illuminated the crowd. He didn't mind waiting.

Then he saw Greta. She was hard to miss with her blonde hair. He stood, hands in his pockets, watching. She was having supper with Cole! His best friend in the world. His heart thumped. It wasn't that he would mind, had he known . . . but neither she nor Cole had bothered to mention it. They were talking, looking very comfortable, and he had to admit they made a striking couple. When she said she wanted to put the past behind her, she'd really meant it.

Should he go in? He shook his head. No, he concluded. Mabel's wasn't the only café in town, it was just his favorite.

Moving as if in slow motion, unaware of others on the busy sidewalk, he suddenly had no appetite. He bought a newspaper from a lad on the street, then turned around and headed back to the store to trudge up the stairs to his apartment. He'd brew a fresh pot of coffee, have some leftover bread and cheese, and spend the evening reading — like he'd done most evenings before those women had upset his routine. He was beginning to consider that his life was better that way. Why take on a wife who was just the total opposite of him in the first place? He'd never be able to please her. He rather liked his unorganized ways. They suited him.

This was all Zach's fault.

The debating continued on in his head while he settled in his easy chair by the window and unfolded the newspaper. The scalding coffee burned his tongue as if in punishment for his negative thoughts, and he bolted up, nearly dumping the mug of coffee as he muttered under his breath.

Out of the corner of his eye, he saw Greta take out her key, then disappear from sight into the store. With just that brief glimpse of her, the debate in his head came to a screeching halt. She was a part of his life now — a part that he wanted to keep. She was like a breath of fresh mountain air every time she entered a room. He loved her unusual accent and how her native language would occasionally slip into a conversation, and he loved how she felt in his arms. How could he live without her now?

But after seeing her look so happy with Cole, he wondered if she wanted him at all. After all, she'd admitted that she had just gotten over his brother. He'd have to find out. But not tonight — she wanted to finish her sewing or endure Agnes's wrath. Yet he was comforted knowing that she was only a few steps away in the room just below him.

Zach was worn out. It had been a longer day than normal for him. He stored the wagon in the barn, then rubbed his horse down and fed him. When he entered the mercantile from the back door, he noticed a light still burning in the front of the store.

What was Jess doing downstairs? All he wanted to do was drop into bed. After he and Caleb cleared a path to his property, he'd hurried back to town and purchased lumber to start a barn and small house. He'd made two loads, then sent Caleb on to help Jess out, but he missed the extra set of hands. Caleb turned out to be a hard worker, and he knew it pleased Jess to no end how it had all worked out. He was certain that Jess saw him as a younger version of Bryan. Jess was so good-hearted and loyal, which made it hard to tell him that Zach was in love with his future bride!

To his surprise, a light was coming from the sewing area, and Greta sat with her head over some material, her foot pumping the treadle as the sewing machine hummed quietly. "Greta, working kinda late, aren't you?" he asked, hating to break her concentration.

She lifted her head and blinked tired eyes. "Oh, Zach. I didn't hear you come in. I've just finished here." She stopped the machine and cut the thread, then knotted it and put the material aside. "You look tired."

"I was just thinking the same of you. Trouble is, *I* smell like a billy goat and you don't." He chuckled. "So I don't want to get too close."

Her laughter rang out. "I promise not to hold you at arm's length." She yawned and stretched her arms overhead. "I'm going back to the hotel," she said, standing.

Zach debated with himself. He wanted nothing more than to go upstairs to bed, but he couldn't let her walk the streets of Central City at this late hour alone. He shifted on his boots. "I'll walk you back then."

"Don't do that. It's just a short distance. I'm not afraid."

"Truth is I'm mighty tired, but I think it's best if I walk you to the hotel. I don't mind at all."

"If you insist."

He waited as she retrieved her coat and packages, then followed her to the door. "Let me carry your bag and you can carry the hatbox. Looks like you did some shopping today. I suppose Cora's already at the hotel? I haven't seen much of her today." They fell into step down the sidewalk while he adjusted his stride to her shorter one.

"Yes, seems she had some mysterious business to attend to, and I saw her leave this afternoon with Jess. But I haven't seen him since I left for supper."

"Hmm . . . guess we'll find out sooner or later, won't we?" This would be a good time to talk to her about his feelings for Cora. But he couldn't do that without finding out if Jess was looking forward to marrying Cora. Best if he talked to his brother first.

"Well, I think I know . . . I saw Cora in his arms and they were kissing this morning, so apparently they're planning to go ahead and get married."

Zach felt like someone had hit him in the stomach. How could that have happened? He stopped and turned to her. "Are you sure?"

"Of course I'm sure. They were near the back of the store, and I was coming through the back door after I went looking for Rascal." She paused. "Is everything all right, Zach?"

A flash of hot anger seeped its way up his neck and into his face. "Sure. I'm just fine." But he was not fine. He continued on down the walk, his hands tightly gripping her bag. How could Cora do that? What happened to her wanting to be his wife and the partner of his ranch? He gritted his teeth, almost forgetting that Greta was walking with him.

Greta slowed her steps on the last block. "Zach . . . I've been wanting to talk to you."

"You've got my undivided attention. What is it?"

She stopped on the sidewalk, gazing up at

him with her big blue eyes. She was just about the prettiest thing he'd ever seen . . . but that was as far as it went with his feelings.

She chewed the inside of her cheek before speaking. "I want to go ahead with our marriage ceremony as soon as possible."

Her eyes held his as he stood dumbfounded, not sure what to say. "You do? I thought we were going to take our time for a few more weeks." His mouth went dry.

She reached for his hand. "I've been doing some thinking. What are we waiting for? I could make the plans for a small ceremony next week. And I can help you build your house. I'm not afraid of hard work."

He swallowed hard. Her hand was soft and warm, but where was the tingle up his spine that he'd had when Cora held his hand?

"I know you're not. It's just that . . . I have a few things I need to take care of first." He knew it sounded lame, but he was too tired tonight to deal with this. She'd thrown him for a loop with this unexpected idea. "This is a bit sudden. Can we talk about it later?"

"All right. But we mustn't wait too long. We don't want Jess and Cora to beat us to the altar, now do we? We are called mail-order *brides,* or don't you remember?"

Zach groaned as she dropped her hand, and they continued on down the street. "How well I remember." When they reached the hotel, he gave her a quick peck on the cheek and a brief good night, then waited for her to enter the building. What had made her get a bee in her bonnet about suddenly wanting to get married next week? Well, it just couldn't happen. Not now. Not ever. He'd speak to Jess when he got home and see where he stood with his feelings for Cora.

But when Zach returned home, Jess was snoring in his bed. Zach considered whacking his brother on the nose for kissing Cora, but he wasn't about to wake him since he intended to be sleeping in less than three minutes himself.

Cora was sleeping soundly when Greta turned the key in the lock. She tiptoed in and was grateful for the hotel's finer accoutrements like the plush carpet so she didn't wake Cora. She'd lost her nerve to ask Cora about kissing Zach and Jess, and she was bone weary. Quietly she set her packages down and hurried through her ablutions. She donned her gown, crawled into bed, and pulled up the fluffy blankets, then stared at the moonlight reflected on the ceiling.

Her head was in a continuing whirl of confusion, and her headache was growing. Finding Cora in Jess's arms had splintered her heart. So much so that she couldn't begin to articulate any words to him once he'd returned this afternoon. The only thing she could do was avoid him. He'd said himself that he was too afraid of his brother's shadow. But hadn't she convinced him otherwise? Then Zach was totally taken aback at the suggestion of their marriage. Hadn't he been eager just a week ago? She shouldn't have practically thrown herself at him tonight. Maybe she should pack up and return to Cheyenne.

Lord, I've never been more confused. I thought I was walking down the right path, but now it seems that pathway has split in two directions. I can only take one — marry Zach or go back home. Give me some sign, some guidance about what to do . . . And please help me be pleasant to Agnes . . . Soon her swollen eyes were firmly shut tight.

It seemed like only moments later when a loud rapping on their door awakened her.

Greta squinted at the clock. It was barely six o'clock. Cora was already awake and dressing and turned to see Greta stirring in bed. "Whoever could be knocking on our door at this hour?" Greta whispered.

Cora shook her head as she stuck a pin into her thick hair. "I can't imagine," she said and walked toward the door. "Who's there?"

"Miss Cora," a frantic voice said through the door. "It's Martha Carey. Please . . . can I speak with you a moment?"

Cora opened the door just as Greta donned her robe. "Martha. Is everything all right?"

Martha stood in the hallway, wringing a handkerchief in her chapped hands. "I'm truly sorry to disturb you at this hour, but you did say if I should ever need anything to let you know."

"Yes, I did. Go on. Are the children okay?"

Martha bobbed her head. Concern was etched in deep lines on her face. "They are. It's Horace. He's in the hospital with a severe case of pneumonia, and I . . . I don't know which way to turn."

Cora took her arm, gently ushered her inside, and closed the door. "Please, tell me what I can do to help."

"It's the children. I've left them alone for two days now, and they're so frightened. The oldest is trying to take care of the little ones." She drew in a deep breath. "Do you think the store could spare you to help care for them while I'm at the hospital for today? I'm so worried about them."

"Have no worry about that. I'm not tied to that store," Cora said, snatching up her coat and handbag. She turned to Greta. "Please let Jess know where I am, will you, Greta?"

"Of course, and if you need anything, just send word." Greta blinked, trying to wake up and grasp the situation.

Cora started for the door, ushering Martha along, then paused. "I'm sorry, Martha, this is Greta Olsen, a good friend of mine."

Martha nodded in her direction as she walked toward the door.

"Nice to meet you, Martha. Your children will be in good hands with Cora."

They were gone in a flash, and Greta was tempted to crawl back under the warm covers, but it was nearly time to get up anyhow. She trudged over to the bathroom and was horrified at the face she saw in the mirror. Puffy eyes stared back at her. Last night she'd slept very little. Frequently she woke to the image of Cora in Jess's arms, made worse by the remembrance of how his lips had felt on her own.

She shook herself mentally and splashed cold water on her face. Enough! Her crying was over. She couldn't change a thing and needed to trust God for her future. The lesson she'd learned was to not always trust her heart, and that just might mean returning to Wyoming.

Greta skipped breakfast and arrived before anyone else at the store. She pulled up the shades, allowing the bright sun to light up the room. She took comfort now in the eclectic smells of the mercantile — beeswax, leather, tobacco, a crate of polished apples, pine floors, and the woodsy smoke smell of the stove. Rascal was awake in his crate, and she opened the door to give him a squeeze. He wagged his tail in delight as his pink tongue licked her hands. Carrying the small ball of fur, she tiptoed down the hallway and opened the back door, then put him out to do his business.

She'd brew coffee when the men came downstairs. She straightened the table and chairs, smoothing the tablecloth and tidying up the area for customers. Since Cora was at the Careys', she shifted her focus to a bolt of cream brocade material and measured out the yards needed for Cora's wedding dress. At least she could do something good for her friend. It wasn't Cora's fault that Jess loved her and she loved him.

She heard a floorboard creak overhead. Someone must be up now.

"I thought I heard noises down here. Mornin'," Jess mumbled. He stumbled down the steps and blinked at her, trying to focus. Pulling his suspenders over his long handles, he smiled and ran his hands over his disheveled hair. "You're here a mite early, Greta."

"I'm sorry if I disturbed you." She walked toward him, thinking she'd never seen him in bare feet or so rumpled. "I was straightening things up a little." She reached around him for her apron and could feel her body tense at his nearness, so she quickly stepped back to the other side of the counter to slip the apron on. "Cora told me to let you know that she's gone over to Martha Carey's to watch her children. Her husband is in the hospital with pneumonia."

"I see. Seems I do remember either Cora or Annabelle telling me Horace had injured his leg and was unable to work. I'm glad she could be of help." His dark eyes held hers across the counter for a long moment. "I'd better run back upstairs and get dressed," he said, scratching the two days' worth of growth on his face. "Don't want to scare you off." His lips curled upward in a half smile.

"Better that you worry about scaring Cora off and not me," she said, turning around so she could start sewing before Agnes showed up. Then she nearly laughed. If she were a betting woman, Greta would bet Agnes would not be coming for her dress until after eleven.

"What's that supposed to mean?" Jess's smile quickly slid off his face, replaced by a somber look.

She spun back around. "I think you know what I mean, so let's just leave it at that." He jerked his head back, frowning, but she moved away. She could feel his eyes staring at her back. When she reached her sewing area, she saw him stomp up the stairs, muttering to himself.

31

Jess didn't care whom he woke as he stomped up the stairs, banged the coffeepot onto the stove, and lit a fire. What had happened to Greta? Ever since she'd returned from Granny's, she'd been unfriendly and detached. While the coffee boiled, he washed his face and combed his hair down, then reached for his last clean shirt. He'd meant to press it, but right now he couldn't care less if it was wrinkled.

Caleb shuffled out of bed with a grunt at Jess and headed down the stairs to the outhouse. Zach sat up in bed and scratched his head. "What time is it?"

"Time to get up," Jess growled. "We have a busy day with freight coming in. We'll be shorthanded too. Cora's gone over to help out the Careys today."

"What for?" Zach asked as he slipped on his britches.

Jess plunked down two mugs of coffee on

the table. "Horace is in the hospital and Martha could use help with those five kids, I reckon."

"Cora enjoys helping people, so I'm not surprised. She told me once that it's her spiritual gift." He buttoned up his shirt, then tucked it into his pants and slipped on his belt.

"Is that so?" Jess wondered when he'd learned that bit of information. "Seems you'd know more about Greta than Cora, wouldn't you?"

Zach took a swig of his coffee before answering. "Maybe. Jess, we need to —"

The door flew open and Caleb strode in, carrying Rascal. "This little booger tried to take off down the alley, but I caught him. Greta would have a fit if he got lost."

"Speaking of Greta, she's already downstairs." Jess poured Caleb his coffee. He opened the cupboard, unwrapped some biscuits from the day before, and placed them on the table.

"Is this all we have to eat?" Caleb frowned.

"You can dunk the biscuits in your coffee. I keep forgetting to stock up on groceries. Zach used to handle that, but he's so busy with his farm that he doesn't have time anymore."

"Did you wake up on the wrong side of

the bed this morning, Jess?" Zach gave him a funny look.

"You might say that," he answered, then broke his biscuit in half and dunked it in his coffee.

"You can have my share," Zach said. "I'm going to Mabel's. Wanna come too, Caleb?"

"You bet!" Caleb hopped up. "I can almost taste that thick slab of ham now."

Zach pulled on his boots, and the two of them made a quick exit, leaving Jess alone, staring into his coffee. Jess admonished himself for snapping at Zach. It was just as much his fault that he could never remember to get done half of what he should on any given day, but then, that had never been his strong suit. But the true reason he was grouchy was the little blue-eyed blonde who made his head reel.

Cora sat on the front porch of the Careys' home with the children sitting in a semicircle around her feet and baby Danny in her lap. Eddy, the four-year-old, sat on the chair arm as she continued to read *Treasure Island* — right where Martha had left off the day before. The children's concentration on the story was evident by their rapt attention, and they barely moved a muscle.

Cora glanced up and saw the baby's eyes

grow heavy as he was lulled to sleep, perhaps by the low pitch of her voice. Amos squirmed in his chair, interrupting as she turned the page. "Miss Cora, do you have any children we could play with?" he asked in his baby-child voice.

Cora paused, staring into Amos's bright eyes. "No. I don't. But someday soon when I get married I hope to," she answered, ruffling his bushy brown hair and making him smile. His chubby hand patted her arm. "I like you, Miss Cora," he whispered.

"Ma told us that you were going to marry Jess Gifford," Amos piped up.

"Shh. Be quiet," Leah ordered.

"No she's not. I saw her kissing Zach down at Clear Creek," Becky blurted out.

"Becky!" Leah admonished her, then turned to stare at Cora. "Who *are* you going to marry, Miss Cora?"

"Well, I . . . don't rightly know . . ." Cora licked her lips anxiously, wondering why the children needed to know the affairs of the heart. Childhood curiosity?

"Yeah, let her finish the chapter," Leah urged.

Cora closed the book. "That was the end of the chapter, children. I'm going to go put Danny in bed, then you all can help me set the table for lunch. How's that?" They nodded, rising from the floor, and Cora was struck by how mindful of their manners the children were. They may have been without means, but it was obvious that the Careys held to their faith and good parenting skills, which no money could buy. Either way, Cora had had a fun day with them and dreamed of the day she'd have her own children to read and play games with.

"Leah, since you're the oldest, would you ask the blessing?" Cora asked later at the supper table. Cooking wasn't one of Cora's natural domestic skills, so Leah and Becky pitched in and helped Cora whip up pancakes topped with thick, heavy syrup for supper. A simple affair, but satisfying nonetheless, and the smaller ones thought it was a great treat.

"I'll be happy to, Miss Cora." Leah prayed for their meal, then for her father.

"Thank you." Cora handed the plate of pancakes around, then helped Eddy cut his pancakes into bite-sized pieces. When she leaned down, he gave her a quick kiss at her temple, and her heart flooded with warmth.

The laughter around the table and the children's chattering was a wonderful change from eating at Mabel's café. Not that she didn't thoroughly enjoy Mabel's cooking, but this was a real family with real issues they were facing. She prayed that Horace would make a quick recovery.

Cora and Becky tidied up the kitchen while Leah got the younger ones ready for a bath. That's when Martha walked in, and they all ran to her with a flood of questions.

"My, my. Let me catch my breath. I walked from the infirmary home and I'm nearly out of breath."

"I'll get you some water," Becky said and took off for the kitchen while the rest waited anxiously for word of their father.

Cora led Martha to the couch, and the children gathered around. "Rest a moment. I'm sure the news can wait a few minutes more."

Martha drank the glass of water Becky brought. "Thank you, Becky. What a thoughtful young lady you are becoming," she said with a smile at her daughter, then directed her gaze to include all the children. "Your father's fever broke and the doctors think he'll be all right, but he will be mighty weak. I'm going to need you all to continue helping each other as before."

"You know we will, Mother." The eldest daughter knelt down next to Martha's chair.

Martha looked up at Cora. "I hope they didn't give you any trouble today," she murmured with a weary smile.

Cora smiled. "They were good and very helpful to an old maid like me. Are you hungry? We have a few pancakes left."

"I'd love that."

"Then you sit right there and I'll bring them to you. I know you must be exhausted." Cora noticed Martha's sunken eyes and the dark circles under them. She'd probably gone days without sleep before taking Horace to the hospital, and she wondered when her last meal had been. By the looks of the dress hanging off her, it couldn't have been for a couple of days.

"Please don't fuss over me, Cora. I'm okay, really. Just need a little bit of rest, I think."

Cora nodded to Leah. "Help me get a tray together for your mother. Then I'll be on my way so she can rest."

When Cora was satisfied that Martha was rested and had eaten, she told the children goodbye. She was pleased with their warm affection and sweet hugs as she left, not to mention Martha's gratitude.

"You're a godsend, Cora. I can't thank you enough." Martha walked her to the door.

"The smile on your face is quite enough, Martha. Please get some rest. If you want me to come back in the morning, I will." Cora lifted her coat and handbag from the hall tree.

"The doctor said he would let Horace come home tomorrow, but he'll be confined to bed for a few days. I'll hitch up the wagon, and the kids will enjoy the ride when we go pick him up. But thank you so much for your help."

"Anytime. I mean that, Martha. Your children have been delightful. I'd better run now." Cora hugged the children again, promised to come back soon, and set off down the road to town, remembering that Jess was to take her back to Granny's after work. This evening if she could, she'd spend more time in the attic to look for the stored dishes. Maybe the Blue Willow would help broker peace between her and Greta once she found out that Cora was in love with Zach.

She was glad that she spent that time with the Carey family today. It only further reminded her of her commitment to help others. She had a soft spot when it came to children, and that gave her a great idea. She couldn't wait to share it with Zach.

Greta, glad that Agnes's dress was finished, began cutting out the pieces of Cora's gown. Since Cora was gone, it was a good time to work on it between helping out with the customers. Sewing was a balm to her cluttered thoughts. She enjoyed taking the pieces to form something beautiful and wearable, and she rather liked the smell of new fabric. Maybe she'd found her niche. If Agnes liked what she'd made, then through word of mouth, others might want her to make something.

Caleb and Zach were unloading the latest shipment of saddles, tack, and blankets while Jess waited on customers. Later Greta would organize the odd assortment of tack and blankets with Caleb. She heard Jess greet Agnes the moment she stepped through the threshold, so she quickly put away the brocade and went to meet Agnes.

"Hi, Agnes." Greta walked over to where they stood chatting. "I've finished your dress and pressed it this morning. Why don't you come back behind the curtain and try it on?"

"I'm ready. Excuse me, Jess."

"I'm sure Greta has fixed the dress to your satisfaction. She's a perfectionist," Jess declared, shooting Greta a half-smile. Greta merely turned and motioned for Agnes to follow her to the dressing and sewing area.

"You seem awfully grim this morning,

Greta," Agnes commented, removing her dress while Greta stood waiting to slip the new dress over her head. "Is something wrong?"

Greta smoothed the dress over Agnes's hips, admiring the now perfect fit. "No, I've just been busy and have a lot on my mind." She turned Agnes around to face the mirror. "What do you think?"

A smile stretched across Agnes's face, and she clasped her hands together. "It's perfect now! You have done a wonderful job. I'm sure when people see it they'll want to know who made it for me."

"Good! I was hoping you'd say that. I'm happy that you're happy with it."

Agnes snickered. "The entire episode has made me rethink what I've been eating. So I hope you'll see me in here to tighten the waist back up again."

Greta surely hoped not — one time of ripping out the top from the skirt was enough — but she smiled at Agnes's admission. It seemed Cole's truth had pricked her conscience.

"You look very nice in the dress, Agnes." Greta unbuttoned the back of the dress and Agnes stepped out of it, then donned hers again.

"I did look good, didn't I?" she answered

smugly. "Maybe it will turn a few heads for me this time."

"No doubt it will. I'll wrap the dress up for you, if you'll follow me up to the counter."

Moments later, after the dress had been wrapped and paid for, Cora returned. As Agnes chattered on about her party, Greta spied Cora talking with Jess through the front glass. He motioned for her to get in the wagon.

"Are you listening to me, Greta?" Agnes turned to see what she was looking at just as Cora and Jess took off. "Oh, I see . . . You're jealous of them. I know you deny any feelings for Jess, but from the look on your face, I believe otherwise." Agnes tapped her on the sleeve with her gloves. "What did I tell you? You simply cannot trust the opposite sex!"

"*Alstublieft!* Please, it's hardly that. I was wishing for a ride in the countryside myself, is all." Greta tried to hide her feelings.

"It's okay, Greta. I won't breathe a word of how you feel. You can trust me. Besides, Zach is going to make a fine husband and rancher."

Trust her? Ha! Greta doubted that would *ever* happen.

Agnes pulled on her gloves and opened

the door, and Greta handed her the package. "See you at church. I better hurry. Cole and I are going back to the ranch."

Greta waved goodbye and wondered just where Jess and Cora were off to again. She had a good mind to follow them . . . but her conscience wouldn't let her.

32

Cora hopped down from the buckboard and rang the bell at Granny's. Moments later Granny came to the door. "Do come in . . . and tell me why my grandson is avoiding me."

Cora laughed. "Granny, he's not avoiding you, he's just doing me a favor. Is it okay if I go on up to the attic? I've been gone most of the day, but I think there's enough light left to search some more."

"Goodness, where have you been?" Granny asked, walking her down the hallway.

"Horace Carey is in the hospital with pneumonia, and I was seeing to Martha's five children."

"I'm sure they were a handful."

"Not at all, which surprised me. They're well-versed in vocabulary and good manners."

"I'm glad you were able to help them out."

"Me too," Cora said, mounting the stairs to the attic. "I enjoyed them so much, and I believe I might have found my true mission in life — helping others."

Granny's face took on a softer look. "Is that so? Well, how wonderful. Each person has their own spiritual gift, you know."

"I hadn't even known there was such a thing as spiritual gifts, but I'm learning that the more I study Scripture. But now I'd better get started. The daylight is wasting away."

"Help yourself to my clutter." Granny chuckled. "When you're done we can have a little snack." Then she scooted on about her business, leaving Cora alone.

The same musty breeze greeted her when Cora shoved open the attic door. Since she'd already looked through the boxes nearest the door, she wandered further back by the window and realized that she'd left it open. At least it wasn't as stuffy today. After going through a stack of boxes and feeling disheartened, she opened the next box to find the treasure she'd been looking for. Nestled in heavy tissue paper lay the Blue Willow dishes. She knew it by the pattern similar to Greta's cake knife. She clapped her hands, then gently removed several pieces to find that the box seemed to hold an entire set. Perfect! Now she wouldn't have to order the dishes. It would be a useful gift but sentimental as well for Greta.

She hurried over to close the window and dragged the box to the door, then decided to take a box of scraps she wanted to ask Granny about. When Jess returned after he closed up shop, she would have him load them in the buckboard. Now, for some of Granny's coffee and pie.

Greta stood back, admiring the window display. She'd placed some pumpkins and gourds together that she'd picked up at the market. Since the leaves hadn't changed yet, she drew and cut leaf shapes from various-colored papers in hues of gold, red, and brown to scatter on the floor and around the window casing. In the center, she'd hung an orange and brown plaid wool dress with matching cape on a mannequin and topped it with a brown velvet hat. In one corner, she placed a new rake with the price tag still on it. But something was missing. Suddenly the idea came to her. She needed a wheelbarrow.

"Caleb? Can you stop stocking shelves for a few minutes and help me?"

"Sure." Caleb hustled over. "What do you need?"

"Don't laugh, but I need a wheelbarrow for my window display."

Caleb gave her an odd look, then shrugged. "Okay . . . we have a few in the back."

"Would you please haul one up here?"

He nodded and went to the back, then returned pushing a wooden wheelbarrow. "Here you go. Want me to set it in the window for you?"

"Please."

He lifted the wheelbarrow up into the raised window. "Is that about where you want it?"

"Yes. Perfect. Thanks for your help."

Caleb stood back, admiring the display. "It looks right nice, Greta. I'll bet that dress catches some lady's eye before the week is out."

Greta smiled at his appraising words. "That's the point, Caleb."

"I agree, mighty nice." They turned around at the voice as Jess walked over. "A letter came for you, Caleb," he said, handing him the envelope. "I think it's from the dean of Agricultural College of Colorado in Fort Collins." Jess winked at Greta.

Caleb snatched up the letter, ripped it open, and read it, and a big smile lit up his entire face. "Wow! I've been accepted! Me!"

he exclaimed.

"I knew they'd take you, son. Your folks would be proud to know you'll be going to school," Jess said, giving him a thump on the back.

"Caleb, this is wonderful. You get a chance to make something of yourself," Greta added.

"I have Jess to thank for this. I'd never dreamed of going." Caleb's face was serious. "It says classes start in September. But I've decided that I need to go home and see my father first. I have to clear things up with him since I left."

"Good idea. I know he'll appreciate that." Jess stepped back to Greta's side. "And I really like the display. It's something I never thought about doing. I guess now is a good time to tell you thanks for the way you handled Agnes. I know she's not easy to work with." He turned to look her in the eye.

"You're welcome, Jess." She studied his brown eyes, looking for some evidence of how he felt, but there was none. Still, she appreciated that he'd acknowledged her creative window display.

Jess slapped his thigh, glancing up at the clock on the wall. "Gotta run out for a bit. Watch the store while I'm gone, would you?

Zach's outside jawing with Silas."

Greta nodded, her spirits suddenly deflated.

"Let me get back to work before Jess decides to keep my pay," Caleb joked, then returned to his chores.

Greta numbly walked back to the sewing area to continue her work while the store was free of customers for the time being. She picked up the dress she was making for Cora. She'd had time to put the pieces together, and it was starting to resemble a wedding gown. Since Cora was close to her own size and stature, Greta had guessed on the measurements. It could always be tweaked a bit here and there if the fit wasn't exact. She could hardly wait to see Cora's face. Greta knew Cora was used to nicer clothing, but this was made from the heart.

She ran her hand over the fabric, feeling the rises that gave brocade its stiff appearance. A bit of lace affixed down the sweetheart neckline presented a feminine, delicate appeal.

It suddenly occurred to Greta that she had no wedding gown of her own to wear. When she left Cheyenne, she'd planned on wearing her pale blue church dress since she assumed she would be having a quick ceremony the day she arrived. Well . . . all that had changed. She'd like to wear a pretty gown such as this, *if* she indeed would be married at all. But for now, it was Cora and Jess who would be celebrating their nuptials. Greta wanted to hear "I love you" before she was ever married to anyone someday.

When Jess stopped the wagon, Granny and Cora were sitting on the porch, waiting for him. Cora waved cheerily, causing a guilty feeling in his chest. She would make a man a good wife, no doubt about it — just not him. He hopped down and strode up the steps.

Granny gave him a hug and pinched his cheek playfully. "I'm always happy to see your dear face. How about a slice of apple pie and coffee?" she asked, sitting back down in her rocker.

"How can I refuse?" he answered. He glanced down at the two boxes by the steps. "I take it you found Mother's china?"

Cora nodded. "Yes. It took some searching, but I did. The other box is full of scraps that I thought would make a nice quilt. It's the one thing about sewing that I *did* learn how to do." She rose from her chair. "I'll go get you some pie. Granny, why don't you sit here with your grandson and chat?" Quietly she slipped through the screen door.

Jess took a seat next to Granny. "How have you been? You look wonderful."

"I feel wonderful! Not many can say that at my age. I'm glad you and Cora thought of the Blue Willow dishes for Greta."

"It was Cora's idea. She saw them in one of our catalogs and thought it'd make a good wedding gift for Greta and Zach."

Granny's eyes narrowed and she leaned forward. "Jess, why haven't you told Cora that you're in love with Greta?"

He was so stunned by the question that it left him speechless, but Granny continued. "Greta told me how she felt about you when she stayed here, and she thought the feeling was mutual."

"It is . . . it was . . . until yesterday when she became distant toward me."

"What happened? What did you do to deserve this?" Granny pressed.

"Nothing, honest! She seemed like a different person a couple of days ago, I tell you." Jess had thought this over many times while lying in bed, and he couldn't think of one single thing he'd done to upset her. "You know, Granny, maybe she's not ready to love after Bryan."

Granny humphed. "That's not true and you know it. The entire time she was here, she had stars in her eyes when she mentioned your name. You listen to me, young man. Greta wouldn't have acted that way and she wouldn't have given me Bryan's locket if she were still in love with him. No one can have a future with the dead. It's the living who must go on."

Jess was used to getting a lecture from Granny, and he knew better than to interrupt. When she was through he said, "Then why would she act that way toward me — almost like a stranger?"

"I don't know," she said, her voice low. "But I do know you have to find out and fix this before you let Cora continue believing you will marry her." Granny paused, smoothing down her apron. "I wouldn't be too sure Cora's in love with you either. Let the Lord guide you, but don't use excuses not to speak up. Time's a-wasting . . . and I'm not getting any younger."

Jess could hear Cora moving toward the door with the pie and coffee, so he leaned close to Granny and whispered, "Then I have to talk to Zach first. I don't want to hurt anybody."

"Then do it, or someone will get hurt," Granny said.

"I promise I'll try to straighten all this out soon. Very soon."

Cora came out carrying Jess's pie and coffee. "Here you are. Do you think you could drive me to the hotel? I'd like to take the china up to my room before Greta gets there, if you don't mind." She leaned against the porch railing as he dug into the warm pie.

"It's no trouble to do that. When we return, it'll be time to close the store anyway. We've had a slow day today, for some reason." He wolfed down the rest of the pie and slugged down the hot liquid. "I'm ready if you are. Sorry, Granny, but we have things to do. See you later." He handed her his plate and gave her a peck on the forehead, making the old lady smile.

He waited for Cora to say goodbye, then he hoisted the box of china and scraps into the back of the wagon. After assisting Cora into the wagon seat, he set off toward Central City again, the cool mountain air descending on them.

Greta completed the dress with the exception of turning the hem. She'd do that after Cora tried it on just to be sure the length was where she wanted it to be. Not knowing when Jess or Cora would be back, she wrapped the dress and grabbed her coat. Caleb said he'd wait until Jess or Zach returned and could lock up — whoever came back first.

As she left, she took time to admire the window dressing and was pleased with it. Several ladies had slowed in their passing to peer in the window earlier, likely surprised because Jess had never taken the time to do any kind of display.

Hurrying down the walk, she planned on waiting until Cora got back to ask if she'd want to have dinner together. When she put her key in the door, it was unlocked and Cora was already there.

"I was hoping you'd come in soon. I had a very busy day with Martha's children, but they were pleasant enough," Cora commented from where she lounged in the chair with her feet up.

"That's good. How is Horace?"

"He turned a corner, and Martha should bring him home tomorrow. They're such sweet people."

"And you're so nice and good to them. What a compassionate heart you have when it comes to others, Cora." Greta laid her package on the bed and removed her coat. "You look comfortable. These new shoes feel tight after wearing them all day." She plopped down on the bed and leaned against the headboard to remove her shoes and rub her feet. "Ahh . . . it feels good to sit down for a change."

"I'm surprised you aren't off having dinner with Zach," Cora said.

"I was about to ask you the same thing since I saw you leave again with Jess," Greta replied.

Cora grinned. "Oh, that. We had something we needed to do." Then her smile faded and she quirked an eyebrow. "But you seem upset about it."

Greta rubbed her foot a little harder than she meant to and winced. "No . . ." She eyed her friend. "Anyway, I have something for you."

"Oh? I like surprises." Cora sat up with an eager expression.

Greta got up and handed her the package. "It's not totally finished yet, but I hope you like it."

"Ooh . . . what is it?" Cora tore the brown paper wrapping off to reveal the gown. "My goodness! How exquisite. Where did you get this?" She stared up at Greta.

"I made it for you. For your ceremony with Jess." Greta stood waiting for Cora to say something.

Cora looked speechless. Tears welled up in her eyes as she stood up. "It's very beautiful. I can't believe you made it for me."

"I thought you'd like it. You'll look lovely,

and I know Jess will agree."

Cora put her arms around Greta and gave her a tight hug, then stepped back and ran her hand over the gown almost reverently.

"Cora?"

"Hmm?" she answered, holding the dress up to herself in front of the mirror. Somehow her countenance didn't seem to fit a bride-to-be.

"I . . . I need to confess something to you. I love you and I hope you feel the same about me. I'm sorry about how I've acted lately toward you and Jess, but the truth is I've found myself caring deeply for the man *you* are to marry, and not the one who's promised to marry me . . . and I'm sorry. I actually thought he felt the same, but I was wrong. I think once you and Jess are married, I'll go back to Cheyenne. But I must admit my confusion, since I saw you kissing Zach before I twisted my ankle."

There! She had finally been honest with her friend.

Cora whirled around, a confused look on her face. "You'll do no such thing! What do you mean you care for Jess? I thought you were in love with Zach!"

"I only wish I was, but since I'm not, I'll get out of the picture so you and Jess can have a happy life — or you and Zach. Which is it to be?" Greta felt heat rising to her face.

Cora started to giggle and put the dress on the bed. "You think I'm in love with Jess?" She turned back to face her.

"Why are you laughing?" Greta thought it was heartless for Cora to be laughing at her admissions. She reached down to get her shoes to leave. She wouldn't stand here and be laughed at.

Cora grabbed her hand. "Listen to me. I'm laughing with joy!"

"Well, good! I'm glad Jess *and* Zach make you that happy! Now let go of my hand!"

"You misunderstand, Greta. I'm *not* in love with Jess. The truth is I love Zach and he loves me!" She beamed.

"What? But Zach hasn't said a word to me! And I saw you and Jess kissing at the mercantile, and his arms were around you." Greta thought she must be dreaming. No wonder Zach hadn't shown any interest in her since that night at Annabelle's.

"I'm sorry, Greta, but you misinterpreted what you saw. Jess was doing me a favor, so I gave him a hug and a kiss, but he didn't kiss me. It was I who kissed him. Nothing more."

"But you've been spending time together and taking off in the afternoons."

Cora walked over to the closet and

dragged a box out. "I was going to wrap this, but maybe it will explain things. Go ahead and look inside. It was to be your wedding present."

Greta dropped her shoes on the floor and frowned, then knelt down and opened the box, peering inside. There was a lot of wrapping, so she lifted some of the tissue off. To her delight, she saw a Blue Willow dish. "Don't tell me that's what's in this box!" She dug around and found more of the same. "Oh my! I really don't know what to say or how to thank you. *Dank U wel!* Thank you!"

"You just thanked me with that beautiful gift of a wedding gown . . . and the truth about you and Zach. And I love you like a sister too. The Blue Willow dishes belonged to Zach and Jess's mother, and Jess was kind enough to take me to Granny's to search the attic for them."

"I'll cherish them." Greta rose and looked at her friend. "But I don't really understand. How do we know this but Jess and Zach haven't said anything to each other? Were they planning on marrying someone they didn't love?"

"My guess is they didn't want to hurt each other or us by loving the opposite mail-order bride." Cora shook her head. "I think it's best if we let them work this out in their own way. It's not our problem. Think about what we went through — both of us arriving as mail-order brides for one man, letters that weren't written by Jess, a musty old miner's cabin, a bear, and Agnes! Don't worry, the truth will come out. And I hope to wear this dress on my wedding day to marry Zach."

Greta bit her lip. "I'm not sure about Jess. I haven't heard him say the three little words yet . . ."

"I have no doubt you will. Give him a little time." Cora took her elbow. "How about we go look for some supper? I'm starving."

Greta smiled back at her friend. "Wonderful idea. But will you tell me one thing?"

"What's that?"

"What do you really think is going on in *their* minds about all of this?"

Cora thought a moment. "Well, I once heard someone say, 'A mail-order marriage is trickier 'n braidin' a mule's tail!' "

Greta and Cora laughed heartily as they left in search of a good, hot meal.

33

Autumn winds continued throughout the next week, bringing with them brisk temperatures, which were eventually kept at bay by the brilliant Colorado sun. It would be a great day for Agnes's barbecue, and nearly everyone in town would be attending. Greta peered out the window to the busy Main Street below. She knew the day would warm up, then cool down again when the sun dropped below the mountain peaks.

She decided on a rose-colored dress that would pick up the hint of pink in the blue-trimmed sunbonnet. The scooped neckline showed her collarbone and bosom to advantage. The bodice had deep velvet inserts of fallow tightly fitted at the waist, with the skirt falling in lush folds down to the top of her shoes.

She should hurry. Jess and Zach would drop by and pick up her and Cora in the covered buggy in case the sudden drop in temperatures proved to be too much for the ladies.

"I'm about ready to go downstairs to wait for Jess and the others," Cora said, pausing long enough to pat a curl into place. She looked at Greta's outfit. "Your new sunbonnet is quite fetching, Greta, and that brim will shade your delicate complexion. Are you about finished dressing?"

"As finished as I'll ever be." Greta giggled. "You look gorgeous in that shade of green, Cora." Greta admired Cora's skin and dark hair against the hue of her green dress dotted with tiny peach flowers. Cora was indeed a striking woman. Smiling at her friend, Greta said, "Ready to go?"

"I appreciate the compliment coming from a woman as pretty as yourself, but this dress pales in comparison to the beautiful wedding dress you made for me. My heart is so full, I think it might burst." Her eyes filled with tears as she spoke.

Greta squeezed her arm. "Now don't go crying and making your eyes puffy before we get to the party. You don't want to be all red-eyed, do you?"

Cora sniffed. "No, I don't. I didn't mean to start blubbering," she said, then blew her nose. "Don't forget your coat. It might be cold on the ride back." Cora handed Greta

412

her coat, then turned to lock their room door.

By the time they arrived downstairs, Caleb was waiting on them in the foyer, wearing a nice pair of jeans and a plaid shirt. "Jess and Zach are out front waiting. You ladies look nice." He twirled his hat in his hands.

"And so do you, Caleb. New clothes, I take it?" Greta asked.

Caleb bowed. "Yes, ma'am — courtesy of Jess and Zach. They said I need to make a good impression on the ladies." He chortled.

"You've impressed me, and I'll bet the young girls will swoon!" Cora teased.

Caleb stood straighter and seemed to puff out his chest with the compliment. He started toward the door and held it open for them as they walked to the waiting buggy.

The wind tore at their skirts, and Greta had to hold on to her sunbonnet to keep it from flying off, even though it was tied securely under her chin.

Caleb hurried them into the buggy, then took a seat up front to drive the team. Jess and Zach sat across from them like two stiff toy soldiers, but they managed a hello and a nod. Greta thought they looked more than grumpy. Maybe they'd had their chat about the brides. If so, it didn't bode well.

"What a chill we have going on today — and it's a trifle windy," Greta said, trying to make small talk. Jess had actually shaved and looked handsome in his stiff white shirt, string tie, dark trousers, and matching coat. Zach looked nice too but was not his usual charming self.

Zach gave her a dull look and said, "In no time, the leaves will be a brilliant orange and red, then watch out for the blast of cold." He looked away at the traffic in the street with seemingly great interest.

Cora caught Greta's eye and pursed her lips, giving her a confused look, then nodded in the direction of the brothers. Greta shrugged.

"Jess, I must tell you that Greta made me a lovely gown to wear at our wedding ceremony," Cora said, baiting him.

Greta waited, but all he said rather thickly was, "That's nice." He squirmed in his seat with his arms crossed.

Zach jerked around and stared at Cora, who ignored his glum gaze.

"And I want to thank the two of you, Jess and Cora, for being so thoughtful of the Blue Willow dishes for mine and Zach's wedding present. It makes me very happy to know that I'll be feeding our children from the same plates that you and Zach were raised on." Greta nearly choked on her words, but she kept her voice steady despite not knowing whether Jess loved her enough to marry her. She'd try to let it play out as Cora suggested, but it was hard.

Jess's eyes focused on her with a soft caress, and he leaned forward. "I hope it will make you happy and that you and Zach will enjoy many a meal on them. We sure did growing up." Without warning, the buggy hit a pothole, jostling all of them about, and Jess fell forward into Greta. She reached out to grab his shoulders, but he recovered quickly. "I'm sorry, excuse me."

Greta's heart rate went up at his nearness and the smell of his aftershave. She was sure that her warm face mirrored her feelings, so she adjusted her skirts and stared down at her hands in her lap. She wouldn't make any more conversation with the men. If Jess or Zach wanted to talk, then let them, otherwise she would just sit quietly. They'd dug their own hole.

"Will Granny be coming to the barbecue?" Cora asked.

"Oh, Granny wouldn't miss a party. You can count on that," Zach muttered.

Greta stole a glance at Cora as she smiled at Zach, whose mouth and jaw twitched in agitation. "Good. I enjoy her company," Cora said. "She always speaks her mind."

"That's true," Jess replied, his eyes resting on Cora.

"I'm looking forward to our wedding ceremonies, and I'm sure we'd both want her there. Right, Greta?"

Greta nodded. Cora was giving them a taste of their own medicine, which would eventually force the truth out of them. She suppressed a giggle as Jess, his face pink, fingered the stiff collar of his shirt, and perspiration soaked Zach's coat and tie.

Their discomfort served them both right! This was proving to be more fun than she'd thought.

Greta couldn't help but notice that Jess's eyes *hadn't* softened when he looked at Cora. Maybe he didn't care for Cora after all. She could only hope that were true, but what if he did, and Cora married Zach once he told Jess the truth? Would Jess be heart-broken? Would Greta be second-best? She sighed so deeply that all three of them looked over at her, so she smiled weakly and looked out at the moving landscape. There was no point in torturing herself. She would simply relax and enjoy the party and her Saturday off from work. Besides, Cole would be at the party and *he* liked her company But it wasn't Cole's attention that she longed for.

Jess felt like a rabbit caught in an iron trap while Greta and Cora cheerfully chattered on about wedding gifts and ceremonies. Zach hardly said a word and sat stiff as a board — so unlike his gregarious nature. He'd hoped to have already talked to Zach, but he hadn't had a minute of free time with so much to do at the store every day. Cora seemed so happy about her wedding dress, and he was doubly surprised that Greta had sewn one for her. She was full of surprises.

Looking at her this moment, he felt his throat go tight. She was as lovely as a rose with her dewy skin. Her pretty dress was fitted in all the right places — so much so that he had to drag his gaze away to look at the shops as they rode past. Cora looked nice as well, but Greta's soft laugh and deep blue eyes made his heart want to sing. Granny was right. He felt awful for not setting Cora straight about his feelings. Would his brother despise him? He didn't think so, but the truth could make for a strained relationship.

If Zach was so excited about marrying Greta, then why was he so sullen this morning? This was not like him at all. Jess squeezed his eyes shut briefly. *Lord, help me say what I have to say to Zach today. You said we shall know the truth and the truth shall set us free. Well, I feel no freedom whatsoever, and this pretense has to stop.*

34

The Circle D ranch came into view as Caleb guided the team over a gentle rise a few miles outside of town. It was a sizeable ranch with several buildings and corrals. Greta thought it appealing with the tall evergreen, spruce, and pines edging the back of the big house, which was built from hewn logs. They rode under a tall iron archway with THE CIRCLE D on a sign overhead, and a winding drive led to the Cartwrights' home. A deep front porch ran the full length of the house, with a profusion of flower beds in beautiful array flanking either side of the broad steps. Though it was still afternoon, lanterns had been strung across the porch railings, reflecting a welcoming glow. People were already milling about the yard or in porch chairs with refreshments in their hands. Several waved as they continued to the pasture's fence, where all the wagons and horses were to be hitched. A very inviting and pleasing setting with an air of excitement greeted them.

Caleb pulled the horses to a halt, hopped down, and tied the reins over the split-rail fence as others before him had done. Jess took Cora's hand to help her down, and Zach offered his hand to Greta. She took it, noticing that he avoided looking directly at her. Once she was down on the ground, he offered his elbow, and they all walked over to the barn where the party was going on.

"Something cooking smells good," Cora commented to no one in particular.

"Sure does," Caleb agreed. "I hear my stomach rumbling."

"What you smell is the roast beef and the pork that's been smoking over the pit for a couple of days, just past the barn in the clearing there." Jess paused to point out the open fire pit, where several cowboys attended the meat with long-handled forks. They basted it with what looked like a shortened mop dipped in sauce as it turned on the spit.

"Cole has his own recipe and is known for his sauce," Zach added.

"Well, I'm not waiting. I'm going after a dish right now. See you around," Caleb said, heading off to the fire pit.

"I can't wait to have a taste." Greta allowed herself to watch the back of Jess's head in front of them, wishing he were holding her arm and not Cora's.

Music and laughter could be heard coming from the barn, and Cole came striding across the lawn to greet them with his infectious smile. Greta thought he looked great. He was an attractive catch for the ladies — tall and well built; wearing well-fitted jeans, a vest, and a blue plaid shirt; and sporting a cream-colored Stetson. She was surprised he wasn't courting someone already.

"Welcome to the Circle D," he bellowed, shaking the men's hands. "I'm mighty proud to have you! Jess, Zach." He cocked his head at them. "And don't you ladies look ravishing. You'll be beating the men off with a stick — mark my words."

"You really know how to flatter a lady," Greta purred, stealing a glance at Jess out of the corner of her eye. He wasn't listening but was watching Agnes approach.

Cole leaned close to Greta and whispered, "I asked Suzanne to come tonight. I'm glad you told me about her." He winked. "She's around here somewhere."

"That's wonderful, Cole. I knew you'd like her. I did."

"I like her a whole lot," he said. Greta gave his hand a conspiratorial squeeze.

"Welcome! Welcome, my dear friends!" Agnes gushed, stretching her hands out to them.

"How are you, Agnes?" Zach asked. "Looks to be a nice party, as usual."

"It will be now that my two favorite Gifford brothers are here," she said, hooking her arms through theirs.

Jess held her at arm's length, studying her dress. "Greta did a great job on your dress, and it's perfect for you."

"I agree, Agnes. You look wonderful. Thank you for inviting us," Cora said.

"Well, I look good because of Greta's skill with a needle." She nodded at Greta.

Greta admired her handiwork and had a moment of pride but pushed it away. "Thank you," Greta murmured. "I aim to please my customers."

"Then you shall have many more." Agnes smiled back. She turned to the brothers. "Come with me and I'll show you the wonderful spread we have laid out. The dancing is later, of course!" She called over her shoulder, "Cole, bring Greta and Cora and follow us."

Greta gave Cora a knowing look as Cole bowed slightly with a grin. He held his arms out to the two of them. "She loves to hand out orders, but this time I truly don't mind having two beautiful women on my arms."

True to Agnes's word, four tables were strung out on one side of the largest barn Greta had ever seen, which left plenty of room for dancing. Every kind of dish Greta could imagine made the makeshift tables sag under the weight of it all. There was fresh corn on the cob, green beans, fluffy rolls, corn bread, pickled beets, sliced tomatoes, chutney, creamed potatoes, and carrots. At the farthest end of the table were platters of fried chicken, barbecued beef, and pork, which had just been taken off the spit. Beverages were at the other end, and there was a separate table for desserts, making Greta's mouth water. A variety of pies, cakes, and cobblers sat waiting to be devoured.

"Well, there you all are! If it's not my handsome grandsons and their brides-to-be," Granny exclaimed as she walked over to them. "Seeing all of you brightens my day. Where is Caleb? You did bring him, didn't you?" she asked, giving Zach a hug.

Jess received his grandmother's embrace as well. "Of course we did. He's checking out the barbecue about now."

"I'm not surprised." Granny laughed. "Both of you ladies look lovely today. I especially like that hat, Greta —"

Agnes interrupted. "Excuse me, Granny. All of you help yourself to a plate of food while I greet the other guests." She walked away to stand near the barn's huge doors as the Potts and Barnes families arrived. Directly behind them were Annabelle and Silas Mead with their children.

"My sister is in her element when she's entertaining folks." Cole reached for the plates on the table and handed them around. "Why don't you all fill your plates? You can sit inside or over on the front porch."

"Ladies first. Granny, Cora, and Greta, you go on ahead," Zach said, giving Greta a nudge.

"I'm not bashful. Come on, Granny, let's fill our plates. I'm famished." Greta made Granny go ahead of her, and Zach and Jess took up the rear. There certainly wasn't enough room on her plate to take a taste of everything, but Greta loaded her dish. "Granny, I should be embarrassed at the amount of food I have." She laughed.

"Pshaw! You could stand to have a little more meat on your bones, honey. Enjoy it, because it's not every day there's a party with a spread like this."

"I hope to have plenty of occasions like this and work it out somehow to give people opportunities to give back to our community. Perhaps Zach and I can change this once we're married," Cora whispered to Greta.

Greta looked at her friend. "Cora, you amaze me. What a wonderful thought. I feel so empty-headed compared to the ideas that are constantly running around in your mind."

Cora smiled and picked up a piece of chicken. "Well, thanks, but I don't have it all ironed out yet. I'm just planning in my head."

"There's an empty table over there," Jess told them. "Or we could sit outside. Which do you all prefer?"

"Let's sit inside, then we'll have a good spot when the dancing begins," Granny said.

"Good idea," Greta agreed.

It wasn't long before the party was in full swing with townsfolk and neighboring ranchers wandering about, talking and enjoying the feast the Cartwrights offered. People were introduced to Greta and Cora, and it was hard to keep the names straight. Greta was having a great time meeting new people, yet watching Jess across the room, talking with friends, made her come to realize how quickly she'd fallen for him.

As she looked on, Agnes strolled over to

his side and spoke to him, and he nodded. The fiddler rosined up his bow, and the band started playing. The next thing Greta knew, Jess was sweeping Agnes around the dance floor to a waltz. Clearly, he didn't know whom he loved, if Agnes could just crook her finger and he'd come running. And she looked awfully pretty tonight.

"A penny for your thoughts," Granny said, stepping next to her.

Greta smiled at the older lady. "Oh, I was just thinking how handsome Jess looked with Agnes . . ."

"Were you?" Granny raised an eyebrow. "Or were you wishing Jess would quit ignoring you?"

Granny was just too observant for her own good. "Mmm . . . too late for that. It seems Agnes has taken my place again, and Zach . . . well, he's dancing with Cora."

"But that isn't what's bothering you, is it? By now you must know how Zach and Cora feel about each other. Jess knows that he has to be honest with Cora."

Greta shrugged. "It really doesn't matter, Granny. I told Cora that I'd stay for their wedding, but after that I'm going back to Cheyenne."

Granny poked her in the side with her finger. "Don't be too rash. I know my grandson loves you but is having a hard time telling his brother. It's fear that drives him."

Greta bit her tongue. They stood on the sidelines, watching Annabelle and Silas twirl about, laughing as if they were all alone in the room. Greta suddenly realized she wanted a marriage like theirs.

Greta was about to tell Granny as much when Cole asked her to dance, giving her a way to escape the conversation. "I'd love to, Cole." He swept her around the room with a big smile plastered on his face.

"Suzanne has agreed to let me court her, and I couldn't be happier." Cole's face softened when he said Suzanne's name.

"That's good news, Cole. I saw you two eating together, and she looked like she was hanging on to every word you said."

"Really? I didn't know, but she and I enjoy talking together, and that's a great place to start, don't you think?"

She leaned back to look up at him. "I do indeed, Cole —"

"Can I cut in on my bride-to-be?" Zach interrupted.

Cole halted their dancing and stepped back, holding Greta at arm's length. "Sure, Zach." He placed her hands in Zach's and walked off the dance floor.

Zach swung her around, holding her in a

tight grip, his jaw working as he looked across the room. Greta followed his gaze and saw Jess and Cora dancing. *You complete dolt! Why don't you say something?*

"Are you having a good time?" Zach asked. "I see Caleb has been a winner with a few of the younger girls."

His palms were sweaty against hers. "It's a very nice party, Zach. Is there something you want to —"

"I'm having a wonderful time too," he replied, but he kept his eye on Cora, who was now dancing with a rancher they'd all met earlier. He stiffened, then looked back at Greta. "I wanted to tell you how much I appreciate all that you do for us at the mercantile. You've changed things for the better, Greta." He was being genuine without his usual trace of teasing.

"I'm so glad you feel that way." Out of the corner of her eye, she watched as Jess cut in on Cora's dance partner, and Zach's fingers tightened around her hand until she winced. "Zach!"

He glanced down at her. "Gosh, I'm sorry, Greta."

"What is wrong, Zach? If you don't want to dance with me, just say so —"

"Excuse me," he said suddenly, leaving her alone on the dance floor. He strode to the other side of the room and tapped Jess on the shoulder just as the band struck up a new tune. "How about giving Cora a little variety in partners for a bit?" he asked.

Greta saw the surprise on Cora's face as Zach's voice echoed across the room. Jess let go of Cora's hands. She watched him ease away while Zach led Cora around the dance floor, holding her close. Greta, somewhat embarrassed, poured herself some punch and tried to fade into the background.

Jess could feel a vein in his neck pulse with blood. *What does Zach think he's doing? I'm the one courting Cora. At least for the time being.* He'd settle this tonight with Zach, one way or the other. Then he'd feel free to speak to Greta, who'd kept her eyes veiled around him tonight but danced with other eligible men, and Zach as well. He tried to pretend it didn't matter, but it did. He wanted her in his arms, but for now, he didn't want to embarrass Cora, so he'd have to act like her husband-to-be.

After Cora had two dances with Zach, Jess decided he'd better cut in again before tongues started wagging. He set his punch down, then as naturally as he could, he waltzed right up to Cora and pulled her back onto the dance floor in a lively square dance where partners constantly changed. They were laughing and having fun until Zach, his face a dark thundercloud, stepped in.

"Let go of her!" Zach ordered.

"What?" Jess stared incredulously at his younger brother.

"You heard me. I've had just about enough of the two of you dancing practically the entire night together —"

"Zach, Cora doesn't belong to you. Calm down." Jess knew how impulsive Zach was, but this took him by surprise.

Zach stepped back, flung off his coat jacket, and began to roll up his sleeves. "I'm gonna have to fight you for her and settle this! Take off your jacket."

The dance floor was emptying as people retreated and the music halted.

"Lower your voice and quit acting like a fool. I don't know what you're talking about." Jess tried to reason, yet he knew Zach was dead serious. But fighting him over Cora? What had happened to him and Greta? Had he missed something?

Zach took a swing at him, but Jess ducked and avoided direct contact with his brother's fist. "Zach!" He straightened. They hadn't had a good go-round since they were kids.

"This is not the place for this. Let's take it out behind the barn." He touched Zach on the sleeve and saw the anger in his eyes, but Zach followed him out.

Granny got up from her chair. "I'm not gonna miss this! Come on, girls!" she said to Cora and Greta, and they scurried out after the brothers.

"This can't continue. Why don't you tell me what's on your mind, Zach." Jess stood with his feet planted firmly apart. He wouldn't take any chances that his brother wouldn't try to punch him again, and he would be ready. Looked like he'd be having that heart-to-heart talk a whole lot sooner than he'd planned, but he certainly hadn't thought it would be in the middle of the dance floor. Zach acted like a loose cannon at times. Jess sucked in a deep breath and tried to remain calm.

Zach crossed his arms over his chest. "For starters, the truth is . . . I love Cora. Seeing you with her and planning to be married has been hard for me to watch. Cora and I have talked, and she feels the same about me, but tonight I just couldn't take seeing her in your arms or keeping my mouth shut anymore!"

Jess had been waiting for the worst, but this was not it. Relief flooded his body.

"Then why did you pretend to court Greta and make plans?"

Zach dropped his arms and ran his hand through his thick hair. "Because . . . I didn't want to hurt you. You're my big brother and I respect you." He drew his lips together in a tight line. "If you loved Cora, then I decided that I couldn't tell you the truth. But then Cora told me how she felt."

Jess leaned back against the barn wall. "So what about Greta? Have you told her how you feel?"

Looking ashamed, Zach glanced at Greta. "No, I've been too chicken until today, but I'd promised Cora that I would. Please forgive me, Greta. I'm sorry for what I've put you through . . ." His voice trailed off, and Greta nodded. Jess noted that she held Cora's hand.

Zach continued in a husky voice. "I should've never sent those letters in the first place without telling you, so I'm to blame for the mess I got us in. However, if I hadn't, Cora wouldn't be here now." He gave Cora a grateful smile, and she returned it with one of her own.

"Zach, I have a confession to make. I planned on telling you tonight and have been praying over this. I'm not in love with Cora . . . and I didn't tell her the truth either. I guess I was hoping things would work out — but I was wrong." He looked over at Cora and said, "I'm sorry," then directed his gaze back to Zach. "I've wanted to talk to you too, but after all that we've been through this last year or so, I was hesitant for fear of causing you more pain. We've both had so much grief with losing Bryan, then Mom and Dad."

Zach stood motionless, a stark look on his face. "You mean . . . you never intended to marry Cora?"

Jess shifted on his feet and pushed away from the barn wall. "Not exactly. In the beginning I did . . . but the truth is I know now that I love Greta." He heard a sharp intake of breath from Greta, but he continued to focus on his brother. "And she cares for me too. I didn't want to cause a breakup since you seemed smitten by her. And the other reason is because Greta was engaged to Bryan before he died. I didn't think I could compete with him, dead or alive." Jess paused and let Zach absorb that piece of information.

Zach let out his breath in a whoosh. "Looks like we've both acted pretty foolishly, haven't we? And at the expense of two beautiful brides neither of us deserve."

Jess gave him a direct look. "Yes, and I

wouldn't blame either of them if they walked out now."

With his comment, Granny humphed. "Most logical thing I've heard from you two so far," she interjected quietly. "Why don't you just square your mistakes and get on with living?" She turned aside, acknowledging Cora and Greta. "It appears that the two lovely brides are still here waiting."

"Granny's right, Zach. We both know how short life can be. And if Cora and Greta will still have us, we have a great future to look forward to." Jess stepped forward, closing the space between him and Zach, and stuck his hand out.

A brief moment passed, and then Zach extended his hand to shake Jess's, his head slightly bowed. While their hands were still clasped, Jess drew Zach to his chest, holding him, then clapped his hand over his shoulders while tears flooded his eyes.

35

Greta sat next to the window in the room she shared with Cora, snuggled in her robe, sipping a delicious cup of hot tea. September was a spectacular time in the Rocky Mountains, the aspen trees spotting the foothills with bursts of color almost overnight. Jess had told her to brace herself for the harsh winter to come, when they'd be shut off from the world.

Reflecting on the changes in her life since leaving Cheyenne filled her with anticipation and excitement. Though Jess was worried she wouldn't want to live above the mercantile store, she assured him more than once that his apartment suited her just fine. She was more interested in helping him run his store, and once Zach built his cabin, he and Cora would move there. Jess had booked a room for them at the hotel for a few nights once they were married, then he'd move her belongings to the apartment.

Zach would be staying with Cora at the hotel now until their place was finished.

She shivered with delight. She would become Mrs. Jess Gifford! She loved the sound of it, and tonight she would be in his arms. She couldn't wait, even though she had been up very late last night with her sister Anna, who had shown up for a visit. The timing couldn't be more perfect, and it thrilled her that a member of her family would be present for the marriage ceremony.

Cora marched over to her. "Are you still sitting there? You're going to miss your own wedding!"

"Never fear that to happen! Here, let me button you up." Greta set her cup down, and Cora turned her back to her. "I'm glad that the gown fits so well."

When Greta was finished with the buttons at the back, Cora turned around. "And I'm honored that I have a friend who would make such a beautiful gown for me."

"You deserve it. And now it's time I slipped my own dress on. I'm glad we decided on a double wedding. So far everything else we've done has been in twos!" She laughed and Cora joined her. Greta untied her robe and walked to the closet for her blue dress.

"Maybe we can start our family at the

same time too!" Cora blushed.

Greta giggled. "That would be an extra blessing from God, wouldn't it? Now it's your turn to help me. I hope Jess likes my dress. I've kept it fresh and pressed just for this day —"

They were interrupted by a sharp rap on the door. "Greta, it's me, Anna," the voice on the other side called out.

Greta smiled. "Coming." She opened the door to find her little sister dressed in her Sunday best for the wedding. "You look very pretty, Anna. Are those flowers for us?"

Anna stepped into the room and held out a nosegay of blue primroses tied with long, trailing white ribbons. "Yes, the primroses will complement your blue dress nicely. And these are for you, Cora."

"They're so pretty, Anna." Greta gave her a peck on the cheek. "*Dank U wel.* I should've known you would remember to get flowers."

Cora accepted the bouquet of large yellow lilies. "Anna, where did you find these?"

"Granny and I went out earlier and picked them. She knew right where to look. I hope you like them. She said the lilies are called avalanche lilies because they grow at alpine slopes after the snow recedes. Jess supplied the ribbon."

"Cora, there's something you need to know. Anna is a plant enthusiast of sorts."

"*Ja,* I am," Anna agreed. "And I have a lot to learn about the plants that grow in Colorado. Oh, there are so many of them."

Greta nodded. "They're beautiful and perfect." She held the bouquet at her waist, pretending to be walking toward a make-believe altar, and the other two cackled.

Anna circled around them, appraising their clothes. "Both of you look beautiful! I'm so glad I came. If Catharine wasn't expecting, she would've come with me for a visit," Anna remarked.

"I've heard so much about her," Cora said. "I hope I can meet her sometime."

Anna seemed animated and excited. About the wedding? Greta didn't think so. She knew Anna better than that. "Anna, you're in very high spirits today, and it's hard for me to believe that it's because of my wedding."

"You're right. Although I'm very happy for you, I'll be traveling to Denver to stay permanently. I'm going to be a mail-order bride to a man there who is a jeweler and clock-maker," she bubbled.

"How exciting! You little nymph — you didn't tell me last night." Greta poked her arm. "I'm very happy for you."

Anna blushed. "It was late and I wanted to keep the topic on your wedding, not mine."

"Congratulations, Anna. I hope you'll be very happy," Cora said.

"Oh, I know I will! And the best part is that Greta and I will only be separated by a few hours by train."

"Girls, we'd better go or we'll be late to our own wedding!" Cora said, excitement flushing her cheeks.

Greta laughed. "Oh, Cora, St. James is just next door, so there's no fear of us being late!" she chided.

"Just the same, she's right," Anna said. "Granny is already at the church, greeting your friends with the Reverend Edwards and making sure everything is ready. So what are we waiting for?"

Jess stared at his reflection in the mirror and straightened his tie, smiling. The new haircut made him look younger, and he hadn't forgotten to shave this morning. Would Greta think he was handsome? He ran the comb through his hair one last time with a trembling hand. It wasn't every day that a man took a wife. He'd donned his church suit and had allowed Granny to pin a blue primrose on his lapel, and he noticed she'd pinned a yellow lily on Zach's. He and Zach weren't used to all this fuss but let Granny have her way. It'd be their only wedding. He could hardly wait to become Greta's husband.

Granny had told him that Greta had planned on going back to Cheyenne if things didn't get worked out between him and Zach. It scared him to think he might've lost her. Thank God he and Zach had cleared the air.

"Jess, you look handsome enough. Staring at your face won't change anything!" Zach teased. "Anyway, I think we need to get to the church before the brides do." He pulled on his suit coat. "We don't want to be the ones to keep them waiting *again,* do we?"

Jess turned around and plucked a piece of lint from Zach's coat. "No, we don't. We may not be so lucky the second time . . . Zach, I want you to know that even though I was totally against what you did writing those letters and then not telling me the ladies would be arriving, I'm grateful."

Zach nodded and hung his head for a moment. "It wasn't me, it was God who gave me the idea that you needed a wife. I figured you'd grow to be an old bachelor still sweeping the store's front porch alone if I hadn't made the decision to force you into finding a wife." He chuckled.

"And I don't think Granny could be any happier!" Jess said. "She seems to really like Cora and Greta."

Zach whacked his brother on the back. "We're doubly blessed, you know. As soon as I can get that cabin built, we'll be moving in there. Cora has already asked me if we could have a separate building to house orphans."

"You don't say? That's great! That'll be something really different for you, Zach. What do you think about it?"

"Life will be different, but with Cora, it'll be worth it. It may be a slow start, but just think of the good a building could do for kids who need a place to go. What better place than open spaces to explore? And we can assign chores that they could handle depending on their age." Zach opened the door and prepared to lock it, then paused to look around. "Where's Caleb?"

"He's been gone. He promised to meet Granny early."

"Humph! I think sometimes she thinks he's her grandson too." He locked the door, and they started down the street toward St. James Church.

Greta stood with Cora and Granny and

listened to the organ playing softly in the background. From the foyer, she peeked through the heavy wooden doors of the church. She saw the new friends she'd made since arriving in Central City and some of Jess's customers already gathered in the pews. Jess and Zach were at the altar with Reverend Edwards. When she saw Jess's profile and noticed his nice suit, fresh haircut, and taut jawline, her heart skipped a beat. Her hand shook as she patted her hair, making sure the pins were secure, then she moistened her lips. She felt her legs go weak momentarily. She was about to say her vows!

"It's nearly time for you and Cora to walk down the aisle," Granny crowed. She was wearing an outrageous hat she'd bought from Suzanne for the wedding. "I'm going to go have a seat now. Anna, you can sit with me. I'm so glad I'm hosting the reception on my newly painted porch, thanks to Caleb."

"Thank you for doing that, Granny, and for taking care of Rascal for a few days." Greta gave the older lady a hug and saw Granny blink back a tear. Anna gave Greta a kiss and left with Granny.

"This is it. I never would've thought we'd be doing this together," Cora whispered.

"And to two brothers! Not only will we be good friends forever, but we'll be family as well." Greta squeezed Cora's arm.

Caleb walked up to them. "Wow! You both are beautiful." He kept his voice low as he said, "I have a small gift for you that I want you to have. I'll be hurrying to catch the train after the ceremony to visit my family before I start college next week, but I wanted to give you both something I made. It's not much, but maybe you'll think of me. I know I'll be thinking of all of you and how you've influenced my life." He placed a small figurine in each of their hands.

"Oh, Caleb . . . a dog. He looks just like Rascal." Greta admired the tiny wooden sculpture. "Thank you." She gave him a brief hug. "You'll be sorely missed."

"What a beautiful angel," Cora exclaimed. "It will be dear to my heart, Caleb." Cora leaned in close to kiss his cheek. "I hope you'll be back to visit. You've become like a part of the family."

Caleb flushed. "I intend to come back at Thanksgiving break. Granny said I could stay with her."

"Then we'll have much to be thankful for. I'm going to tuck my dog into my bouquet for now." Greta pushed the figurine into the nosegay of primroses.

"I'll do the same," Cora whispered.

"Oh! The music is growing louder. You'd better hurry and take your seat, Caleb. It's almost time for us to go," Greta urged.

He gave them a farewell hug and hurried inside, propping the doors open for them to enter just as Mendelssohn's "Wedding March" rang out in a crescendo. Everyone stood in respect as Greta and Cora strolled down the aisle to meet their respective grooms.

With great emotion but with tears in check, they spoke their vows before God and man. When it came time to give the brides their wedding bands, there was a moment of panic while Jess searched his pockets.

"Jess, you told me you'd take care of getting the bands. Where are they?" Zach asked through clenched teeth, clearly irritated.

Greta looked at Cora and smiled. She wasn't surprised at all that Jess had forgotten to bring them. She may as well get used to this. A few people in the pews twittered, and she heard a chuckle.

"I . . . well . . . it seems I forgot to get them." Jess apologized with a shrug while the reverend, his eyebrow cocked, stood waiting to continue the ceremony.

Caleb sidled up to them. "I kinda figured

you wouldn't remember," he said quietly, then handed a ring to Jess and Zach. Zach winked and Jess muttered a thank-you.

Zach gave Cora's ring to her, and Jess slipped Greta's band on her finger, looking at her with tenderness. His hands were warm to her touch . . . warm just like his heart. He whispered, "I love you," and her heart swelled as she mouthed the words back to him. The reverend smiled, and after a prayer of blessing, he said the men could kiss their brides.

Jess's smoldering gaze sent a tingle up her spine. He kissed her, not lingering, and gave her a squeeze about the waist as they all turned around to be presented to the congregation. Greta smiled at everyone present and wondered if her face reflected the excitement she was feeling. All was well. She was Mrs. Jess Gifford! There would be time later for more affection, no doubt.

36

Greta saw Jess's brown eyes widen in approval when she entered the bedroom of their hotel suite. She'd spent extra time on her toilette in the bathroom, brushing her hair until it spilled in soft, shiny waves down her shoulders. Catharine had given her the cream silk gown and robe set as a wedding gift before she'd left Cheyenne.

"Ahh . . . my beautiful *wife*," he murmured hoarsely. His eyes swept over her form, perusing the outline of her shape from where he sat waiting by the window. She drew in a nervous breath and moved toward him. When he spoke the word *wife*, it was almost like a caress.

He'd changed from his suit into a woolen robe, but his feet were bare. *Is there anything underneath?* she wondered with a quiver in her belly. Noticing her look, he grinned mischievously. He held out his arms, enfolded her in an embrace, and pulled her onto his lap.

"Greta," he whispered huskily in her ear. His breath was hot against her skin. "You look ravishing in that gown." His hands stroked her arms, and their eyes locked for a long moment.

"Mmm . . . thank you, my *husband.* It was a gift from Catharine," she replied, looping her arms around his neck and feeling the muscles there tighten. It felt good to be able to claim the word *husband,* and she liked the sound of it when it rolled from her lips.

His smile broadened, and he tenderly reached for her. "You are such a gift. One that I longed for . . . prayed for." His lips brushed her temple, then moved to the curve of her neck, and she leaned back with a whimper, allowing her eyes to drift closed. He nibbled her earlobe, then she turned slightly, her eyes traveling to his full lips.

"I do love you," he breathed.

"*Ja* . . . yes, I love you too. I was happy to hear you say those three little words to me today, but you can continue to say them through the years. I shall never grow tired of them."

Smiling, Greta leaned in close, teasing him with her lips, and he tried to capture them with his until finally she let him.

Their kiss was slow, long, and full of

desire, as he fingered the delicate blue ribbon on her gown.

AUTHOR'S NOTE

Contributing to the rich and colorful setting of the American West, mail-order brides and women in general influenced the creation of schools, libraries, and churches and established hearth and home. It didn't take long for men who traveled west of the Mississippi to realize their need for the "gentler sex," and soon mail-order brides became prolific. Although many Dutch and Swedes settled in Minnesota, I took the liberty of having my heroine from Holland travel out West, looking for love and adventure.

My love of Blue Willow china, given to me by my brother when I was a child, led me to write this story. I use Blue Willow dishes every day and never tire of their design and beauty. In the Blue Willow Brides series, I use a common thread of Blue Willow dishes to weave a story around the bride and her sisters. There are several legends of the Blue Willow story in the center of the plates. In my story, I use the one most commonly associated with the dishes.

Central City, Colorado, where my story takes place, was known as the richest square mile on earth by 1859 as the result of the gold rush strike in 1858. This area in the seat of Gilpin County was called the Cradle of Colorado. John Gregory, a man from Georgia, discovered enormous deposits of gold at Gregory Gulch between Black Hawk and Central City, thirty-five miles west of Denver.

When I lived in Denver, Central City was one of my favorite places to visit. It's nestled between Clear Creek and the base of the Bald Mountain summit of the Rocky Mountains. Many of the historic buildings are there today, but gambling casinos have taken over the sleepy mountain town, much to my dismay. In 1870 the population had fallen to 4,000, but at the height of the gold rush, 60,000 people lived in and around Central City. Today the population is about 645.

The Teller House, where my heroines had a brief stay, still stands proudly on Eureka Street. It was built in 1872 by Henry Teller, one of Colorado's first senators and a well-known attorney, whose office was across the street. At one time it was known as one of the finest hotels west of the Mississippi. I met the late actor Richard Crenna there while he was filming *Centennial.*

The Teller House was one of the first hotels with plush carpet from Brussels and rooms trimmed in rich walnut. In 1936 a local artist painted a picture of a woman's face on the wooden floor of the Teller House bar. I saw the painting firsthand, and it makes for interesting conversation. It is well-known as the "face on the barroom floor."

The townsfolk paved the sidewalk in front of the hotel in silver ingots when President Ulysses S. Grant visited in 1873. In 1874, fire destroyed most of the city's business district, but the Teller House, made of brick, withstood the fire and helped prevent its spread to other areas of town. Later, businesses were rebuilt by brick and stone, as required by the city. The Teller House is now a popular steak house and casino.

Major John N. Andrews was a real commander in charge of Fort Bridger, and I took the liberty of using his name on the letter to Jess Gifford.

St. James Church, where Greta and Cora marry Jess and Zach, is the oldest church in Colorado and is still standing today. It looks exactly the same as it did in late 1871 when it was completed.

The Agricultural College of Colorado started its veterinarian department in 1900, and the college's name was changed to Colorado University in 1935.

Lastly, in case you didn't guess, my hero, Jess, suffered from ADD (attention deficit disorder), which was recognized as early as 1798 but wasn't labeled as such until 1902. I have several friends and family members with this disorder, so I wanted to write about it with a light hand by using my character. For further information for someone you know who has ADD, please visit the national ADD website: http://www .add.org.

ACKNOWLEDGMENTS

My sincere appreciation to the following:

Doris and Dianne, my sisters who support all my writing efforts. I love you!

My brother, Sam, for introducing me to Blue Willow dishes by giving me a tea set for Christmas when I was eight years old. Here's to you in heaven.

Mag's Peeps, my prayer warriors — Sheri Christine, Karen Casey, Connie Crawford, Linda Hoffner, Kelly Long, Gaye Orsini, and Lynn Underwood.

My critique partner, Kelly Long, for your friendship, constant support, and love that keeps me focused.

Dottie Poythress and the ladies on staff at the BookMark of Johnson Ferry Baptist Church.

Andrea Doering, my wonderful editor, and the entire Revell team who bring my novels to life.

Angelina, Maggie, Peter, and Sarah, my grandchildren who fill my life with constant joy, as well as much-needed distractions!

Julie Lessman, for her friendship, encouragement, and most of all her prayers.

All my readers everywhere, who champion me with their words of encouragement.

Natasha Kern, my agent, for her friendship and valuable advice.

The Lord, who is my rock and my salvation.

ABOUT THE AUTHOR

Maggie Brendan is a bestselling author. She is a member of the American Christian Writers (ACW), the Authors Guild, the American Christian Fiction Writers (ACFW), the Romance Writers of America (RWA), Faith, Hope & Love (FHL), and the Georgia Romance Writers (GRW). Maggie led a writers' critique group in her home for six years and was quoted in *Word Weavers: The Story of a Successful Writers' Critique Group.* She was a guest speaker at a Regional Church Bookstores and Libraries conference in Marietta, Georgia, on the value of Christian fiction.

A TV film version is currently in development for her first novel, *No Place for a Lady,* book 1 of the Heart of the West series. *Deeply Devoted,* book 1 in the Blue Willow Brides series, received a 4-star review from *Romantic Times.*

Maggie is married, lives in Georgia, and

loves all things Western. She has two grown children and four grandchildren. When she's not writing, she enjoys reading, singing, painting, scrapbooking, and being with her family. You can find Maggie on her website, www.MaggieBrendan.com, and on her blog, www.southernbellewriter.blogspot.com. She is also a resident blogger on www.bustles andspurs.com.